THE

DUKE
OF
KISSES

USA TODAY
BESTSELLING AUTHOR

DARCY
BURKE

The Duke of Kisses
Copyright © 2018 Darcy Burke
All rights reserved.

ISBN: 194457641X
ISBN-13: 9781944576417

This is a work of fiction. Names, characters, places, and incidents are the product of the author's imagination or are used fictitiously. Any resemblance to actual events, locales, or persons, living or dead, is purely coincidental.

Book design: © Darcy Burke.
Book Cover Design © The Midnight Muse Designs.
Book Cover Font Design © Carrie Divine/Seductive Designs.
Photo copyright: © Period Images.
Editing: Linda Ingmanson.

For Duchess

You are still the queen of the housecats.

Prologue

❧·ε·3·❧

Stour's Edge, Suffolk, England
December 1817

FRANCES SNOWDEN GLARED at the rabbit hole but quickly acknowledged she was angry with herself, not the tiny animal she'd foolishly followed through the copse and up the hill and over an icy stream.

Blast, she was an idiot. She'd seen the rabbit hunkered down near a tree. It had seemed to be shivering, and so she'd decided to scoop it up and take it home before it succumbed to the elements. But as soon as she'd moved close, the animal had scampered away.

Satisfied the rabbit would be fine, Fanny watched it run until it stopped. Then it sat down and began to quiver again. That had started what seemed to be a game of cat and mouse as Fanny went after it, and it ran away, then stopped again. Over and over until it had disappeared down its hole.

"Well, I suppose I did see you safely home," Fanny muttered. "You're welcome!"

She pulled her woolen cloak more tightly about her and looked up at the muted sky as the first snowflake struck her square on the nose.

"Oh, to be that snowflake." A masculine voice rent the quiet, drawing Fanny to spin about toward the source of the sound.

A tall gentleman lounged against a tree as if he frequented hills in the middle of a snowstorm with careless ease. Er, *possible* snowstorm. Fanny squinted her eyes toward the heavens once more and wondered just how far from Stour's Edge she'd strayed.

"Miss?"

There was that voice again, reminding her that the snow and her unknown location were perhaps not her most troubling problems at present.

"I'm on my way home—to Stour's Edge," she added hastily.

A single dark brow the color of the chocolate she'd taken to drinking each morning since coming to live with her sister arced into an upside-down V as he pushed away from the tree and sauntered toward her. The wide brim of his hat shaded his features, but they were clearly visible, from the chocolate hair visible at his temples to the strong line of his jaw. "I see. You must be the Duke's bride."

"I am not."

The man's dove-gray eyes flickered with appreciation. "I see. How nice."

Was he flirting with her? Fanny had next to no experience with that. Mr. Duckworth had tried such nonsense with her, but his efforts always seemed far more…lascivious. She would forever thank her sister for saving her from certain doom. Without Ivy inviting her to come live at Stour's Edge, Fanny would undoubtedly have found herself the next *Mrs.* Duckworth. The third, in fact.

Best to just let this gentleman know she wasn't the sort of woman he might think. "I'm afraid I'm not adept at flirting, nor do I have any interest."

"Was I flirting?" He moved closer, his athletic frame moving easily. "I didn't intend to. But I never do, and then a beautiful woman happens across my path, and I simply can't help myself." His lips curved into an arresting smile.

Fanny's breath caught. He was the most handsome

person she'd ever clapped eyes on. And he was looking at her as if he maybe thought the same thing about her.

Except, he'd just said he flirted with all beautiful women, which meant this wasn't a singular event for him, as it was for her. And really, she wasn't beautiful. Far from it. She had freckles and her lips were too full, as her mother was fond of pointing out. "You're definitely flirting," she said warily.

"And you are on your guard. As you should be. You're a bit far from Stour's Edge, however. Are you certain that is where you are from?"

He doubted her? Actually, perhaps it was best that he did. This was a scandalous encounter, and it would behoove her to keep it from becoming known. Which meant she couldn't tell anyone about it, and she didn't want *him* telling anyone about it either.

"I think I'll just be on my way." She turned from him and started down the hill. She made it about twenty feet before she stopped and frowned. She had absolutely no idea where she was going. *Blast it all.*

"Are you lost?"

The question came from far too close behind her, and she jumped. She quickly turned and backed up at the same time, moving quickly and without care for her location near the top of the hill. Just enough snow had accumulated that she slipped.

And tumbled down the hill.

She landed in a heap at the bottom, her eyes closed and her body smarting from rolling over a few times on the way down.

"Hellfire!"

The proximity of his deep voice made her open her eyes. The concerned, yet still unbelievably handsome, face of the stranger hovered over hers.

"Are you all right?" he demanded, his gaze darkening to the color of iron.

Fanny moved her fingers and toes. "I think so." Her backside stung most of all, and she was acutely aware of the frigid temperature of the ground beneath her. "It's quite cold down here."

He knelt beside her, but quickly clasped her waist and pulled her to stand, rising to his feet in front of her. "Better?"

And now she was acutely aware of his hands on her and the delicious, almost entirely foreign sensation of being held.

She quite liked it.

"Yes," she said rather breathlessly, realizing she sounded like a ninnyhammer and not caring in the slightest.

"I insist on seeing you home." He looked up at the sky as the snow seemed to be falling in larger flakes than it had just five minutes before. "Stour's Edge, you say?"

She was cold and now wet, and for some reason, she felt safe with him. "Yes."

He gave a firm nod, then wrapped her arm over his. "We'll walk briskly. If you can."

She nodded, then wiped at the dirt and grass that seemed to cover her cloak. He helped her, his hand moving over her hip and then her backside. The moment he made that contact, their gazes connected.

"Sorry," he murmured before averting his gaze.

They walked in silence for a few minutes, a hundred questions tumbling through her head and an equal amount of sensations coursing through her body.

He glanced over at her, a snowflake landing on his dark lashes and melting almost immediately. "I know we haven't been properly introduced, but it seems we should take care of that."

"It's a bit scandalous, isn't it?"

"No more so than my caressing your backside."

Caressing. Oh dear. Those hundred sensations doubled.

"I'm Frances." She decided it was best to just keep things simple. He didn't need to know she was Fanny Snowden, sister-in-law to the Duke of Clare.

"I'm David."

"Pleased to meet you, David." For all she knew, he was a footman at a neighboring estate. She doubted that, however. While her experience with anyone outside her tiny town of Pickering in Yorkshire and its environs was limited, she could tell he was Quality. Or at least good at mimicking it.

"What brought you so far from home?" David asked.

"Providence, thankfully." She realized belatedly he didn't mean *that* home. She blamed the fact that she'd just been thinking of Pickering. Though she'd been at Stour's Edge for nigh on six months, apparently she could still think of her lifelong home as home.

He gave a soft laugh. "Because you met me?"

Now she realized how that may have sounded. "No, I didn't mean that. I meant... Oh, never mind. I am abysmal at polite conversation. I've almost no experience with it."

"Are you in service?" he asked, voicing about her what she'd just been thinking of him.

She seized on the opportunity to mask her true identity and have a way to explain why he couldn't escort her to the house. "Yes, I'm a housemaid." She looked at him askance. "What about you?"

"In service?" He started to shake his head but then stopped. "Not precisely. I'm serving as apprentice to a steward."

"That sounds exciting."

He turned his head toward her. "Indeed?"

"Oh yes. To be responsible for so many things... You must be quite intelligent."

He shrugged. "My father always told me so."

"My father always told me I was a featherbrain."

"Well, that sounds rather rude. Also, I find that hard to believe—that you're a featherbrain, I mean." He said this with utmost certainty. "Although, you did wander far from home in a snowstorm."

"It wasn't snowing then, and I was trying to save a rabbit." She exhaled. "I'm afraid I'm terribly softhearted when it comes to animals. My father also told me I was far too kind. Once, he made me abandon a litter of puppies after their mother died."

David gasped. "That's atrocious."

She nodded, glad for his support. "Yes, but I sneaked back out to where they were and rescued them anyway. One of the neighbors had a dog who was almost finished nursing her pups, and she was more than glad to adopt the four little babies. Ironically, my father took one of those dogs several months later, never realizing it was one he'd left for dead." She shook her head. "He loved that dog more than any of us, I think."

"What an astounding tale. I would say you have a kind heart, not soft. There's a difference, I think."

She swung her gaze to his. "Do you?"

"I do."

They stared at each other a moment before she nearly tripped over a rock. He caught her, his free hand clasping her hand while he gripped her arm. "All right?"

"I'm also rather clumsy."

"Then allow me to assist you over the stream, though I gather you made it across by yourself earlier."

They'd arrived at the slender but swift-moving brook. "It was a miracle, really."

He laughed, then withdrew his arm from hers. "I'll go first and help you." He leapt over the water with ease, and she decided she could watch him do that a thousand times. In her mind's eye, she would.

He held his hand out to her. "Ready?"

She clasped his appendage, and he brought her over the stream with a fluid grace she didn't possess on her own. "I'll wager you're a fine dancer," she said.

He grimaced. "Barely passable, I'm afraid."

She grinned at him. "I'm a *disaster*."

His eyes gleamed as he chuckled. "You're a *treasure*, Frances."

Heat rose in her face, but she suspected her cheeks were red from the cold and was relieved he couldn't see her blush.

He tucked her arm over his once more and they started on their way, keeping up their rapid pace. "Do you often get lost?" he asked.

Only when she struck off in a new direction and then only sometimes. Snowstorms were particularly helpful if one wanted to lose one's way. "No, but then I just left home for the first time less than six months ago." She wished she hadn't revealed that much. But he was so easy to talk to.

"You're new to your employment, then?"

"Yes. What are you doing out in the middle of a snowstorm?" she asked, hoping to divert the conversation away from herself lest she bore him with the story of her life.

"I was just taking a walk. Then I saw you running up the hill, and I was curious."

"So you followed me?"

"Guilty." But the look he cast in her direction didn't reflect even a tinge of regret.

She was glad and more than a little...tantalized. "Well, I suppose I must be grateful since without your help, I would be lost and cold."

"But dry. I can't imagine you would have fallen without my intervention." Now she detected a dash of remorse.

"That's a nice theory," she said wryly, "but I did tell you I was clumsy."

"I suppose we'll never know," he mused. "Come, let's move a bit faster, or we'll both be soaked to the skin."

She had a sudden vision of him in clothing that was plastered to his muscular, athletic frame. Muscular? Yes, she could tell from his arm and the way he'd lifted her effortlessly from the ground and assisted her across the stream. Athletic? Evidently, given how quickly he'd made it down the hill after she'd fallen and the fact that he hadn't lost his balance as she had. Besides all that, she had eyes, and she could see he was broad-shouldered and long-legged.

"Do you often go for walks?" she asked, thinking he must.

"Every day. At least once. Like you, I have an affinity for animals. In my case, it's birds."

"Indeed? What are your favorites?"

"It's very hard to say." His response was solemn, as if he were deeply considering her question. "I find myself drawn to birds of the marsh—it's their long legs and long beaks, I think. There's something very graceful about their composition and demeanor. Avocets are beautiful. As are godwits."

"I know next to nothing about birds." But she suddenly wished to correct that and planned to scour West's library for every book on ornithology she could find.

"I could teach you," he offered softly.

It was the nicest, sweetest, most alluring offer she'd ever received.

Too bad she couldn't accept. He was a steward's apprentice, and she was the sister-in-law of a duke, destined for a grand Season and probably a marriage to a prince. Or at least a duke. That was what she and Ivy joked about, at least.

Ivy! She had to be worried sick.

"How far are we from Stour's Edge?" Fanny asked.

"About a quarter mile, I should think." He pointed in front of them. "There. You'd see it if not for the copse of trees and this thickening storm."

She recognized the copse from earlier and from the walks she'd taken since coming to Stour's Edge. When they reached the trees, she stopped. "We should part here, I think."

"You probably don't want to be seen arriving with me," he guessed accurately.

"I don't think that would be wise. I've been gone too long as it is."

"Are you sure you can find your way?" he asked.

She nodded. "Yes, I'm quite oriented now. I meant it when I said I don't usually get lost."

He glanced up at the sky, blinking. "It really is snowing hard. You should go."

"I should."

And yet neither of them moved. They stood there facing each other, arms still clasped, cloaked in white, seemingly alone in the world.

"Pity there isn't mistletoe," he said softly.

Oh, he wanted to kiss her!

Good, she wanted him to kiss her too.

She edged closer until they almost touched, chest to

chest. "Let's pretend there is."

He pitched his head toward hers, and she closed her eyes just before his lips touched hers. They were cold but soft. His arms came around her, and he held her close.

The kiss continued, awakening all her senses and arousing them so that, to her mind, there was just him and her and the snowy quiet enveloping their secret embrace. When his tongue licked along her lips, she opened for him, driven by curiosity and a sweet hunger she'd never experienced.

Once inside, his tongue met hers, and he coaxed her fully, showing her what it meant to really be kissed. She'd always wondered, and now she knew.

It was over far too soon, and the cold that he'd banished from her for a few, brief minutes came rushing back, reminding her that she was cold and damp and needed to get inside.

He brushed his gloved fingertips along her cheek. "I refuse to say good-bye, so I'll just say, Happy Christmas."

She refused to say good-bye too, even though she knew it was. "Happy Christmas."

Then, before she could lose her courage, she turned and fled.

By the time she reached the door to the drawing room at the rear of the house, she was breathless, both from her dash through the snow and her encounter with David.

Ivy met her at the door, her forehead creased. "Fanny! I've been so worried." She pulled her sister inside and wrapped her in a fierce hug. When she drew back, she looked down at Fanny's snow-covered cloak. "You're soaking wet."

"And now you are too," Fanny said with a touch of irony.

"So it would seem." Ivy raised her gaze to Fanny's.

"Where have you been?"

"Trying to save a rabbit."

"Of course you were," Ivy muttered. Her gaze snapped to Fanny's skirts. "Did you fall down too?" She shook her head. "Never mind. You need a warm bath. At once."

"Yes, Ivy." Fanny leaned forward and kissed her sister's cheek before departing the drawing room. On the way, she waved at Lucy and Aquilla, Ivy's two dearest friends, who were on the floor with their baby boys and Ivy's daughter, Leah.

After dinner that night, they tried the Queen's tradition of lighting candles on a tree. When they were lit, Fanny gasped in wonder.

Ivy, holding Leah against her chest, moved close to Fanny's side, smiling. "It's beautiful, isn't it?"

"It is."

"Who knows where you'll be this time next year," Ivy said with a touch of sadness. "You may be married. I'll miss you, especially when we've just found each other." Ivy had left home more than a decade ago and had only renewed contact with Fanny and the rest of their family last fall.

"I'll miss you too. I may *not* be married, however. Maybe I'm meant to be a spinster."

Ivy laughed. "No, not you."

"You nearly were."

"Yes, and as you can see, you can never be too sure about the path you're meant to take." Her gaze settled lovingly on her husband, West, the Duke of Clare, who stood chuckling with his friends, Lucy's husband, the Earl of Dartford, and Aquilla's husband, the Earl of Sutton.

Fanny thought about the path she'd taken that day and decided that while it had been a small moment, it had been an important one. She doubted she'd be able to shake David from her mind. Nor did she particularly want to. Indeed, she hoped she'd encounter him again.

In the meantime, she had ornithology books to study.

Chapter One

◆Ɛ•Ȝ◆

London, April 1818

DAVID LANGLEY, SEVENTH Earl of St. Ives, stood in the doorway to the subscription room at Brooks's Club and resisted the urge to spin on his heel and quit the establishment. Before him, gentlemen milled about or sat at tables where they drank and gambled. This was a world in which he'd never felt comfortable, a world in which he'd never spent much time.

It was his father's world.

And now, having assumed his father's title, it would be David's too. He'd known this day would come, of course, but he'd thought it would be years from now. His father had been a healthy, robust man in his early fifties until a minor injury—a bloody *splinter*—had taken him.

The hell with it.

David abruptly turned to leave and ran straight into another gentleman.

"Beg your pardon," the man said, recovering and stepping back.

"The fault is mine," David said, irritated with himself for being both hasty and careless. He shouldn't leave. He should try to find a place. "I'm St. Ives."

The other man, who was of a similar age, offered a sympathetic nod. "Sorry to hear about your father. I'm Anthony Colton. Please call me Anthony as my father is Colton."

David had studied Debrett's and knew Colton was a viscount. This must be his son. "Pleased to make your acquaintance."

Anthony squinted at him briefly. "Did we meet at Oxford?"

"God, no. I attended Cambridge." How could he not when it wasn't very far from his childhood home?

Laughter greeted David's horrified reply. "So you're a heathen. Excellent. We'll get along famously, then. Come, have a drink with me." Anthony didn't wait for David to accept or decline, but started toward a table.

David followed, and a few minutes later, they were ensconced near the wall with glasses of brandy. "I've never been here before."

Anthony's brows climbed his forehead. "To Brooks's? You don't say."

"I was never intrigued by London," David admitted. "I prefer the country."

Anthony sipped his brandy. "Why is that?"

David shrugged. He wasn't about to launch into a discussion of his passion for ornithology. "Society events never appealed to me. I am terrible at dancing."

"Dancing." Anthony winced. "You just reminded me that I promised my sister I would go to the Anderton ball tonight to dance with her and her friend."

"You're a kind brother."

"My sister's a bit of a wallflower, and her new friend is just about the worst dancer I've ever seen. Dancing with her is a dangerous endeavor for one's toes."

David laughed. "How unfortunate. For everyone involved."

"Come with us!" Anthony urged. "Felix will be joining me here momentarily, and we'd planned to go together. But three is always better."

"Felix?"

"The Earl of Ware," Anthony said. "We've been friends

forever. Or nearly so. You'll get along famously. And he's exactly the man you need to know since you're new to London. Felix knows everyone and everything Important. He's a trendsetter and an event maker. If you're fortunate enough to be in his group—and you shall be—you'll be invited and included everywhere. Plus, he's just damn fun."

The notion of attending a ball on his first night out in London didn't particularly appeal to David. Hell, it didn't appeal to him at any time. "While I appreciate the invitation, I'm not sure I'm quite ready to wade into deep waters."

Anthony chuckled. "That's precisely what you'll be doing too. Look at it this way, if you come tonight, you'll be dipping your toes in with friends who will happily whisk you away at the earliest opportunity. It's really the best way to make your entrée."

"I don't even have an invitation to this ball."

"Only because they didn't know to invite you since you're new to town. Trust me, that won't matter to Anderton. He'll be thrilled to have the new Earl of St. Ives at his home." Anthony was quite persuasive.

David regarded him with a dash of skepticism. "I needn't stay?"

Anthony shook his head, then fixed him with a mischievous stare. "But you may want to. You'll presumably be on the hunt for a countess, and there are plenty of charming and attractive young ladies."

Yes, he would marry, but he wasn't on the hunt. Furthermore, he couldn't seem to stop thinking of the young woman he'd met at Christmastide. But Frances was a housemaid, and dwelling on her alluring wit and delectable lips did him no good. Perhaps this ball would be just the thing for him to fully inhabit this role of earl that he'd seemed reluctant to accept. It was past time, his father would say.

"All right. I'll go."

Anthony's gaze lit, but it wasn't focused on David. His attention was fixed over his shoulder, causing David to turn his head. "What splendid timing," Anthony said.

Another gentleman approached their table. He was a bit taller and leaner than Anthony, his hair darker, and his face longer. This had to be the Earl of Ware.

"Felix, come meet our new friend, St. Ives."

St. Ives wasn't a name he was used to being called. He'd been Viscount Woodhurst forever. The past seven months had been an adjustment, and he still wasn't fully where he needed to be. Wherever that was.

David started to rise, but Ware waved him back down. "No need to get up," he said. "Pleasure to meet you, St. Ives."

"The pleasure's mine." David indicated the empty chair to his left. "Care to join us for a few minutes?"

"Indeed. My fortification is on its way." Ware deposited his slender frame into the chair.

"He means brandy," Anthony said. "But I'm sure you deduced that."

A footman brought a glass to the table, and Ware raised his tumbler in toast. "To our new friend, the Earl of St. Ives. May you find whatever your heart desires here in London, and may your debauchery be both clandestine and satisfying."

Ware laughed and tapped his tumbler against Anthony's, then turned to do the same to David. "Welcome."

David took a drink as he pondered the toast. Debauchery? "Er, what is it you do here in town?"

"I think you frightened him," Anthony said. "Ignore

Felix. He likes to be provocative."

"No, I *am* provocative. There's a difference."

Anthony rolled his eyes but smiled at the same time. "He's also harmless. To us, anyway. Do not, however, get on his bad side."

"Duly noted." David took another sip of brandy before setting his glass back on the table. "What else do I need to know? I'll be taking my seat in the Lords day after tomorrow and going to court next week."

"Ah, the pomp and circumstance," Anthony said. "Court isn't terribly taxing, and it must be done. As for your seat in the Lords, I will leave that to Ware since I have yet to take mine and won't for many years to come."

Anthony's father was still alive, and perhaps young and fit as David's had been. The grief he carried pushed him to say that Anthony couldn't rely on *anything*, but he wouldn't darken the mood. Instead, he turned to Ware. "Any advice?"

"None." Ware's mouth stretched into a brief but somewhat humorless smile before he took a drink of brandy. His green eyes seemed a bit cool, but he turned his head quickly, looking over his shoulder, so that David couldn't be sure if he'd seen any emotion at all. When he turned back around, he leaned forward a bit and lowered his voice. "Rumor has it young Hornsby plans to call out Royston for breaking his sister's heart."

"Good Christ," Anthony said. "I would defend my sister's honor to the death, but you can't fault a man for not wanting to court a young lady."

David looked between them. "What's the issue?"

Ware angled himself toward David. "After dancing with Mr. Bernard Royston on two occasions, Miss Dahlia Hornsby developed an infatuation for said gentleman. When a courtship was not forthcoming, she is said to have been devastated. Her brother, Barnard—do not confuse him with *Be*rnard—Hornsby, pledged to defend her honor."

"But her honor wasn't besmirched. Or am I missing something?" David expected London to have rules that he hadn't encountered before, but this made no sense.

"No, you have the right of it," Anthony said. He fixed his gaze on Ware. "Is Hornsby here? Is that why you turned to look?"

"I thought I heard that he was, and I'd hate to miss the scene if there is to be one."

Anthony slid an amused glance toward David. "Felix could organize the event and ensure a vast audience—if Hornsby wanted one."

"Will he actually call Royston out, and will Royston accept the challenge?" David had heard of men dueling for nonsensical reasons, but surely someone would inject some much-needed reason with these gentlemen. "Have they no one to talk sense into them?"

Anthony shrugged. "Who's to say what will happen?" He consulted his watch. "We should go, even if it means missing the excitement." His tone was regretful as he picked up his brandy and tossed the last of it down his throat.

"*I* don't have to go," Ware said. "You've got St. Ives here to dance with Sarah."

Anthony looked over at David. "Sarah's my sister. Do you mind partnering her?"

Hell in a handbasket. His dancing skills left much to be desired. He simply couldn't remember all the damn steps. "I don't mind, but I should warn you that I'm not very good."

Anthony grinned. "Brilliant. She isn't either. Though she's a far sight better than her friend." Anthony's shoulders twitched with a shudder. "I should have worn extra stockings to protect my feet. Or, better yet, my riding boots." He looked toward Ware. "I demand a thorough and animated description of Hornsby's challenge."

Ware's answering stare was tinged with cynicism. "Would I give you anything else?"

The answering bark of laughter from Anthony made David smile. The camaraderie between the friends was rather contagious. "We'll see you back here later." He glanced toward David. "At least *I* will. I suppose I shouldn't speak for St. Ives."

"I am yours to direct this evening." David was glad to have made their acquaintance.

"Until later, then," Anthony said, rising. "We can take my coach to the ball, if that meets with your approval?"

"Yes. I walked here."

Both Anthony and Ware stared at him, their jaws slack. "You *walked* here."

"My house isn't far," David said, feeling a bit defensive. He liked to walk.

Ware shook his head. "Most gentlemen don't walk to their club, particularly in the evening." He picked up his glass. "How else can you show off your vehicle and your horseflesh?"

Oh yes, London had different rules. David only hoped he could tolerate them.

A while later, he walked into the Anderton ball after having been introduced to the host and hostess by Anthony. As he'd said, Anderton—and his wife—was delighted to have David in attendance and apologized for not inviting him. Which was silly since he hadn't even been in town.

The ballroom gleamed with a thousand candles

reflected in the jewels adorning many of the women in attendance. Music drifted from the far corner, mingling with conversation and laughter. It was simultaneously alluring and revolting. It wasn't that he didn't like people. He just didn't normally see this *many*. And especially not when they'd all be interested in him.

"We needn't stay long," Anthony, who along the way had urged David to call him by his first name, said. "My sister and her friend Miss Snowden are expecting us."

"And is there any chance you may court this Miss Snowden?" David asked as they made their way along the perimeter of the ballroom.

"I hadn't thought of it, to be honest. I haven't yet reached the stage where I wish to pursue a wife." He winked at David. "Though, she is quite pretty and possessed of a charming wit. I could do far worse."

"But your toes would suffer," David said with a chuckle.

Anthony joined him in laughter. "They would." He craned his neck toward the corner. "Ah, there they are." He wove his way through the crowd with rapid intent.

Two young women stood apart, their heads bent together. David could plainly see one—clearly Anthony's sister, with her dark hair and pert nose. The other was mostly turned away from him, but he registered her bright red-gold hair and the elegant sweep of her neck above a finely trimmed blue and ivory gown.

There was something about her…

As they neared, the young lady turned. David's breath stalled in his chest. It was *her*. The housemaid. *Frances.*

But she clearly wasn't a housemaid. Yet she was most definitely Frances—her eyes widened in clear recognition and stark surprise.

He didn't much care that Anthony was supposed to

dance with her or that his toes were about to become mincemeat. He bowed before her. "Good evening. May I have the next dance?"

◆E◆3◆

FANNY'S HEART THREATENED to beat a hole clean through her chest. David was here. Were stewards invited to balls? She didn't think so. Oh, but he was *here*.

And he looked splendid in his black evening finery. His dark hair was a bit shorter than the last time she'd seen him, and there was something different about his eyes. They were still gray, of course, but they held a flint she hadn't seen before. She might even have described his gaze as cool.

Realization struck her a moment later than it ought. He thought she was a housemaid, and clearly she wasn't. He knew she'd lied.

Her heart beat even faster.

Anthony chuckled. "Hold on a moment, proper introductions must be made. St. Ives, may I present my sister, Miss Colton, and her friend Miss Snowden." He gestured to Sarah and Fanny in turn. "Ladies, allow me to introduce you to the Earl of St. Ives."

The *earl*?

And he dared look at her as if she'd committed an offense. Fanny dipped into a curtsey. "Pleased to meet you, *my lord*." She put the barest emphasis on the last two words, but looked at him pointedly and knew he caught it. "I'd be delighted to dance, but I'd reserved this for Mr. Colton." The plan was for Anthony and the Earl of Ware to come and dance with her and Sarah. Ware was supposed to dance with Sarah so she wouldn't have to dance with her brother. Only Ware wasn't here.

Sarah voiced Fanny's thoughts. "Where's Felix?"

"Being Felix," Anthony said. "I brought my new friend St. Ives instead. He's just come to town and needed to experience a ball. What good is going to a ball if you don't dance at least once?"

"Well, if he's taking Felix's place, he should dance with me," Sarah said. She flashed a smile at her brother. "I can't imagine you want to dance with me any more than I care to dance with you."

They had a loving sibling relationship, but Sarah didn't often dance, and Fanny well understood why she'd prefer to do so with David. St. Ives. Oh bother, he was already David in her head, and so David he would remain.

And when Sarah found out he was the man Fanny had kissed at Christmastide... That revelation would have to wait until later. In the meantime, she wouldn't upset her friend's plan even if she was disappointed not to have David to herself so she could get to the bottom of his lies.

Fanny gave David an apologetic smile. "You must dance with Sarah."

He had to agree or he'd appear an ass. "Of course." He held his arm out to Sarah. "Shall we?"

Sarah curled her hand around his sleeve with a grin. "Yes."

Anthony bowed to Fanny. "Shall we as well?"

"Indeed." Fanny took his arm, and the quartet made their way to the dance floor, where the prior set had just ended.

"It's to be a quadrille," Sarah said. She tilted her head up to look at David. "Do you enjoy the quadrille, my lord?"

His gaze shot to Fanny as he answered, "As much as one can."

He'd told her he was a terrible dancer. What the devil

was he doing dancing at a ball, then? The same thing she was doing—being a bad dancer didn't mean you didn't like it, and it certainly didn't mean that you didn't hope, one day, to become better. At least that was how it was for Fanny.

"I've been practicing," she whispered to Anthony.

"Is that what you were doing in the country?" he asked. "I thought you were visiting a friend."

"I was." Fanny had returned to Yorkshire to visit her oldest friend, who'd just given birth. It had been a wonderful visit, but she'd been eager to leave her parents' house and return to London—or, more importantly, to Ivy's house, where she felt much more…loved. "But I also worked on improving my dancing."

"Excellent. Just the same, I shan't be getting too close." He laughed softly, and his eye held a twinkle.

They joined another pair of couples and formed their square. Fanny and Anthony stood opposite Sarah and David. The music began, and they bowed and curtsied to each other. Thankfully, the other couples went first, which gave Fanny the chance to review the steps in her head. Hopefully, she wouldn't turn the wrong way and crash into anyone. It had been a while since she'd made that mistake.

When it was their turn, she started her steps, dancing forward and back, circling Anthony and then moving to the middle of the square, where she met Sarah, who gave her an encouraging smile. "You're doing well," she said, keeping her voice low.

Fanny didn't dare respond. She was having a difficult enough time not watching David, and she needed to focus on her steps. Then it was time for her to take David's hand. Her gaze slammed into his, and for a moment, she was entirely lost in their gray depths. The touch of his hand in hers sent a jolt of electricity through her, reminding her wholly and keenly of his kiss and the fact that she longed to feel his lips on hers again.

He released her hand, and, in a bewildered haze, she spun about in mistake. Realizing her error, she turned back and smacked directly into his chest. She'd been moving quickly with the music, and the force of their connection sent him staggering backward. He fell against one of the other young ladies in their square, and in his effort to steady her, they all went crashing to the floor.

It was, without question, the worst dancing disaster Fanny had ever caused, and she'd instigated quite a few.

The dancers around them stopped and stared while Anthony and the other gentlemen in the square sought to help Fanny, the other woman, and David to their feet. Once they were vertical, everyone exchanged hapless expressions.

"Shall we continue?" Anthony asked, as if she hadn't just brought the entire ballroom—or very nearly—to a standstill.

"Are you sure you dare?" she asked him in an attempt to hide her embarrassment.

"I dare," David answered after straightening his clothing. He sent her a look of warm encouragement. "And you should too. Come."

The music hadn't stopped, and the other squares had gone back to dancing. The other two couples waited, including the woman Fanny's clumsiness had sent sprawling. "I do apologize," Fanny said to her.

She was a bit pale and appeared put out to say the least. Her partner, however, leapt to Fanny's cause. "Accidents happen. You've given us quite a story to tell this evening." He laughed good-naturedly, and soon, everyone was laughing.

Still, Fanny wanted to melt into the floor until the ball was over, then creep back to her sister's house—the one far away in the country, *not* the one in London—and never return. Affixing a smile to her lips, she resumed her position in the square, and they did their best to start up again.

Unfortunately it just wasn't to be, and it wasn't entirely Fanny's fault. She moved hesitantly, waiting to follow what the others did. But no one did anything save Anthony. As he danced to the center by himself, the rest of them burst into laughter.

Perhaps this would make a good tale after all.

At last the music ended, and they parted ways with the other pair of couples. Anthony escorted her back toward the corner. "I must thank you for a most memorable evening, particularly for St. Ives. What do you think of London now?" he asked David with a chuckle.

"This was not a good example of London," Fanny said, throwing him a frown.

"I think," David said, "that if you'd allowed *me* to dance with Miss Snowden, you'd have been the one sprawled on the dance floor." His tone was droll, and Anthony laughed again.

"So I would have. I'll owe you one. Now, we must return to the club. Hopefully, we haven't missed the spectacle."

"What spectacle?" Sarah looked at her brother in suspicion.

"It's nothing to do with me," he said to Sarah before bowing to Fanny. "Until next time, Miss Snowden."

"I don't think there will be a next time. I may put my dancing slippers away for good."

Sarah patted her arm. "You've said that before. You'll feel better tomorrow." She smiled prettily toward David.

"It was lovely to meet you, my lord. I do hope we'll see you again soon."

"The pleasure was entirely mine." He bowed to Sarah and then to Fanny, his gaze lingering on her as he rose back to his full height.

Fanny could scarcely believe he was real. She'd begun to wonder if he'd been a dream. She'd looked for him for weeks before coming to London, never imagining she'd find him here. As a bloody earl.

The gentlemen took their leave, and Sarah immediately sidled closer as they watched them depart. "Oh, he is very handsome, even if he's not much of a dancer. He barely knew the steps, did you see? His gaze was completely fixed on what Anthony was doing. I daresay that disaster wasn't entirely your fault." Sarah patted the curls near her face. "*Very* handsome. And an earl to boot."

"Yes, an *earl*," Fanny said, irritated that she hadn't been able to ask why he'd lied to her. She watched him move through the crowd, his dark head visible above most.

She'd been about to tell Sarah that he was David, the mystery kissing steward Fanny had told her all about, but the revelation crumbled to ash in her mouth. Why tell her new, very dear friend that the man she found attractive was the man Fanny had kissed and fantasized about these past four months?

Sarah was lovely and charming, the daughter of a viscount, and in search of a husband. It was also her fourth Season, and she was far more in need of one than Fanny. In fact, Fanny didn't *need* one at all. She had no parents prodding her to wed. Oh, her parents had tried prodding her in that direction until her sister Ivy had rescued her from her dull life in Yorkshire and laid a new future before her. That future included a home with Ivy and her family as long as Fanny wanted it.

Did that mean she would so easily relinquish the man she'd dreamt about?

He and Anthony disappeared from the ballroom, and the surroundings suddenly seemed dimmer.

"What are you thinking?" Sarah asked. "You watched my brother the entire time he made his way through the ballroom."

"Not your · brother," Fanny said softly, apparently abandoning her earlier intent to keep David's identity secret. "I was staring at David."

"David?" Sarah sounded perplexed.

Fanny turned her head to look at her friend. "*David.*"

Sarah's eyes rounded as realization struck. "David!" Her jaw dropped, and she looked back toward where they'd exited the ballroom. "You never said he was an earl."

"I didn't know until tonight." Not being able to query him about it was driving her mad.

"Your mystery steward just became more mysterious," Sarah said.

Indeed he had. And she had every intention of solving the puzzle.

Chapter Two

❦

THE SPOTTED FLYCATCHER perched on the tree outside David's study window made him smile. Perhaps living in the city wouldn't be so tedious. Especially knowing Frances was there.

He still couldn't quite believe his luck—both to have found her again and to find she wasn't, in fact, a housemaid. He'd thought of her often since kissing her, an act he ought to regret but couldn't bring himself to, and had worked to put her from his mind. He could have no future with a housemaid, but with the sister-in-law of a duke…

"My lord?"

David turned to see his secretary, Graham Kinsley, standing in the doorway. "Why are you still calling me that?"

"I shall always call you that," Graham said, stepping over the threshold.

"I wish you wouldn't," David grumbled. He sat down at the desk while Graham took the chair angled to the side.

"Here is your correspondence, including a rather robust stack of invitations." Graham set the missives on the desk.

"Robust?" David asked.

"You're the new earl in town," Graham said. "Curiosity is bound to run amok."

"Put like that, it sounds dreadful."

Graham's dark gaze took on a sardonic cast. "You think *all* of this is dreadful."

"I didn't think I'd have to do this so soon."

"Neither did I," Graham said, reminding David that he was only slightly more enthused about any of this than he was. Four generations of Kinsley secretaries had worked for four generations of the Earls of St. Ives. When David's father had died in October, Graham's father had retired his position, leaving it for Graham to take over. And so here they were, raised together from boyhood and now conquering this together too.

"Do you want to decide which invitations to accept, or do you require my assistance?" Graham asked.

"What do we know? Can they wait until my mother arrives?" He hated these kinds of details and couldn't imagine Graham liked them either.

Graham's ebony brows twitched. "Do you really want her choosing what you do?"

"She knows better than I do." She'd actually spent considerable time in London, unlike David.

"I know you've never particularly cared about social events in the past, but now you must." Graham blinked at him. "On second thought, forget I said that. You don't have to go to a damned thing if you don't want to."

But he wanted to. How else would he be able to see Frances? "I'd like to go to a few things. I mean, I *should*."

Graham narrowed his eyes. "Why?"

David should have realized Graham would pick up on his sudden interest in something he'd never paid much attention to. "I met some gentlemen last night—including the Earl of Ware. They've offered to help me acclimate."

"So see them at the club. If I were you, that's where I'd focus my time." Graham had always been more of a pleasure seeker than David, who'd been far more discreet, at least when it came to women. At Cambridge, Graham's reputation for revelry had been legendary. "Unless there's some other reason you want to go to a ball. Or a rout."

"What the devil is a rout again?"

"You're avoiding the question."

David gave him a bland smile steeped in sarcasm. "I didn't actually hear a question."

Graham laughed. "Fine, don't tell me."

There wasn't any point in enlightening him about Frances. Not now anyway. They'd shared a kiss and lied to each other. He was likely mistaken to harbor any hope.

"I thought we'd go to Tattersall's on Monday to select a sporting vehicle," Graham said. "I still recommend a phaeton."

"So you can drive it."

Graham shrugged. "Perhaps. You like phaetons."

"I did until I crashed one." That had been David's reputation at Cambridge—driving fast. He'd been unbeatable until he'd botched a turn, distracted by a heron. He had to be the only man whose attention could be stolen by a bloody bird. There was just something about them and what they represented: freedom.

"It's past time you got back on the perch."

The butler, a flat-faced man Graham had hired last month, arrived in the doorway. "I beg your pardon, my lord, but you have a pair of visitors. The Earl of Ware and Mr. Anthony Colton."

David rose, which prompted Graham to stand too. "You can stay here and deal with that," David said, gesturing toward the pile of correspondence on the desk. It still felt odd, having his friend work for him, but they'd known this would come to pass. Again, it had just occurred sooner than they'd thought. David looked at Trask, the butler. "I'll meet them in the drawing room."

"Very good, sir." Trask offered a quick bow before taking himself off.

David rounded the desk and looked to Graham. "Are you certain you find this arrangement acceptable? I could find another secretary."

"And what would I do instead?" Graham arched a brow. "I lack funds, position, and interest in anything else. If I ever win a sizeable pot that would allow me to pursue a life of indolence, you can find a new secretary." He laughed, clapping David's shoulder as he moved around him to sit behind the desk.

Shaking his head with a faint smile, David went upstairs to the drawing room. Ware and Anthony stood near the windows overlooking Bolton Street.

"Afternoon, St. Ives," Anthony said, turning. "We're on our way to the park and wondered if you'd care to join us."

David noted their horses were in front of his house, with one of his grooms attending them. "I'm not dressed for riding."

"We didn't think you would be. We can walk today, knowing you've no quarrel with that activity." He and Ware exchanged smiles that prompted David to let out a brief chuckle. "Tomorrow we'll ride, unless you decide you hate the park."

He looked between them. "Is there something to hate?"

Ware lifted his shoulder. "Besides matchmaking mamas and overeager husband hunters? Not a thing."

"Ignore him," Anthony said. "He's sensitive to anything to do with marriage."

Ware nodded rather somberly. "It makes me violently ill."

David laughed. "I will endeavor to remember that. Let me just fetch my hat and gloves."

Ten minutes later, they were on their way to Hyde Park along Piccadilly. "I thought you were supposed to go at five o'clock," David said. It was only half four.

"It's close enough," Anthony answered. "Felix has to conduct a meeting at a quarter before the hour."

"What sort of meeting?" David knew he was lacking when it came to London habits, but meeting in the park was one he hadn't even heard of.

"I'm starting up weekly races," Felix said as they neared Hyde Park Gate.

David had learned last night that Felix was *the* facilitator of amusement. "Aren't there clubs that race?"

"Yes, but exclusive clubs are so *boring*." Felix stretched the last word a bit.

"I see." David would likely have a phaeton by then. He hadn't felt an urge to race in some time, but the desire swept over him rather fiercely for a moment. "I used to race."

Felix's brows shot up. "Did you? Well, then it's good you came with us so you can attend the meeting." He gave his walking stick a jaunty flick as they walked into the park through the gate.

"Down by the Serpentine?" Anthony asked.

At Felix's answering nod, they made their way in that direction. David had been there a few times, but not in years. He followed their lead down to the bank of the water. Right away, he began cataloguing the waterfowl—coots, moorhens, and a few tufted ducks.

A handful of men had gathered, and David listened with one ear while he focused on the birds. A pair of mated swans glided into view. David made a mental list so he could write down all he'd seen when he returned home. He could see that morning walks to the park might become his habit.

Then his attention was drawn to something else entirely. A trio of women coming down a different path toward the Serpentine, one of whom was Frances Snowden.

He'd hated not being able to speak with her more privately last night. He wasn't going to let that happen again today.

Having lost all interest in the racing meeting and knowing Ware and Anthony would inform him of what he'd missed, David made his way to intercept the women. He recognized Anthony's sister as one of the other two, but the third was unknown to him.

"Oh, Lord St. Ives, how do you do?" Sarah asked.

"Well, thank you. I couldn't resist coming over to greet you." He looked at her and, more pointedly, at Frances who was unabashed with her interest in his arrival. Indeed, her gaze raked over him, initiating an inconvenient heat in the vicinity of his groin.

He transferred his attention to the third woman, lest he develop an entirely inappropriate reaction. It wasn't his fault—Frances was lovely, her blue-green eyes as rich and lush as a peacock's feather and her slightly parted lips looked like fresh strawberries he wanted to suck the juices from. These thoughts were not helping.

"Good afternoon," he said to the unknown woman.

Sarah gestured toward the pretty, auburn-haired lady beside her. "Allow me to present the Marchioness of Northam. Lavinia, this is the Earl of St. Ives." Had she emphasized his name? David couldn't be sure.

And then he was.

The marchioness's eyes took on a perceptive gleam. "St. Ives, what a pleasure to make your acquaintance." Her tone held a note of unmistakable glee. It was evident Frances had told them all about him. But had she told them *everything*?

He bowed. "The pleasure is also mine." His gaze

drifted toward Frances, and he tried to think of how to get her alone. Or at least a bit away. So they could have a much-needed discussion.

Was it really necessary? She'd lied. He'd lied, or omitted the entire truth anyway. Did any of that matter?

"I'm going to sit on a bench," Miss Colton announced. She curled her arm through the marchioness's. "Come with me, Lavinia."

Any doubt as to whether they were aware of the connection between David and Frances was completely demolished. As the two women walked toward a nearby bench, David turned to Frances. "That wasn't very subtle." He kept his voice low, though he wondered why he should bother. "Do they know everything?"

She shrugged. "They know you aren't a steward." She fixed him with an irritated stare.

"No more than you're a housemaid." He offered her his arm. "Shall we walk for a spell?"

The moment she placed her hand on his sleeve, he suffered another shock of heat, and he was suddenly overwhelmed with the memory of her soft lips and the intoxicating scent of lilies of the valley.

He guided her along the bank of the Serpentine. "It's good to know you didn't lie about everything," he murmured. "You really are a terrible dancer."

Frances squeezed his arm and sucked in a breath. "You aren't much better—on either count. You're an *earl?*"

He looked down at her upturned face. "And you are clearly not a housemaid."

"It seemed…prudent to mislead you," she said defensively.

"Why?"

"Because if I told you my brother-in-law is the Duke of Clare, you never would have kissed me."

Another flash of heat. Why did she have to bring that up? As if he wasn't thinking about it. He looked quickly over his shoulder at the two women sitting on the bench and farther down the bank at the group of gentlemen talking. "Keep your voice down."

"No one can hear me," she said. "And even if they could, it would only be Lavinia and Sarah, and they already know you kissed me."

He exhaled, trying to keep his wits amidst his frustration—both from the conversation and his troublesome desire. "Frances—" He looked down at her again. "Is that really your name?"

"Everyone calls me Fanny."

"I can't call you Fanny."

"Why not? I can't keep from thinking of you as David."

This dialogue was veering into territory that was beyond acceptable. He was never more acutely aware of his new and rather cumbersome title. "Let me understand. You told me you were a housemaid because you wanted to entice me to kiss you."

"Not at all. I was being cheeky a moment ago. But it's true. If you knew who I really was, you wouldn't have kissed me, and I rather enjoyed it. As I recall, I tried to tell you I was from Stour's Edge, and you didn't seem to believe that could be true." She gave him a pert look. "So I told you what I thought you wanted to hear."

She was right, damn it. He'd seen her walking and had followed her, which had turned out to be a good thing since she'd been lost. But stalking after a young lady was somehow worse than stalking after a housemaid. And yet it wasn't. They were both equally cringe inducing. "I heartily apologize."

"For what?"

"For all of it. Making assumptions, kissing you,

generally behaving like an ass."

She smiled broadly, with a hint of coquetry. "I thought you were incredibly charming, and if you apologize for that kiss again—you already did it once, and that was one time too many—I'll kick you in the shin."

He stopped, turning toward her. "Why not just threaten to dance with me?"

She laughed, and he was, for a brief moment, transported back to that snowy December day where he'd felt absolutely smitten.

"Fine, I'll dance with you, then—a waltz so you need only suffer me for a short time instead of an entire set."

He could think of far worse fates. "We have an accord." And now he was quite tempted to apologize a third time. But he didn't.

They continued along the bank. "Why did you tell me you were a steward?"

"It wasn't a complete lie. The steward was reviewing things with me because I had just become the earl in October. In hindsight, I didn't quite feel like an earl at the time, so it was easier to just not be one." He still didn't quite feel like one.

Her gait halted, and he slowed with her. She laid her other hand over his arm so that her grip encircled him. It was both comforting and enticing. "Your father died recently?" she asked softly. At his nod, she touched his sleeve. "I'm so sorry."

"Thank you. It was rather sudden." And utterly devastating. "I hadn't planned on being the earl this soon."

He'd wanted to write a book about the birds of Huntingdonshire. He'd wanted to travel to all the various islands around Britain to study waterfowl in particular. He'd wanted to study migratory patterns and breeding habits. He'd thought he had at least another twenty years before he'd have to assume the title. Every other Earl of St. Ives had lived to be eighty or more. In fact, David's father had only been the earl two years.

"I hadn't planned on being the sister-in-law of a duke…ever. But here we are."

He stared down into her eyes and was overcome with the same sensation he'd felt four months ago—an overwhelming desire to kiss her. "Yes, here we are."

She leaned into him, and he began to bend his head. The flurry of wings nearby when a small gaggle of greylag geese landed in the water reminded him they were in public and he couldn't kiss her, let alone shouldn't.

She seemed to realize the same thing, for they jerked back simultaneously. She took her hand from his arm, and suddenly she tilted. Her eyes widened. She was falling backward. David lunged to reach for her, but he was too late.

The loud squawking of geese filled the air as Fanny hit the water with a splash.

⊷℥•ℨ⊶

THE WATER WAS very cold. Fanny gasped as she windmilled her arms through the water, taking in a mouthful of it for her trouble. Spitting and sputtering, she was aware of strong hands clasping her waist and pulling her up.

Those same hands swept her out of the lake. David's arm came underneath her knees, and she threw her arms around his neck and held on with everything she had.

He sloshed through the shallow water to the bank and continued walking. "Where is your coach? I dearly hope you arrived in a vehicle or that you live close to the park. I would drive you home myself, but I walked here." He sounded supremely disappointed in himself.

She gauged the firm set of his jaw and the chill in his eyes. "This isn't your fault."

His gaze tipped down to hers. "I'm certainly not blameless."

"Why, because you wanted to kiss me again?"

"Fanny, you really need to speak more quietly."

Lavinia and Sarah had rushed over to meet them. Both wore matching expressions of horror mixed with concern, but given the way they glanced between Fanny and David, they'd clearly heard what Fanny had said. Yes, perhaps she should think before she spoke. Thankfully, it wasn't anything she wouldn't have told them anyway.

"Are you all right?" Sarah asked.

"Quite." She smiled for good measure, because really, aside from the soaking, she was rather pleased to be in David's arms.

"You're drenched," Lavinia said with a frown. "Fortunately, I drove my new curricle today. Unfortunately, it's over near Grosvenor Gate. I'll hurry to fetch it and bring it around." She looked to David. "Can you carry her to the drive over there?" She pointed back along the bank of the Serpentine.

"Certainly," David answered just as several gentlemen arrived, led by Anthony and Felix.

"How can we help?" Anthony asked.

"Lady Northam has a curricle near Grosvenor Gate in which to transport Miss Snowden home," David said. "One of you can likely fetch it faster than she can."

"I'll go," Felix offered, taking off at a run before anyone could respond.

Fanny leaned toward David's ear and whispered, "You should put me down."

He started walking toward the drive, and she noticed he stayed far away from the water's edge. "I'll set you into the curricle when it arrives. I don't want you catching cold."

"So you're keeping me warm, then?" His thoughtfulness certainly warmed her. "I'm getting you all wet."

"I'll survive." He winced, and the reaction made her frown.

"What's the matter?"

"I shouldn't have said that."

"Why not?"

"A splinter brought my father down. What's to say a wet coat won't see me to my end?"

Fear laced through her. "You don't really believe that. Do you?"

"Not rationally, no. I suppose it's possible, but it's unlikely." He gave his head a shake. "This is a dismal topic, and I insist we depart from it."

"Whatever you wish. Though sometime, I hope you'll tell me about your father."

He glanced down at her, but his expression was unreadable.

The entourage of people, including Sarah and Lavinia, followed them to the drive. Heeding her own advice— and David's—Fanny kept her voice low. "You don't have to keep carrying me. I must be rather heavy. I'm too tall, and my dress must weigh an extra half stone at least now that it's wet."

"I doubt that, but in any case, you aren't heavy at all."

As he paused to adjust her weight in his arms, she wasn't sure she believed him. But she didn't protest again. Instead, she inhaled the scent of pine and clove that clung to his jacket. "You smell divine," she whispered near his ear.

"Fanny, you must stop doing that." His voice was low and urgent.

"What, whispering in your ear or telling you that you smell nice?"

"All of it. Particularly since my clothing is—" He snapped his mouth closed. "Never mind."

She wanted to ask what his clothing was, but they'd reached the drive, and Sarah moved around to Fanny's lower half and wrung water from the hem of her gown.

"You don't have to do that, Sarah. You'll ruin your gloves," Fanny said.

"They're just gloves."

Lavinia winked at Fanny. "She's saving the interior of my new curricle."

Fanny laughed, then focused her gaze on David, whose jaw was still tense. "Since you walked, does that mean you live close?"

"On Bolton Street."

"Lovely. Clare House is in Berkeley Square. In case you wanted to know." It was a shameless solicitation for him to call on her—if he was paying attention.

He slanted a look at her, his lips twitching briefly. "I did, in fact." Good, he *was* paying attention.

Felix drove the curricle toward them. He came to a stop nearby, and Lavinia's groom jumped from the back to help Lavinia into the vehicle.

David carried Fanny to the curricle, and Fanny saw a crowd of people coming down the drive, some on horseback, and even a few vehicles that were nearly upon them.

"Blast it all," she murmured.

He followed her gaze just before he set her into the vehicle. He looked toward Lavinia. "Hurry and go before the vultures descend."

Lavinia nodded as she picked up the reins. "Right."

"Thank you," Fanny called to him as Lavinia steered them away.

Fanny was suddenly cold and wrapped her arms around herself to ward away the chill.

"I'll get you home as soon as possible. I'm getting quite good at this. Beck has been giving me lessons." Lavinia said this with a sparkle in her eye and a note of giddiness in her tone. She'd been married a few weeks, and her bliss was on display for all the world to see. She glanced toward Fanny very briefly. "What was going on with you and David—I should really call him St. Ives, but since you told us about 'David' from the start, that will be difficult—down by the water?"

"I have trouble with that too. I'm afraid I can't think of him as anything other than David. I hope I don't forget propriety and address him the wrong way."

"You mean the way you two nearly forgot propriety before you fell into the lake?"

"Whatever do you mean?" Fanny belatedly recalled that Lavinia had heard her say that he was about to kiss her. Regardless of what Lavinia might have seen, she knew the truth of it. "Never mind. You know what was going on. Why even ask me?"

"Because I wanted the full story, not just what I could see."

So she had come to a conclusion without hearing what Fanny had said. Fanny tipped her head toward Lavinia. "And what did you see?"

"Two people about to kiss. Again. Is he going to court you?"

"We didn't discuss it. I'm afraid my clumsiness prevented further conversation."

"He should court you. Or stop kissing you." Lavinia shook her head. "Don't listen to me. I am not a paragon of virtue."

"No, you aren't. If memory serves—and only because you informed us *after* the fact—you were kissing Beck long before there was any formal courtship. Did you even *have* a formal courtship?"

"As I said, I am not a good example." Lavinia turned them from Piccadilly up Berkeley Street. "You should stay home tonight to ensure you haven't taken a chill."

She was probably right, but Fanny didn't want to. She wanted to go wherever David would be. Unfortunately, she didn't know where that was. "I doubt Ivy will let me anyhow. She mothers everyone."

"Good. You require mothering this evening." Lavinia drove into the square and pulled in front of Clare House.

Lavinia's groom rushed from the back to help Fanny descend. She walked toward the house, her feet squishing in her probably ruined half boots.

The butler, Tarenton, opened the door, and his face immediately registered shock. He turned and barked at a footman to fetch the duchess.

"I'm fine, Tarenton, just damp." That was a rather gargantuan understatement.

Lavinia had followed her into the house. "Do you want me to stay?"

"No, Ivy will take care of me," Fanny said as another chill tripped across her shoulders. "Though I do think a hot bath will be in order." She sent a smile toward Tarenton, who took himself off to presumably set things in motion.

"We'll check on you tomorrow." Lavinia gave her a concerned smile before turning and quitting the house.

Fanny realized she was dripping on the marble floor

and made her way through the hall to the wide staircase. Ivy was already on her way down, her jaw gaping in horror.

"What on earth happened?" She rushed to the bottom and put her hand on Fanny to guide her up the stairs. "You fell in the Serpentine, obviously," she said, answering her own question.

Fanny lifted her sodden skirts as she climbed. "How is it obvious?"

Ivy's answering look of sarcasm nearly made Fanny laugh. "You were at Hyde Park. You like to walk down by the Serpentine. And you're you."

"Meaning I would fall in."

"I'm honestly surprised it hasn't happened before now."

Now Fanny did laugh. She was so glad to have found her sister after so many years apart. Ivy had left their household when Fanny had only been ten, and Fanny had missed her dreadfully.

"You need a hot bath," Ivy said as they reached the first floor and continued up toward the second, where the bedrooms were located.

"Tarenton is seeing to it." Fanny realized this was the second time—out of three encounters—that she required a bath after being with David.

"Good. Then you'll drink hot tea and broth and whatever else to ensure you don't become ill. Cook will make you a toddy. Then you'll rest."

"Is it too much to hope we'll still go out this evening?" Fanny asked.

Ivy blinked at her as if she'd just asked to fly to the moon. "Yes."

Fanny exhaled. "I thought as much. Still, I had to ask."

"How, exactly, did you fall into the lake?" Ivy would

ask until Fanny told her what happened.

"I was walking with a gentleman."

Ivy cast her a dubious glance. "Walking or falling?"

"Walking. I tripped." She certainly wasn't going to tell Ivy the truth of the matter. She'd never even told her about meeting David, let alone kissing him. Though Ivy was happily married to a wonderful man, she still believed most men to be pigs. Fanny was certain her sister would categorize a man who'd followed her onto Stour's Edge property and kissed her as such.

They arrived on the second floor and went toward Fanny's chamber which overlooked the square. Ivy opened the door and ushered Fanny inside toward her dressing room. "And who is this gentleman so I can be sure to have West scold him about allowing you to fall into the Serpentine?"

"West will no more scold him than you'll allow me to go out later."

Ivy laughed. "True. Still, I'd like to know who he is so I can glare at him surreptitiously."

Fanny peeled her wet gloves from her puckered fingers. She looked at Ivy in question.

"Just drop everything on the floor."

Fanny's maid, Barker, an efficient woman in her middle thirties, arrived. "I'll get the fire going, and they'll set the bath up in front of it to lessen the chance of a chill."

Ivy inclined her head toward the maid. "Thank you, Barker." She returned her attention to Fanny, who was fumbling with the ribbon of her bonnet. It was the driest part of her, but her hands were too cold to function anymore. Ivy took over, untying the ribbon and removing the hat. "Who was the gentleman?"

"The Earl of St. Ives. He lifted me from the water and carried me to Lavinia's curricle."

"He *carried* you?"

Fanny heard the concern in her sister's voice and sought to placate her. "He was doing me a courtesy."

Ivy turned Fanny around and began to unlace her gown. "Huntwell, St. Ives's seat, isn't far from Stour's Edge—maybe fifteen miles. How interesting that he was the one to rescue you."

That explained, somewhat, why Fanny had encountered him in December. Though fifteen miles wasn't walking distance. What had he been doing at Stour's Edge that day?

She'd find out next time she saw him, and she was certain she would. Something was happening between them. She could hardly wait to see where it led.

Chapter Three

❦3❦

DAVID HADN'T EXPECTED to see Fanny that evening, but he'd gone to two routs and a ball just in case he was wrong. He was not. He was, however, quite popular, as his rescue of the Duke of Clare's sister-in-law was on everyone's lips. As a result, he'd suffered far more conversation with strangers than he'd ever hoped to engage in. Thankfully, Anthony and Ware had accompanied him and had known precisely how to extricate them all from the situation.

At last, they were ensconced at a table in the corner at Brooks's sipping brandy, and David was finally able to relax.

"This is grueling," David said. "I don't know how you keep up." He was exhausted from making polite conversation and feigning interest. There was, perhaps, a reason he spent most of his time outdoors with little to no company.

Ware peered at him in curiosity. "You didn't make it look difficult. In fact, you seem an accomplished flirt."

David snorted before he took a drink of brandy, welcoming the smoky liquid tantalizing his tongue. "Flirting doesn't take effort."

For whatever reason, flirtation had always come naturally to him. It was an easy method of communication—flatter and amuse, then duck away. And in a few cases, take the flirtation to the next stage.

"True," Ware said. Anthony nodded in agreement. "But are you more than that?" Ware waggled his brows at David.

Anthony chuckled. "He doesn't strike me as a rake, Felix. Though he did look rather interested in Miss Snowden. He all but abandoned your racing meeting."

"I saw that." Ware sniffed in mock annoyance.

"If I have to choose between racing and women, I'll choose women." That hadn't always been the case, but after his accident, he'd welcomed their distraction.

Anthony raised his glass. "Amen." He took a drink, then narrowed his eyes briefly toward David. "You seem taken with Miss Snowden. First, you wanted to dance with her instead of my sister, then you went straight for her at the park."

Was he? He was something, and he probably shouldn't be.

Ware looked past David toward the door. "Oh hell, here comes Clare."

David resisted the urge to turn. "He's coming this way?"

"Yes, he looked around, saw us—likely, you—and is making his way in our direction."

"We won't abandon you," Anthony said. "Clare's an affable sort anyway. Did you know he was called the Duke of Desire?"

"I did not." And why on earth would he?

The duke arrived at their table. He was an imposing figure with broad shoulders and ink-black hair. But then he smiled, and David glimpsed the "affable" man beneath the formidable exterior.

"Good evening. I'm Clare." His voice was as dark and potentially dangerous as the rest of him. He glanced at the other gentlemen. "Ware, Mr. Colton."

"Evening, Clare," Anthony said.

"Care to join us?" Ware invited, gesturing to an empty chair next to David.

"I would, thank you." The duke moved behind David and sat down.

David turned to him. "I'm St. Ives."

"Yes. My sister-in-law's daring rescuer. I wanted to thank you for your quick thinking."

"How is she doing?" David asked, hoping he didn't sound too eager.

"Very well, thank you. My wife also wishes to extend her gratitude."

A footman stopped by the table, and the duke requested a glass of whatever they were drinking. Clare turned back to David. "You're new to town?"

"Yes."

"I'm sorry about your father. He went so quickly, or so I heard."

"He did." The pain was still fresh enough that David had to work to keep the memory at bay. He sought to redirect the conversation. "Ware and Anthony have been introducing me to London."

"Well, you can't have a better guide than Ware. He knows all the best amusements, and if he can't find one, he'll make one." Clare tipped his head toward the earl. "What do you have planned that I should be aware of?"

"Nothing you should attend," Ware said with a sly smile. "Unless you're looking to return to your premarital reputation, and I would doubt that."

Clare laughed as the footman brought his brandy. He nodded in thanks before responding. "I assume you're planning some sort of hedonistic party—I hear you're quite good at those."

"I went to a few hosted by Viscount Lockwood for inspiration, though mine are not nearly so large or, I hope, scandalous."

Clare and Anthony both laughed, and David's curiosity

was piqued. "Who is Lockwood, and why are his parties scandalous?"

"He hovers near the edge of Polite Society," Clare said. "I like him, however, even with that nasty scar."

Ware picked up his brandy. "His parties are exclusive and only for the sexually bold."

Clare nodded. "That's an apt description. I've been to a few myself. Anonymity is key, though I admit I went once without a mask. Why hide my identity when everyone already assumed I went?" He glanced toward David before sipping his brandy.

"You have a point." Ware leaned back in his chair. "You've never been, have you, Anthony?"

His shoulders twitched. "No, and I don't plan to. The notion of shagging one of my mother's friends hidden behind a mask is enough to make me cringe."

They all erupted in laughter before David asked, "So, Ware, you are offering an alternative to Lockwood? No masks?"

"People can wear whatever they like. Mine are unmarried gentlemen and Cyprians only."

"Ah, so I wouldn't be invited in any case, which is just as well," Clare said. "Will you attend, St. Ives?"

It was an innocuous question, but David recognized it for what it was: a query into the sort of man he was. Clare had been stealing looks in David's direction as they'd discussed Lockwood's libidinous parties, as if he'd been gauging David's reaction. It seemed he was judging David's worthiness. His respect for Clare shot up.

"That sort of party doesn't particularly appeal to me," David said.

Clare regarded him for a moment, then gave a single nod, perhaps in approval. "I see."

"I'm also planning some racing events in Hyde Park,"

Ware said.

"Are you?" Clare's dark brows lifted. "Dartford will be delighted."

"Of course. We can't have a race without him."

"He wouldn't allow it." Clare grinned, turning toward David once more. "Dartford is a friend of mine—he adores racing. And anything else that would make your heart pound. He's called the Duke of Daring for a reason."

David had studied Debrett's and knew Dartford was an earl. "Why is he called a duke?"

"They're nicknames," Clare said. "Started by my wife, actually." There was a note of pride in his voice. "And her friends, including the Countess of Dartford. They call us The Untouchables and assign us names befitting our reputations."

Such as the Duke of Desire. David only nodded. A thought occurred to him and gave him a sudden queasy feeling. "Do I have a name?" He couldn't imagine he did. He hadn't done anything to gain a reputation at all.

"Not that I'm aware of. Ivy—my wife—will know. I'll ask her and let you know." He scrutinized Ware for a moment. "Do *you* have a name?"

"The Duke of Distraction?" Ware looked around the table for their reactions.

"The Duke of Amusement," Anthony put in.

David had nothing to contribute, so he didn't. His mind was trying to determine what he might be called and came up with nothing save the Duke of Birds, which, while accurate, was an awful nickname.

"The Duke of Pleasure." Clare's eyes narrowed slightly, and he laughed. "I'll ask my wife if you have a name too. If you don't, I'm sure she and her friends could come up with one, though I believe their naming days are behind them."

"Please assure her that I don't need one," David said.

"Just so." Clare finished his brandy and stood. "Thank you for the company. I am anxious to get home to my wife and daughter. Have a good evening, lads." He turned to David. "Pleasure meeting you, St. Ives. I'm sure I'll see you soon." It didn't appear to be an open invitation to call on Fanny, but David knew that was precisely what it was. This had been an interview of sorts, and apparently, he'd passed.

This made him inordinately pleased but also a bit queasy. He was supposed to be meeting another young woman—and he would. Soon. He pushed the nagging thoughts from his mind. He inclined his head and lifted his glass in a toast. "Likewise."

Anthony and Ware said good night to Clare, and he turned and wove his way out through the tables.

"He came to assess your worthiness." Anthony directed his gaze at David.

David drank the last of his brandy and set his empty tumbler on the table. "So it would seem."

"Do you have an interest in Miss Snowden?" Anthony asked.

"I might." It was the most he was willing to admit out loud. Yes, he was interested. But there were...complications. Again, that bothersome sensation pulled at his brain. He wasn't avoiding it—he wasn't. He was simply adjusting to his new role and making acquaintances, including Miss Snowden's.

Ware peered at him over his brandy glass. "And are you really not interested in my upcoming party, or were you just staying that to impress Clare?"

"I'm really not interested, though I don't begrudge you such entertainments." He flicked a glance toward

Anthony. "Or you. I hope that doesn't mean we can't be friends."

Anthony laughed. "Of course it doesn't."

"Speak for yourself," Ware said loftily. "I only associate with lecherous scoundrels." He exhaled. "But now that Beck has married and completely abdicated any bit of depravity he possessed, I suppose I must accept decent friends too."

"He's referring to his good friend the Marquess of Northam. You placed Miss Snowden in his wife's curricle this morning. They were recently wed. We'll introduce you to him if he ever shows up at a Society event again." Anthony shifted his gaze to Ware. "He'll come to a race."

"Most definitely. Especially since my races will include women—he's more likely to attend anything if he can bring Lavinia along."

"Ah, love." Anthony lifted his glass in a toast, then frowned at their empty tumblers. "You're both out."

"A solvable problem, thankfully." Ware drew the attention of a footman, and a moment later, they all had fresh drinks.

Anthony raised his new glass. "Where was I?"

Ware snorted as he reluctantly lifted his glass. "Nattering on about love."

"Ignore him." Anthony rolled his eyes. "Ware will never marry, and honestly, who would want him anyway?"

"No one, which is precisely the point." Ware grinned widely before he took a long drink.

"St. Ives, on the other hand, seems amenable to the institution." Anthony slid him an inquisitive glance. "Or at least courtship."

David was more than amenable. He expected to marry. But as with the earldom, he just hadn't expected to be faced with it this soon. However, with the earldom came responsibility and that damned persistent *thing* he'd promised. He was nothing if not a dutiful son.

He tipped his glass to his lips and swallowed a mouthful of the smoky brew. Just once, he'd like to break free.

❦

AFTER FOLDING THE last pair of stockings, Fanny set them atop the stack only to have the entire tower slouch to the side and slide from the table. "Oh bother!"

Ivy swept into the drawing room and eyed the pile of stockings on the floor. "Problem?"

Fanny sighed. "No, just a Fanny Moment." That was what they'd taken to calling her bouts of clumsiness or misfortune.

"Well, this one is certainly drier than yesterday's." Ivy smiled as she joined her in picking up the stockings. Taking several, she sat down at the small round table opposite Fanny and began to refold them. "Are you coming with me to deliver these to the orphanage?"

Nodding, Fanny said, "Yes, if you don't mind. I wanted to speak with Mrs. Frawley." She managed the establishment with assistance from several patronesses, including Ivy.

"Oh?" Ivy's interest was clearly piqued.

"I've been thinking I want to start something," Fanny said. Her sister had been dedicated to helping both orphans and unmarried mothers and their children for some time. Having spent time in a workhouse herself, Ivy understood the hardships that faced people who were alone in the world. Unfortunately, Ivy had been exactly that person after their parents had turned her out when she was seventeen. Fanny continued, "A kind of workhouse where women can come to learn a trade that they can then do somewhere else. They can learn to sew or to read and write or to become companions."

Ivy's gaze softened. "What a wonderful idea." She'd been a companion. A patroness from the workhouse where Ivy had lived had seen her intelligence and grace and arranged for a position. "That you have embraced my charitable endeavors so warmly and completely is a gift I deeply treasure."

"You're an inspiration," Fanny said, carefully stacking her folded stockings. She hadn't known the truth of Ivy's departure and the ensuing ten years of her life until she'd come to live with Ivy and West last summer. She couldn't help feeling angry and bitter about her parents' treatment of Ivy and the way they'd lied about why she left. They'd told her she'd taken a position as a governess, when in reality, they'd thrown her out after she'd become pregnant by a gentleman who'd vowed to marry her. He hadn't, of course. He'd abandoned her completely, which was why Ivy despised men. *Most* men. She adored West. And he worshipped her. It might have been nauseating if it wasn't like a fairy tale come true.

"Where do you want to locate this workhouse?"

Fanny had given this much thought. "It makes sense to have it in London, but I was also thinking it might be nice to have one in the country. There are so few opportunities for women to improve their station. Honestly, I think I'd like to start one in Yorkshire. Just think if something like this had been available to you."

Ivy wiped a hand over her eye. "The babe makes me such a watering pot." Ivy and West were expecting their second child at the end of the summer, and Leah wasn't even yet a year old.

"I'm surprised you aren't taking a nap while Leah is

sleeping."

"I wanted to make sure everything is ready to go to the orphanage tomorrow. But now that I see you have everything well in hand, perhaps I'll do that."

Fanny folded the last of her stockings and scooted the pile next to Ivy's. Having learned her lesson, she didn't stack them on top of each other. "I'm happy to help. I'll fold the other linens and box up the other donations."

Ivy rose, the slight swell of her stomach barely discernible beneath the drape of her moss-green muslin day dress. "You are the very best sister anyone could want."

The butler, Tarenton, appeared in the doorway. "Your Grace, there is a caller. For Miss Snowden."

Ivy exchanged a look with Fanny before asking, "Who is it, Tarenton?"

"Lord St. Ives."

Fanny's heart skipped just before it picked up speed. She'd so been hoping he would call, and yet she didn't want to deprive her sister of her nap.

"Show him up," Ivy said without hesitation.

The butler nodded and left.

"But you want to rest." Fanny stood.

Ivy waved a hand. "I'll just sit here while you take a walk outside. That will allow me to rest—the chaise in the corner is quite comfortable—and give you privacy with Lord St. Ives. Just promise me you'll remember everything I told you about men."

"That they're focused on one thing, and most don't care a whit how women feel about it. They take what they want, and we can be damned."

Ivy smiled in approval. "Exactly. It does seem St. Ives may be in a small minority. He performed quite well under West's scrutiny last night."

Fanny's eyes rounded—and her heart skipped again, but for an altogether different reason. "What did West do?"

"Oh look, he's here." Ivy gave Fanny an apologetic glance as she turned to face their new arrival.

David removed his hat and bowed deeply. "Good afternoon, ladies. Duchess. Miss Snowden." He leaned first in Ivy's direction then Fanny's.

"Good afternoon, Lord St. Ives," Ivy said. "I was just telling Fanny that you ought to take a turn in the garden since it's such a lovely afternoon."

David's gaze met Fanny's, and she gave him a tiny nod. "We can go out this way." She gestured to the doors that led to a terrace that overlooked the garden. Stairs led down to a path that circuited the enclosure behind the house. "Allow me to fetch my bonnet." Thankfully, it was resting on a table nearby since she'd already gone outside earlier.

As she tied the hat beneath her chin, David offered another small bow to Ivy. He replaced his hat on his head, then came to Fanny and presented his arm.

Her heart tripped faster again at his proximity. His scent of clove and pine filled her nose and only heightened her awareness. They were quiet until they walked outside.

"How are you today?" he asked.

"I'm so glad you called," she said at precisely the same moment.

They laughed, and he guided her down the stairs to the garden.

She clutched his arm perhaps a bit too tightly, but she didn't care. She wasn't going to slip and fall down the stairs in another Fanny Moment. "I'm perfectly fine, thank you. Ivy made sure I was warm to the point of discomfort for the remainder of yesterday."

"I see. Your sister cares for you a great deal."

"She does. I'm quite lucky to have her. She's more than adept at dealing with my Fanny Moments."

"Fanny Moments?"

"As you've noticed—and I believe I told you when we first met—I'm rather clumsy."

"I had noticed, and truly, you didn't need to tell me at all. You tumbled down a hill the first time I met you." His brow creased as they started along the path. "And at our second meeting, there was that dancing disaster where you fell again. You also fell down the third time I met you. By God, descending the stairs was a risk we should not have taken."

She laughed. "I refuse to live in fear. I simply try to be more careful. Sometimes it works and sometimes it doesn't."

"Well, I do hope it isn't me. I'd hate to be the cause of any misfortune."

"It isn't you, I assure you." They strolled through the roses that were not yet in bloom. "I understand my brother-in-law may have interrogated you last night. What happened?"

He made a noise in his throat that was part laugh and part grunt. "Interrogated is perhaps too strong a description. He wanted to meet me, to glean whatever he could about my character."

She tipped her head to the side and looked at his profile. The angles of his face were sculpted elegance—from the subtle jut of his forehead to the slender slope of his nose to the curve of his lip. "And what did he glean?"

"You'd have to ask him, but I believe he found me acceptable. It was a pleasant, genial encounter."

"So you passed his test, whatever it was." That West

had somehow determined David should be tested and that David recognized it too only strengthened her belief that something was happening between them.

"I seemed to, but West's good opinion means nothing without yours." His words sparked a heat in her belly that spread through her.

"If you'd spoken to me like that yesterday, there wouldn't have been any concern that I would be chilled."

His gaze met hers, but he quickly pulled it away and laughed. "I wouldn't have—there were too many people. You, on the other hand, have no problem saying things regardless of the audience."

He was referring to her discussion of their kissing. Or almost kissing. "They're my friends, and they won't say anything, nor will they judge. I have, however, learned my lesson. I will refrain from discussing kissing with you in public. I must also request that you refrain from almost kissing me in public. That will make my task so much easier."

They were near the back corner of the garden, a fair distance from the house, but still within view if anyone cared to look. He stopped and turned toward her. "I want you to understand that I do not go around kissing young women."

"Thank you for telling me."

"And I really shouldn't start now." He started walking again, albeit more slowly than they had been.

"You actually started back in December," she pointed out. "If you're having an internal debate as to whether you should kiss me again, would it help to know that my sister isn't watching us? She's reclining on a chaise far from the windows. She's expecting a child later in the summer, so she's very tired."

He sent her a brief glance, his lids low over his eyes.

"You're not helping my resolve."

She smiled cheerfully. "I'm not trying to."

"*Fanny.*"

She waited for him to say more, and when he didn't, she decided she'd robbed him of speech. Perhaps if they were stationary, he might be more inclined to kiss her again. Especially if they were at least partially shielded from the house. "Come, let's sit for a moment." She steered them toward a bench that was tucked behind and beneath a tree that provided a bit of privacy.

Reluctantly, she took her hand from his arm and sat down on the smooth stone. He joined her, stretching one leg out. "How are you finding London?" she asked, thinking that if they stopped talking about kissing, he might forget he was trying not to and stumble into it.

Was she trying to manipulate this entire encounter to obtain another kiss? It certainly seemed that way. She was not very good at this demure-young-lady business.

"A bit complicated. Though I did take a walk early this morning. I'm enjoying the birds in Hyde Park."

Of course, birds! "Yes, I've noticed that too. I admit I've taken up bird-watching since meeting you. I kept hoping I'd encounter you at Stour's Edge again. What were you doing so far from Huntwell that day?"

He turned slightly toward her. "We have a parcel of land that adjoins Stour's Edge. It's only about three hundred acres, and I should probably sell it to Clare. However, my uncle keeps a small lodge there where he hunts. Or used to in his younger days. Now he goes there to paint. I sometimes visit to watch for birds. And to be alone."

"Do you prefer that?"

"Sometimes." His answer seemed a bit noncommittal. "Why do you live with your sister? Is it because she's sponsoring your Season?"

"Yes, and because my life in Yorkshire with my parents was unfathomably dull." Particularly after her dearest— and really only—friend had married two years ago. Fanny suppressed a shudder when she thought of how she could be married to the odious Mr. Duckworth. "I hail from a small town called Pickering. It's just north of Nowhere, right next to Nothing."

His mouth ticked up in a slight smile. "Sounds heavenly."

"It isn't. Or at least, it isn't with my family. With the right person, it might be. There is an astounding number and variety of birds. I'll return at some point. I wish to start a—never mind." She was beginning to learn that she didn't need to tell everyone everything, and doubted he'd care to hear about her workhouse idea.

"I shall make a point of visiting someday, especially if you're going to be there. Were you going to say something else?"

He looked at her with such avid curiosity that she wondered why she would keep anything from him. "I plan to start a workhouse that will help unmarried mothers and orphans. We'll train them to find positions outside the workhouse to give them the best possible life."

His gaze swept over her face with warmth and admiration. "You're still testing my resolve, Fanny." The words came out soft but with a scalding heat.

She edged closer, scooting an inch or two along the bench. "I wasn't trying just then, but I'll take what I can get."

"I really should resist." He leaned closer. "But you make it blessed difficult."

She tipped her head back as he loomed over her. "And

I'm trying to be a proper young Society miss, but I'd much rather kiss you."

"Then we are in agreement there." He hesitated the barest moment before muttering something she couldn't quite understand. Then his lips claimed hers and his arms came around her back, pulling her closer.

She'd dreamed of this moment so many times but had long ago given up hope. Until she'd seen him at the ball the other night. Then her imagination had taken flight once more, and now here they were. She put her hands on his chest and slid them up his coat as his lips opened over hers.

Sensation threatened to sweep her away when her tongue touched his. The memory of his kiss had filled her for four long months, but the reality was more intense than she imagined. There was wet heat and a surprising urge to thrust into his mouth and claim what she wanted. She felt brazen and seductive. Powerful. But also a willing recipient of his boldness, of *his* seductive power. He might not make a habit of kissing women, but he was certainly skilled.

One of his hands cupped the back of her neck as he tilted her head and slanted his mouth over hers, gaining deeper access and joining them more intimately. With his other hand, he pulled her flush against his chest so that her breasts tingled from the contact. Indeed, her entire body came alert with sexual curiosity and need. An image of herself throwing her leg over his lap and straddling him invaded her mind and set off a burst of heat between her thighs.

She clutched at his neck, returning his kiss with all the fervor bursting inside her. The hand on her neck moved to cup the side of her face as he drew away—not far, just enough to look into her eyes. His had darkened to flinty steel. "Fanny, this is dangerous territory."

"It's lovely territory. I'm keen to explore more of it." She pressed on his neck, urging him to kiss her again.

With a soft groan, his mouth crushed hers, his tongue licking along her lips and his teeth grazing her flesh. She gasped while his thumb stroked her cheek and his tongue plundered her mouth. Their first kiss had been sweet with a bit of spice, while the second had been audaciously exciting. This was something wholly different. This was primal and urgent, utterly demanding. He insisted upon her response, and her body required satisfaction.

He pulled away again, this time breathing heavily and putting space between them. "I think that's enough for today."

Disappointment chilled her, but she knew he was right. She wasn't entirely sure what would happen next, but she knew it oughtn't take place on a bench in her sister's garden. Even so, she could think of no better place. She'd met him outside and associated the smell of earth and the sound of birds with how it felt to be in his arms.

She took in the rigid planes of his face and allowed her gaze to dip over his frame. Men were at a distinct disadvantage, for their arousal was often plainly visible through their garments. She wondered if hers was in any way. She felt a woozy desire, a need that pulsed between her legs, but surely none of that could be seen. "How do I look?" she asked, barely recognizing the low rasp of her kiss-drenched voice.

His attention sharpened, indicating he might have been suffering the same woozy state. "I beg your pardon?"

"I'm trying to determine if you can see how I feel. The way I can see you." Her gaze dropped again to his crotch.

He smiled. "Ah. You are rather observant."

"It's hard to miss," she said wryly.

He leaned close and whispered, "Just imagine if we were standing. Then you'd feel it against you."

Molten fire dripped through her, tightening the desire she felt below her belly. "Now who's testing our resolve?"

"You make it far too easy." He turned from her and inhaled deeply. "No more kissing."

"Ever?"

"Not today."

She was still disappointed, but acknowledged that was the smart plan. "Well, if I can count on kissing you each time I see you—or at least nearly—I shall be quite content. Though, I may have to give you one of my sister's Untouchable nicknames. The Duke of Kisses, I think."

He turned back toward her, his gaze sharp with alarm. "Oh, bloody hell, *no*. I do not want one of those. Furthermore, you can't call me that to anyone, for they'll wonder how you came up with it."

He had a rather good point. "You're aware of these names, then."

"Clare mentioned them last night. I'd be mortified to have a nickname."

"I'll do my best to ensure you don't—at least publicly. To me, you are already the Duke of Kisses, I'm afraid." She brushed a speck from his shoulder and allowed her hand to linger. "But it's our secret."

"Good." He stood and held his hand to help her up.

She took it, wishing they weren't wearing gloves. Or hats. Or clothes at all.

Rising, she tucked her hand over his arm for the walk back to the house. "Are you presentable?" she asked with a soft laugh.

"I will be. Just watch your mouth—don't say anything provocative."

"I would never do that." At his bark of laughter, she added, "On purpose."

He slid her a dubious glance. "I'm not sure I believe that, but I must rely upon your good grace."

"When will I see you next?" she asked, already eager for the encounter.

"Where will you be tonight?"

"A small dinner party. Unfortunately, nowhere you'll be or can be." She frowned. "Tomorrow? You could come to the park. And tomorrow evening is the Newcastle ball."

"I'll do my best to be in the park, but I will definitely make an appearance at the ball. You can help me decide if I should purchase a phaeton on Monday."

"You absolutely should, and I hope you'll drive it to the park. I can't wait to see it. Perhaps you can teach me to drive it."

He laughed again. "Fanny, the idea of you driving a high-perch phaeton strikes fear deep into my heart."

She swatted at his arm, grinning. "Perhaps it will be the one thing at which I will be graceful and thoroughly adept."

As they neared the stairs, he gave her a heated stare. "I can think of at least one thing at which you are quite adept."

"Oh, now you're breaking your own rules. That isn't well done of you."

His mouth spread in a smile that turned her knees to water. "No, it isn't." He made no apology, and she suddenly understood why some females swooned. "Let us hurry. I need to take my leave before I reach an embarrassing state once more."

"We wouldn't want that," she murmured. She did, in fact, want that and looked forward to the day when she could coax him to that state and let the consequences be damned.

Chapter Four

AS HE SETTLED into his coach for the ride back to Bolton Street, a smile teased David's mouth. He'd never met a woman like Fanny. She was so genuinely charming and unabashedly alluring.

And yet a voice in the back of his mind—his father's voice—kept reminding him that he had a duty, a promise. A promise he'd made to a dying man...

He closed his eyes and rested his head back against the squab, allowing that memory to wash over him, but just for a moment. He never could have foreseen meeting Fanny again here in London or the strong connection he felt to her.

The coach pulled to a stop in front of his house, and he didn't wait for the footman to open the door before jumping out and striding inside. The butler, Trask, welcomed him into the hall. "The countess and your uncle have arrived, my lord."

He'd been expecting them, but his current frame of mind didn't encourage company. Perhaps he'd be fortunate to learn they were resting. "Where are they now?"

"Awaiting your arrival in the drawing room."

Of course they were. Quashing his annoyance—which was really directed at himself—he handed his hat and gloves to Trask. "Thank you."

Ascending the stairs, he did his best to push his frustration aside and summoned a smile as he walked into the drawing room. "Welcome to London, Mother, Uncle."

His father's brother stood upon David's entry. Uncle Walter wasn't as tall as David's father had been, but his hair was less gray and his eyes more so, and his frame more athletic. In some ways, David supposed he took after him, but then they did share blood.

Uncle Walter came forward and clasped him in a brief but warm hug. Walter had never married and had moved into the dower house at Huntwell when David's grandfather had died a few years ago. It was unclear where he would live once David's mother moved there. But then that wouldn't happen until David took a wife.

The unsettling sensation he'd had in the coach and really several times over the past few days—of promises not kept—stole over him before he tucked it away.

David went to his mother and leaned down to kiss her cheek. He took in her dove gray costume. "You've moved on from black, I see."

A handsome woman with blue eyes and brown hair streaked with gray and white, she smoothed the skirt of her gown over her knee. "It was time."

David felt a twinge of sorrow. He didn't like to think of things moving on without his father, but of course, they must. "Did you have a pleasant trip?"

"Yes, thank you." She smiled up at him and patted the space beside her on the settee. "Sit and tell me how things have been."

David dropped onto the settee, and his uncle took a chair across from them. He wanted to tell them about Fanny, that he'd met a young lady he wished to court, but he hesitated. "Very well. I am acclimating to things as you'd expect. I've made a few friends who are shepherding me through."

"Who are these friends?" his uncle asked.

"The Earl of Ware and Mr. Anthony Colton—his

father is Viscount Colton." And because it would impress his mother, he added, "And the Duke of Clare."

His mother nodded in approval. "Well done. Who else have you met? Have you made the acquaintance of Miss Stoke?"

And there it was. David tensed. "I haven't yet."

Mother's brow furrowed. "Why not? They are expecting you to call."

"They will understand I am busy adjusting to my new role."

"Of course they will," his uncle said, sending a glance toward the countess.

"Don't wait too long," Mother said. "It's good that I came to help you. Aren't you anxious to get on with things?"

Apparently not as keen as his mother was. "What things?" David knew bloody well what "things."

"You're in dire need of a countess. You've wasted time with your birds long enough."

Not nearly.

"Is this why you came out of mourning? To pester me about marriage? While I plan to wed, when I do so isn't your concern. Nor to whom."

"I am still in half mourning. I will only attend a few Society events, and I don't plan to dance, of course. But this isn't about me." She frowned at him and looked over at his uncle while giving an infinitesimal nod toward David. Clearly, she wanted him to intervene. David braced himself, for he knew Walter would.

His uncle cleared his throat and fixed David with a serious stare. "You made a promise to your father. And he made a promise to Yardley Stoke."

"I can't be required to fulfill a promise my father made before I was even born."

"Don't be ridiculous. Marriages have been arranged for centuries," his mother said, still frowning. "This was very important to your father, and if you can't honor his promise, then honor yours."

It had seemed an easy thing as he'd held his father's hand in those final hours. The infection had taken complete hold of him, and his moments of lucidity had become few. But during one such respite, his eyes had been clear when he'd asked David to honor a very specific request: marry the daughter of his dearest friend. They'd attended Cambridge together and had hoped to unite their families one day. While David hadn't ever met Miss Stoke, his father had, and he'd sworn she was beautiful and intelligent and would make him an excellent countess. His father had hoped she and David would fall in love as soon as they met. Then he'd retreated into his delirium once more, speaking of romantic, endless love and happiness that knew no equal.

David fought against the duty and the love he felt for his father tugging at him from within. "This is not an arranged marriage."

Uncle Walter spoke with a carefully bland expression that didn't reveal how he felt about the matter—which he often employed—and David didn't know. "Perhaps not legally, but your father thought of it as such, and I believe Stoke does as well."

"Does he?" David wasn't certain of that either. In fact, his father had said official promises had not been made—not to Miss Stoke and not to her father. Still, there was perhaps an expectation, and if he didn't mean to at least attempt to see if he and Miss Stoke would suit, he should inform them immediately.

David abruptly stood, eager to quit the room and this conversation. He missed his father dreadfully, and he hated the idea of disappointing him. And yet, how could he turn away from the incomparable Fanny?

His mother looked up at him, her lips pressed in a perturbed moue. "Where are you going?"

"I've a meeting with Graham."

"Oh." She seemed mollified by this excuse—David hoped Graham was about. "Do give him our best."

"Of course. He'll join us for dinner." He bowed to her, then turned to his uncle and inclined his head before stalking from the room.

He descended the stairs with speed and purpose, agitation propelling him to his study, where, thankfully, Graham sat at his desk poring over ledgers. He looked up as David walked in.

"I hear the countess and Walter have arrived."

"Yes."

Graham started to rise, but David waved him back down. "Sit. I'm getting a drink. Do you want one?"

"When would I refuse?"

Never. David went to the sideboard and poured two glasses of the whisky he'd brought back from a trip to Scotland two years ago. He delivered one to Graham, who received it with an appreciative nod. "To what do I owe the pleasure of drinking with you at this hour?"

David slumped into the chair next to the desk with his legs sprawled out in front of him. He took a long draught of the liquor and briefly closed his eyes as he rolled it over his tongue before swallowing.

He turned a weary expression toward Graham, who sipped his drink. "I have a vexing dilemma."

"Allow me to help. If I can."

"I've met someone."

Graham nodded slowly. "I suspected as much. You were being rather evasive yesterday regarding your social interest."

David arched a brow as he stifled a chuckle. "Social interest?"

"You've never had any before, and suddenly you wanted to attend a bloody ball? I didn't believe that for a moment. It had to be a woman." He sipped his whisky and sat forward in his chair, setting the glass on the desk before him. "Who is she?"

"I met her over the Christmas holiday while I was out for a walk. She's the sister-in-law of the Duke of Clare."

Graham blew out a breath with a slight whistle. "Well, that ought to have pleased your mother."

"I didn't tell her. She immediately brought up Miss Stoke."

Graham's ebony brows shot up, and he nodded. "Of course she did. And honestly, if you'd told me about this woman yesterday, *I* would have brought up Miss Stoke."

David scowled at him. "Not you too."

"You promised your father you'd marry her." Graham paused before continuing. "I know how much you loved him, how much you miss him, but that was a promise you never should have made."

A bitter taste vaulted into David's throat. "That's easy for you to say. Your father is still among the living."

Graham's dark eyes narrowed. "My father wouldn't have asked me to marry someone I'd never met."

Anger roiled in David's chest. "No, he'd just browbeat you into taking a position you never wanted."

Graham picked up his glass and took a leisurely sip, but his gaze glittered with suppressed irritation. "If I didn't want to be here, I wouldn't."

"If you had somewhere else to go."

Graham slammed his glass onto the desk, causing whisky to slosh up over the edge and send droplets across the ledger he'd been reading. "Don't direct your frustration at me. This is your mess to untangle, not mine."

David sat up straight and glared at his best friend. "Then help me bloody untangle it!" He rarely raised his voice. In fact, he had rarely surrendered to any emotion until the grief of his father's sudden death had overtaken him. Since then he'd been a bit more volatile—prone to things such as raising his voice or kissing young women he shouldn't.

One young woman.

Fanny.

He fell back against the chair and took another drink. "I'm being a prick."

Graham's black brows slanted up. "Yes."

"I want to honor my father—you know I do. No one was more important to me than him." His voice was low and nearly cracked. He swallowed and wetted his suddenly dry mouth with more whisky.

"Of course I know that. Just as I know that marriage should not be entered into lightly." Graham spoke from experience, given that his mother had left his father and abandoned Graham when he'd been just four. She'd claimed she hated being married and simply left.

"I've no plans to marry anyone."

Graham looked at him over the rim of his glass. "Not yet, but you will."

Feeling perhaps more irritated than when he'd arrived, David stood and left the study. He took the back stairs to his chamber on the second floor rather than chance meeting his mother or uncle. He still held his whisky and finished it as he entered his room.

Setting the glass down on a table, he pulled at his cravat to expose his throat. He took a deep breath in an effort to still the conflict in his mind. He wanted to court Fanny. He felt beholden to at least meet Miss Stoke. Perhaps she'd be vapid or cruel, and he could dismiss her immediately.

He doubted she was either of those things. If Father had liked her and thought her worthy of marrying his son, she was likely a model young woman. He ought to at least meet her.

And if he liked her?

Cursing, he strode into his dressing chamber and poured water from the ewer into the basin. He splashed the tepid liquid over his face, mindless of it trickling down his neck.

He couldn't torture himself like this. He'd made no promises to Fanny and hadn't made any directly to Miss Stoke or her father. He would make his own choices.

Why, then, did he feel as if he were trapped in a cage?

❧·3·☙

FANNY SURVEYED THE arranged seating in the drawing room. In a few minutes, guests would start arriving to hear Fanny's proposal for a workhouse. She'd extended invitations to listen to a "new charitable endeavor" and looked forward to discussing her idea in detail. She was a bit nervous wondering if they'd support her.

Ivy came into the drawing room, her hand resting on the curve of her stomach. "Leah is with her nurse, so I am yours to command. Has anyone arrived yet?"

"No, but I expect them at any moment." Fanny was prepared for ten or so guests, including Sarah and Lavinia and their friend Miss Jane Pemberton, as well as Ivy's friends, Lucy, the Countess of Dartford, Aquilla, the Countess of Sutton, Emmaline, the Marchioness of

Axbridge, and Nora, the Duchess of Kendal. Nora's mother-in-law, the Countess of Satterfield, was also expected and was perhaps bringing some other ladies.

Aquilla arrived first. Fanny knew her well and wasn't at all bothered when she and Ivy bent their heads together and exchanged stories of motherhood. Sarah came next with her mother, and Fanny went to greet them.

Mrs. Tabersham and Jane came in right after Sarah and Lady Colton, and after exchanging a few pleasantries, the younger women separated from the mothers.

"How was the Newcastle ball?" Fanny asked. She hadn't seen Sarah since the dinner party they'd both attended Friday night.

"Oh, like any other ball," Sarah said. "Jane and I amused ourselves trying to discern which gentlemen were wearing padding. There seemed an excessive amount of abnormally thick calves."

Jane's eyes sparkled with mirth. *"Excessive."*

Fanny grinned. "I'm sorry I missed that. Leah was having trouble with her tooth coming in, and Ivy didn't want to leave her." Fanny didn't blame her, though she'd been disappointed to miss the ball. The ball? She didn't give two figs about the ball. She'd missed seeing David. "Was the Earl of St. Ives there?" She tried to sound casual in front of Jane, who wasn't aware of the near courtship between them. Was it nearly courtship? Or did kissing make it an actual courtship?

"Yes, he was there," Jane said. "I didn't see him dance. He was with an older woman and a gentleman."

Sarah glanced toward Fanny. "Anthony said that was his mother and uncle. They'd just arrived in town the day before."

The day before? That was when Fanny had seen him, and he hadn't mentioned it. Perhaps they'd arrived while he was here. And perhaps they were why he hadn't shown up at the park the following day. After missing him at both the park and the ball, Fanny had hoped to see him at church yesterday. Unfortunately, he hadn't been there either.

"Do you have a special interest in the earl?" Jane asked, smoothing a hand over the back of her upswept blonde hair.

Fanny darted a look toward Sarah to see if she should say anything, but Sarah only offered the barest shrug, which said, *I have no idea.*

Thankfully, she was saved from having to answer by the arrival of Nora and Lady Satterfield. They were accompanied by another pair of ladies who appeared to be mother and daughter. Fanny greeted them as they entered the drawing room, and Ivy joined her.

Lady Satterfield smiled warmly. "Thank you so much for your kind invitation. I'm delighted to be a part of such a wonderful endeavor. As I mentioned I would do, I brought some other interested parties, and I do believe Mrs. Greville will also be joining us. And perhaps a few others. I hope you don't mind that I shared the meeting with so many."

"Of course not," Fanny said. "The more hands we have, the faster this will come to fruition." She looked toward the women who'd accompanied the countess.

"I am remiss," Lady Satterfield said. Her gaze went deferentially to Ivy. "Duchess, allow me to present Mrs. Yardley Stoke and her daughter, Miss Arabella Stoke." She turned to the Stokes. "This is the Duchess of Clare and her sister, Miss Fanny Snowden."

"Pleased to meet you," Fanny said. "I'm so glad you came today."

"We are always eager to help those in need," Mrs. Stoke

said.

They moved aside as others began to arrive, and Fanny spent the next several minutes welcoming everyone. Just as they were about to begin, the tap of a walking cane hitting the floor at intervals brought a smile to Ivy's face. Fanny knew it would be her former employer.

The Viscountess Dunn walked in, surprisingly spry for a woman nearing seventy. She was petite but possessed a personality twice her size. Her sharp brown eyes assessed the room before landing on Ivy. She smiled widely. "Duchess."

Ivy went and embraced her in a hug. "It's so lovely to see you. How was your trip?"

Lady Dunn had been in Cornwall enjoying fairer climes for the past several months. "Pleasantly boring. I am glad to be back. I won't go for so long again. As it was, I cut my time short by a fortnight. I was delighted to hear of this meeting from Lady Satterfield."

The aforementioned countess came forward to greet her. "I didn't think you'd come—you only arrived yesterday."

Lady Dunn lifted her cane. "Bah. I wouldn't miss a thing hosted by my dear Ivy, or her sister." She sent a warm smile to Fanny. They'd met last summer when Lady Dunn had paid a visit to Stour's Edge to meet Leah. "But I am a tad late, and I don't wish to delay your business. Let us get on with it!"

As Ivy guided the viscountess toward a seat, Fanny overheard Lady Dunn say, "I am not surprised Clare has filled you with child again. You brought that man's life to a careening halt. Please give him my love."

Ivy laughed softly. "Of course I will. He'll be sorry he missed you."

Taking her place in front of the assembled guests,

Fanny suddenly felt a bit nervous. What if no one wanted to support her idea? For some reason, she was afraid that a workhouse would be less appealing than a hospital or foundling home.

"Thank you all for coming today," she said loudly. "As you know, my sister and I are devoted to the support and care of those in our society who are less fortunate."

As Fanny spoke the words, her skin prickled with unease. Looking around the opulent drawing room, she saw a collection of women who wore rich fabrics and were adorned with beautiful and, in many cases, unnecessary accessories. A selection of tea and cakes was laid out on a table that bore silver and crystal. It was all so…expensive. While Fanny hadn't been poor, she'd come from a much different background, as had Ivy. One in which they had chores to complete and learned to sew for utilitarian purposes, not just to embroider. She exchanged a look with Ivy, who gave her a tiny, encouraging nod.

Fanny continued, "There are many places where someone may seek care or shelter, and in some cases support to help them provide for themselves. I would like to launch an endeavor that will provide care and shelter, but also hope for the future. How many of you have visited a workhouse?"

Several of the attendees lifted their hands or nodded.

"Then you know that those in the workhouse perform a service in exchange for their food and shelter. I would like to found a different sort of workhouse, one that will train the inmates in a field in which they could then find employment. We would train them to be governesses or teachers, cooks or maids, seamstresses or weavers."

"How can we be sure they would find employment?" Nora asked.

"That's one thing the staff will need to be able to do—help these souls find a permanent position. My hope is that our involvement will support that effort."

Mrs. Stoke lifted her hand. "Are you suggesting we provide references for these women?"

Lady Dunn turned her head toward the woman. "That's what it sounds like to me, and I think it's a wonderful idea."

Mrs. Stoke's face turned a dull shade of pink. "I wasn't sure," she said quietly. "It is a good idea."

"Thank you." Fanny wanted to smooth any ruffled feathers. "I appreciate your questions as well as your votes of confidence." She smiled pointedly at both Mrs. Stoke and Lady Dunn.

"How did you arrive at this innovative scheme?" Lady Satterfield asked.

For a moment, Fanny's brain arrested. Her gaze darted to Ivy. Her green eyes met Fanny's in unspoken communication. Ivy's history in a workhouse was a secret they hoped would remain buried.

Fanny offered a bright smile and a shrug. "It came to me as I worked with my sister on various charitable efforts. Growing up in Yorkshire, I saw plenty of young women who would benefit from formal training." That was certainly true. Her and Ivy's background was firmly working class. Their father made furniture and was proprietor of a cabinetry shop, and they lived on a farm that provided most of their food.

The conversation continued, and by the end of Fanny's presentation, everyone in the room was excited about her project. The final question, from Emmaline, asked where the workhouse would be located.

"It seems as though it should be here in London," Fanny said. "Yet I can't help think of where I am from in

Yorkshire."

Aquilla looked around the room. "Perhaps we can start one here and, based upon its success, because of course it will be successful, we can then establish one in Yorkshire."

There were universal murmurs of agreement, and Fanny felt a swell of pride and excitement. "Wonderful," she said. "The first thing we must do is find a suitable location."

"Or build one," Lady Dunn said. "Though I daresay that would be rather expensive."

"Yes," Fanny agreed. "We will definitely need to raise a good deal of funds."

Ivy stood. "My husband will be assisting us with the financial organization." This was, unfortunately, necessary. It was frustratingly impossible to have an entirely woman-run endeavor. However, if any gentleman would help in the least intrusive way possible, it would be West.

"I'm sure Ned would be eager to help," Aquilla put in. Fanny recalled that Aquilla's husband was heavily involved in supporting asylums and could actually provide useful assistance.

"Thank you," Fanny said. "And now, please enjoy some refreshments! There is ratafia and lemonade along with cakes and biscuits at the back of the room."

Most of the women stood, and conversation immediately picked up.

Miss Stoke came toward Fanny with a tentative smile. "This is such a wonderful project. However did you find the courage to propose it?"

"I don't think it was courage. More likely blind naïveté." Fanny laughed. "In all honesty, I credit my sister. Ivy has such a compassionate and devoted heart."

And without assistance from a benevolent person such as these women here today, her life would be quite different. As would Fanny's. She'd be married to Mr. Duckworth and probably fat with his child.

"I'm sure it helps that she's a duchess," Miss Stoke said. "Money and position allows many things." There was no bitterness or jealousy to her statement, but Fanny wondered at its origin. She was correct, of course, so perhaps it was nothing more than an honest observation. Still, Ivy was so much more than her title or wealth.

"It does, but Ivy would be the first to tell you that it's precisely because of those things that she has a duty to help."

Miss Stoke's mouth spread into a pretty smile. "I agree. I am very much looking forward to helping, however I can." She leaned closer and kept her voice low. "We don't have a very lofty position, but my parents are hoping my marriage will change that."

"Are you betrothed?" Fanny asked politely.

"Not yet, but I will be. To an earl." Her eyes shone with anticipation, and Fanny had to keep herself from saying she hoped she would be too. It was far too soon to expect a proposal from David, but she certainly wished for things between them to progress.

"I shall look forward to the announcement," Fanny said. "And your participation in our endeavor. You should meet my friends Lady Northam, Miss Sarah Colton, and Miss Jane Pemberton." Fanny escorted her to where the trio stood together and made the introductions.

Some time later, when the room was finally empty of guests, Leah's nurse brought her in to see Ivy, who scooped her daughter up with a happy smile. "How is my girl?" Ivy nuzzled the baby nose to nose, then looked over to the nurse. "How is the tooth coming?"

"I think we're through the worst of it," the nurse said.

Leah grabbed the front of Ivy's dress and tugged, causing Ivy to chuckle. "Someone is hungry, I think." She shot a glance to the nurse. "I'll bring her up in a bit. Thank you."

The nurse inclined her head before turning and leaving the room. Ivy lowered herself onto the settee and dropped the front of her gown to expose her laced-front corset, which she quickly and expertly loosened. Tugging down the top of her chemise, she gave Leah free access to her breast to which her daughter happily latched on.

Fanny sat in a chair adjacent to her sister. "That went very well."

"It did. Are you excited to get started?"

"I am." She couldn't stop thinking about the question regarding how she'd come up with this idea. "When Lady Satterfield asked—"

Ivy didn't even let her finish the thought. "I could tell it gave you a start. It did me too, but I've stopped worrying about whether people will find out."

"You wouldn't care?"

"I would, but only insofar as it would reflect poorly on Leah and her sibling." She cradled her daughter gently and looked down with a loving gaze that pulled at Fanny's heart. She never recalled her mother looking at any of them that way. Ivy speared Fanny with a confident stare. "The only people who know of my background are you, West, and a small number of my dearest friends. And Bothwick, of course, but he's too afraid of West to ever say anything."

Viscount Bothwick was the man who'd stolen Ivy's innocence, promising to marry her and getting her with child, then abandoning her. "He's all but gone from Society," Fanny said.

Ivy nodded. "Ever since West called him out in Bath a year and a half ago. Everyone thinks he simply insulted me and the fact that I was a paid companion. Our…history remained secret and will continue to be so."

Fanny was still relatively new to Society, but she knew if a duchess were found to have been a former inmate at a workhouse and had given birth to a bastard, the resulting scandal would shake the ton to its core. Thankfully, it seemed that would never come to pass.

Chapter Five

THERE WERE SO many people at the Webley rout, David could barely move. Still, he sliced his way up the stairs, using the advantage of his ascension to scan the hall below. There was no sign of Fanny.

He continued up to the drawing room where the crowd was a bit less dense. At last he located her, standing near the windows overlooking the street below. Her tall, lithe frame was exquisitely draped in an ivory gown trimmed with indigo ribbon and pearls. That same color ribbon wound intricately through the curls piled atop her head. Single pearls dangled from her ears, and a strand of them nestled against her throat. She was elegant and beautiful and seemed utterly untouchable.

Untouchable. That was supposed to be him, but right now, the word fit her better. At least from his perspective. She was also captivating and alluring, and he wanted her. And yet he should turn his attentions elsewhere. The promise he'd made burned in his mind.

Fanny turned her head, and their eyes connected. He walked through the crowd toward her, as if drawn by a powerful magnet. When he drew near, he belatedly realized she wasn't alone. Her sister stood at her side, and David bowed first to her and then to Fanny.

"Good evening, Duchess, Miss Snowden."

"Good evening, Lord St. Ives," the duchess said. "If you'll excuse me for a moment, I wish to speak with a friend." She glanced toward her sister before gliding away.

David looked after her before turning toward Fanny. "That's the second time your sister has left you alone with me."

Fanny laughed. "I hardly call *this* alone. It's a wonder we can draw a full breath."

"It's worse downstairs," he said, relaxing in her company. She never failed to put him at ease.

"Why do you think we came up here?" she asked jovially. "In any case, we won't be staying long. It's far too warm and close, and Ivy is uncomfortable in her current state."

David assumed she meant because the duchess was carrying. "Then I am doubly grateful to her for giving us a few moments."

She turned completely toward him, her gaze seeking his. "I missed seeing you at the park the other day."

"I'd intended to be there, but my mother and uncle arrived as I called on you. I've been a bit busy with them and with other nonsense."

Her brows arched briefly. "Nonsense?"

"All the things earls must do. I have an even greater respect for my father and wish I'd paid more attention to what he wanted to teach me before he died." Regret pierced through him. "I really thought we'd have more time."

"I'm sorry you didn't," she said softly. "I know what it's like to wish for more time with a loved one."

"Did you lose someone?"

She blinked as she glanced away. "No. I mean, yes. I'm sure your father would be very proud."

"That's what my mother says. With her and my uncle— my father's younger brother—here, I've been thinking about him more than usual."

"All of it good, I hope."

He smiled. "Yes. I've been walking in Hyde Park in the morning. My father and I used to take morning walks together when I was a child. That's how I became interested in birds. He always pointed them out to me, and then I would learn as much as I could about them to impress him with my knowledge."

Her eyes sparkled beneath the candlelight. "And did you?"

"I think so. He certainly tried to find every book about birds and ensure it was in our library."

"It sounds as though he loved you very much."

He had. David's heart squeezed. He wanted to change the subject. "I was disappointed when I couldn't find you at the Newcastle ball."

"My niece was suffering from cutting a tooth, and my sister didn't want to leave her. Without a chaperone, I had to remain at home."

"Devilish unfair, really. If you were a man, you could've gone by yourself."

She laughed in agreement. "Indeed." Her lids dropped a bit as she looked up at him, lending her a seductive air. "I was very sorry to miss seeing you at the ball. I was looking forward to abusing your toes."

Now he laughed. "Then I should be delighted you weren't there." He lowered his voice and leaned forward slightly, looking directly into her shining blue-green eyes. "To be clear, I was *not*."

She held his gaze for a moment before glancing about the room. "Are your mother and uncle here?"

"Yes. I left them downstairs." Hopefully, they would stay there. He didn't want to have to introduce everyone and move on, as would probably be expected. For whatever reason, whenever he was with Fanny, he could pretend he wasn't the earl and that his life was far less complicated.

Someone jostled David from behind, pushing him

forward so that he nearly crashed into Fanny. He clasped her waist to steady her. She lifted her hands and clutched at his shoulders. It would be a simple thing to lower his head and kiss her. Bloody hell, he *was* the Duke of Kisses. At least where she was concerned.

"Beg your pardon," the man who'd bumped him said with an apologetic grin. His gaze drifted to where David and Fanny touched. They both quickly dropped their hands.

Fanny rushed to say, "I'm fine." She looked up at David. "Thank you, my lord, for keeping me from falling."

"Terrible crush," the man said before moving on.

"I would glare at his departing back," Fanny said, "but that was rather nice."

As she flashed David a charming smile, his eye caught his uncle stepping into the drawing room and scanning the crowd. David assumed he was his uncle's mark and sought to avoid being spotted. Offering his arm to Fanny, he said, "Shall we walk?"

"Here?" She placed her hand on his sleeve. "If you can manage it. This really is very crowded. West and Ivy and I didn't plan to stay long."

David steered them toward the back of the room so they could duck out onto the terrace if necessary. "The Duke is here?"

"Yes, but he is also downstairs. Lord Webley wanted to speak with him about sheep."

"Sheep? Sounds like a conversation I should probably be a part of. We have sheep at Huntwell, and my father had been thinking of increasing the flock."

"Do you want to go find them?"

"Trade you for sheep? God, no."

Her laughter floated around him. "That's very nice of

you to say. Oh, here comes Ivy. It must be time for us to leave."

David was loath to let her go, but he must. And not just because her sister was bearing down on them. Turning toward her as she took her hand from his arm, he offered a bow. "It was a pleasure to see you this evening."

Her gaze settled warmly on his mouth, and he had the distinct impression she was thinking about their kiss. *Kisses.* "I hope it won't be long until I see you again."

"That is also my hope."

The duchess glanced at David but spoke to Fanny. "It is time for us to take our leave, I'm afraid."

"Yes, let's." She curtsied to David. "Good evening, my lord."

The duchess inclined her head toward David, then they picked their way toward the door. They passed relatively close to Uncle Walter, whose gaze now settled on David with purpose.

Exhaling in resignation, David met him near the center of the room. "Looking for me?"

"Yes. Your mother wanted me to fetch you back downstairs." He turned, expecting David to follow, which he did.

David couldn't help but stare at Fanny as she and her sister descended the stairs a few people in front of him and his uncle. He watched as they joined up with the Duke and made their way to the door, which was open to admit new arrivals.

"She's waiting for you over there," Uncle Walter said, gesturing to where his mother stood in the hall. She was not alone. Two women—one close in age to her and another who was young—stood with her. David instantly knew who they were—the Stokes.

His gaze drifted back to the door in the hope of

catching one last glimpse of Fanny. She was near the door, her head turned up toward him. Their eyes locked for what seemed forever but was in reality the barest moment, then she turned and was gone.

How he longed to follow her. But he had obligations, and they could no longer be avoided. He walked with his uncle to where his mother stood.

She gave him a reproving look before fixing a pleasant smile across her lips. "David, allow me to present Mrs. Stoke and her daughter, Miss Arabella Stoke."

They curtsied to him, and he bowed.

"This is my son, the Earl of St. Ives." The pride in her voice was unmistakable, and David had to remember that above all, she loved him and wanted him to be happy.

"I'm delighted to make your acquaintance finally," David said.

"Yes, finally." Mrs. Stoke laughed. "Yardley always planned to bring us to Huntwell for a visit, but it just never came about. We've been to London a few times, but you weren't with your father."

No, because he preferred the country. He directed his attention to Miss Stoke. She was far more petite than Fanny, with light brown hair and deep green eyes. "How do you find London?"

"It's exciting, my lord. There is so much to do and see."

"And what of that interests you?" David asked.

"I like visiting sites that predate the Great Fire. I appreciate history."

"She also enjoys riding in the park and dancing," Mrs. Stoke said with a laugh. "It's too bad there isn't dancing here, or you could see for yourself."

"I would say that's to Miss Stoke's benefit, for I am a rather awful dancer, I'm afraid."

His mother laughed too, and it was apparent the

mothers were doing their best to make a match. "He's not awful at all. And he just purchased the most gorgeous phaeton. You can see yourself in the shine of the black lacquer."

Mrs. Stoke's eyes gleamed with fascination. "One horse or two?"

"Two, of course," his mother answered. "Spectacularly matched bays. Their black tails are the exact color of the lacquer."

David was about to suggest that his mother take Mrs. Stoke for a ride but decided this was not the time or place for sarcasm.

"How splendid," Mrs. Stoke exclaimed. "I'm sure Arabella would be delighted to take a ride."

Blast. Now he'd have to avoid taking his phaeton to the park unless he wanted to take her for a ride. He'd wanted to take Fanny for a ride.

Blast again. He owed it to his father and the Stokes to give Miss Stoke a chance. And where did that leave Fanny?

Exactly where she was and had been. He'd made no promises to her. He suddenly longed to be as far away from this rout—and any other rout—as possible. He flashed everyone what he hoped was an amiable smile. "Please excuse me, but I've an appointment to keep at my club." He looked specifically at Miss Stoke. "I'm sure I'll see you again soon." He glanced toward Mrs. Stoke and then his mother, bidding them both good night before turning to go.

Walter walked with him a few steps. "Your club? We were supposed to attend another rout."

David gave him a beleaguered stare. "Must we? I've already met Miss Stoke, and wasn't that Mother's objective?"

A burst of laughter drew both of them to turn their heads toward the base of the staircase.

The Earl of Ware stood with a group of people who were all focused, rapt, on him. "The first race will be Wednesday, and we'll start with the ladies."

A woman next to Ware put her hand on his arm. "Truly?"

"Why should you miss all the fun?" Ware asked playfully.

The woman let out a rather undignified squeal, and everyone laughed. Whether they were laughing at her or simply buoyed from Ware's exciting announcement was unknown, but neither did it matter. Ware's gaze met David's. "Ah, here's my friend St. Ives. Have you all met him?" Ware made quick introductions as he beckoned David to join the group, indicating he should move to Ware's side.

When he finished, David leaned close to him and whispered, "Is there any chance you're leaving soon?" David belatedly realized he'd just left his uncle standing several feet away and hadn't bothered to include him in the group.

"In fact, I am. Why, do you want to tag along?"

"Yes, please. My mother and uncle are here, and they require my coach to attend another rout."

"And I can see you're done with routs for the evening." Ware chuckled. "We'll depart momentarily."

David smiled in gratitude, then went back to Walter. "I'll leave with Ware. You and Mother can take my coach."

Uncle Walter nodded. "Your mother only wants what's best for you."

"And that's Miss Stoke?"

"Your father thought so."

David flinched. "I'll see you tomorrow."

Before Walter could respond, David went back to Ware, who had just extricated himself from the group. "Where are you going, Ware?" a young buck asked.

"It's a mystery. Why don't you all place bets?" Ware's mouth curled into a sardonic smile as he collected his hat from a footman and exited the town house.

David took his hat from the same retainer—how they were managing accessories for people was beyond him—and followed Ware into the cool night.

"Will they really place bets?" David asked as they descended the steps to the pavement.

"They might." Ware shook his head. "Bloody ridiculous lot."

"But they hang on your every word."

Ware sent him a look heavy with cynicism. "Which is why they're ridiculous. Who the hell am I?"

Ware led him up the line of vehicles to a carriage with bright yellow trim. The coachman nodded at Ware and opened the door.

Ware climbed inside and sprawled on the forward-facing seat. David followed, depositing himself on the opposite side. "Thank you. Where are we headed?"

"I was considering a brothel, but perhaps that isn't on your agenda."

"Er, no." Since he was presently torn between two women, he didn't think he could possibly entertain a third, even if it was only for physical release. "I thought I'd go to the club."

"Fine by me." Ware turned to the open door and instructed the coachman to drive them to Brooks's. The door closed with a snap. He set his hat on the seat beside him. "We can gamble a bit, and if you change your mind about joining me for feminine companionship—well, not *joining* me, but accompanying me to an establishment—you are welcome to do so."

"I appreciate the invitation."

Ware cocked his head to the side as the coach jostled forward. "Do you? I think you'd rather stick a needle in your ear than come along."

"I'm a bit overwhelmed this evening. Too many women on my mind already."

"Well, that could be either wonderful or bloody annoying. Sounds as if it may be the latter."

"I find myself in a predicament and am unsure how to proceed." He knew how he ought to proceed—spend time with Miss Stoke and see if they would suit. In the meantime, he should stay far away from the temptation of Fanny. "The business of finding a wife is more complicated than I would prefer."

Ware twitched. "Don't ask me for advice. I have none to offer."

"Right, you don't plan to take a wife. Aren't you concerned about passing on your title? Your legacy?"

Ware snorted. "Trust me when I say no one would really want it." He waved a hand. "There's an heir somewhere along the line. I'm not concerned about the future of the title. Perhaps you shouldn't be either."

David wasn't sure if there was an heir besides himself. Uncle Walter had never married and had no children, and he and David's father had been the only sons in that branch. They must have cousins, but David didn't know who they were. Not that it mattered since David had every intention of doing his duty. But just the idea that he could choose a different path… He looked over at Ware. "You don't feel beholden to provide an heir?"

"Absolutely not. I'm aware that makes me an aberration, but there are many things that do that." His lips twisted into an enigmatic and almost sinister smile. "Now, tell me you're going to drive that stunning new phaeton in Wednesday's race."

The thought of racing again eclipsed his preoccupation with Fanny and Miss Stoke. Perhaps that was what he needed—a distraction. A calm stole over him, and he leaned back against the squab with a small smile.

"I wouldn't miss it."

Chapter Six

THE DAY OF the race was pleasant but cloudy, and every so often, a stiff breeze picked up and shook the trees. It also made the ribbons on Fanny's bonnet tickle her face.

Lavinia was playing chaperone for both Fanny and Sarah, which seemed a bit laughable since just a month or so before, they'd all needed chaperones. Lavinia's marriage had made her suddenly responsible. Or something like that. Society's rules were absurd.

They'd squeezed themselves into Lavinia's curricle. Her groom and, more importantly, her husband were riding behind them.

"Have you been practicing for the race?" Sarah asked Lavinia.

"A bit. Beck has been teaching me how to turn at a higher speed than I normally would." She glanced over at them, her brow creased. "It's much more difficult than you'd think."

"Oh, I don't know about that," Fanny said. "I think it sounds terribly challenging. But then I'd expect to topple the thing over."

They laughed, but Fanny hadn't been joking. Sometimes her clumsiness, though typically harmless, was rather frustrating.

Lavinia cast her a sidelong glance. "Are you hoping to see St. Ives today?"

"Always," Sarah answered with a laugh.

Fanny had gone walking in the park the past two mornings at varying hours in the hope of seeing him. At least she knew he'd be at the races today. Or so she believed. It seemed Fate wasn't always interested in ensuring their paths crossed, and yet how else could one explain the way they'd met?

Fanny decided to ignore the topic of David altogether. She was looking forward to spending time with her friends and cheering Lavinia. She wouldn't pin her hopes on seeing David. "Will there be wagering today?"

Lavinia drove them into the park. "Beck thinks so."

"Well, they'd better allow women to wager too," Sarah said with a sniff. "I brought money." She picked up her reticule and shook it.

Lavinia narrowed her eyes. "If we're driving, we're wagering." And if Lavinia put her mind to it, there would be no question. She possessed an indomitable force of will.

Several people were already congregated with their vehicles. It was just past noon, and Felix was directing the spreading of blankets and placement of hampers. "Did Felix arrange for food?" Fanny asked.

"Felix arranges for everything," Sarah said. "He's the consummate host. It's a wonder he doesn't host his own ball."

"Doesn't he need a wife for that?" Fanny asked.

Sarah waved her hand. "Not according to Felix. He doesn't need a wife for *anything*."

Lavinia coughed. "I would beg to differ…" They laughed as her meaning was clear—at least to Fanny.

And apparently to Sarah too, for she said, "I'm fairly certain he doesn't even need a wife for *that*. Rumor says he doesn't want for female companionship."

After parking the curricle, Lavinia's groom helped Sarah and Fanny to descend, while Beck assisted his wife. Fanny noted the way his hands lingered on her waist as well as how close they stood together. She turned her head to scan the people gathered, searching for David. Sarah had been right. She was always looking for him.

And there he was, driving his sparkling new phaeton. He barely drew to a stop before he was swarmed with people fawning over his vehicle. Probably over him too. He was new to town and an earl, which made him infinitely interesting to a Society that feasted on information and gossip.

Though she was eager to go see him, Fanny stayed with her friends, which prompted Sarah to ask why she wasn't going over to him.

"He looks rather busy," Fanny said.

"And yet do you see how he's looking around?" Sarah was right again. His gaze sifted through the crowd until it landed on Fanny. Even at this distance, she detected the faint smile teasing his lips, and her heart missed a beat.

The Earl of Dartford drove up next in his flashy high-perch phaeton, passing by them to park next to David. He carefully helped Lucy, his countess, down.

"I didn't realize he'd emblazoned 'Daring' on the back," Sarah said with a laugh. He was still called the Duke of Daring, which referred to his adventurous activities.

"I wonder if Ivy has seen it," Fanny mused since Lucy was one of Ivy's closest friends. "Let's go take a look." That would distract her from David.

She and Sarah linked arms and went to where the Dartfords stood next to the vehicle. Several others had come over to speak with them, but Lucy immediately broke away to greet Fanny and Sarah. "Have you come to watch?" she asked brightly.

"Yes," Sarah said. "Lavinia is going to race her curricle."

"How exciting!" Lucy adopted an apologetic tone. "I am also racing, and I'm afraid this phaeton is hard to beat." She gestured to "Daring."

"You're driving Dartford's phaeton?"

Lucy narrowed her dark eyes. "Oh, it doesn't just belong to him." She laughed. "When I married the Duke of Daring, I'm afraid I became the Duchess of Daring rather effortlessly."

"Who are we supposed to support now?" Sarah asked.

"Both of them." Fanny looked over toward Lavinia, who still stood near her curricle with Beck. Felix had joined them. "But if you're wagering, put your money on Lucy," she whispered.

Sarah laughed but nodded with determination. "I'm going to ask Felix how I can do that." She took herself off, leaving her with Lucy, who was eyeing David's phaeton, which was next to theirs. "St. Ives has a beautiful new phaeton. But it needs personalization." Lucy winked at Fanny who imagined the word "Kisses" in bright red letters along the back of David's phaeton. Perhaps she'd suggest it.

Fanny blinked at Lucy. "I look at these vehicles and wonder how in the world you don't pitch right over the moment you attempt a turn."

"It is rather challenging, but that's what makes it fun—learning how to master the sport. Andrew designed the suspension himself so that it would take corners more smoothly at higher speeds."

"Did he? How enterprising."

Lucy's gaze settled on her husband. "He's rather brilliant." As if they were somehow connected, the earl turned his head and sent his wife a provocative smile that made Fanny feel as though she were intruding. He beckoned for Lucy to join him.

"Will you excuse me?" Lucy asked.

"Of course." Fanny walked around the flashy phaeton

and came face-to-face with David.

He grinned at her, and again her heart skipped. "Good afternoon, Miss Snowden."

"Good afternoon, my lord." She glanced toward his vehicle. "Your new phaeton is splendid. Would you show it to me?"

"It would be my pleasure." He offered her his arm.

She placed her hand on the sleeve of his bottle-green coat. "Are you truly going to race? You just purchased this phaeton. How can you possibly be ready?"

"I am not new to racing," he said, surprising her. "In my younger days, I was rather obsessed with it. I did practice yesterday, and I'm happy to say it all came back to me rather easily."

"You were obsessed with something other than birds?"

He looked down at her with a glint of mischief in his eye. "It's been known to happen." The response seemed tinged with innuendo. She found herself wondering when they could possibly kiss again. She hoped it would be soon.

She'd been about to tell him that she'd gone walking in the park in search of him, but a bell sounded, prompting them all to turn toward the source.

Felix stood on a small platform and spoke through a horn to amplify his voice. "Good afternoon, racers and spectators! If you'd care to place a wager, come over and see Mr. Kinsley." He indicated a gentleman seated at a small table to his right. Sarah was there, and Kinsley was writing something in a ledger.

"That's my secretary," David said.

"Mr. Kinsley?"

David nodded. "Ware was in search of someone who was available to record the wagers and keep the funds. Graham is a wonder with numbers. With anything, really.

The man's intellect is astonishing."

"Wherever did you find him?" Fanny asked.

"Kinsleys have been secretaries to the Earls of St. Ives for generations. After my father passed away last fall, Graham's father retired."

Kinsley didn't look like the bookish sort. Though he was seated, the impressive breadth of his shoulders was evident. He tilted his head up toward Sarah and smiled in such a way that every woman in the park would have sighed if they'd seen it. Fanny certainly did.

"Oh dear, don't tell me you're going to develop a tendre for him too," David said.

Fanny laughed and turned her head to him. "Definitely not." How could she when her heart was already being pulled in another direction?

Felix continued with his announcements. "The first race will be the ladies and will begin shortly. If you plan to race, I should already have your name recorded in the ledger. If you have not entered your name, please do so immediately." He flashed a smile before continuing. "Gentlemen who are racing, please also ensure your name is recorded. Ladies, please report to the starting line, and we'll draw names for race assignments!"

Fanny looked up at David. "What does that mean?"

"Each race will be two people. The winners of the race will advance to next week's races. Ware imagines a tournament over a handful of weeks." David cocked his head. "He's tireless when it comes to amusements."

Fanny watched as Lavinia drove her curricle to the start. "I'm nervous for Lavinia. How can a curricle compete with a phaeton?"

"Maybe she won't have to." David turned to her. "I'm afraid I must leave you to go enter my name."

"That's all right," she said. "I'm going to join Sarah."

"Then you can walk with me." He guided her to where Sarah stood near the wagering table.

Fanny took her hand from his arm. "Good luck!"

He bowed. "Thank you."

Fanny went to Sarah and watched him walk over to Felix.

"I see you found him," Sarah said.

"By accident. I walked around Lucy's phaeton, and there he was."

"I'm sure," Sarah murmured with a smile.

"Did you place your wager?"

"I can't yet," she said. "As soon as they draw the racers, I can wager. I'm hoping Lucy and Lavinia aren't racing each other."

"I hope so too. Though if they aren't and they both win, they could end up facing each other next week."

"Yes, I just heard that Felix intends to do this until there's a champion."

Fanny laughed. "It's a modern-day jousting tournament."

Sarah grinned. "And with women too! How revolutionary."

They chatted while waiting for the race to begin, focusing mostly on discussing the ladies' hats. "Is there such a thing as a racing hat?" Sarah wondered.

"Not specifically that I'm aware of."

Felix returned to his platform with his horn and announced the four ladies' races. Luck was with them, for Lucy and Lavinia were not racing each other. Sarah went to place her wager and quickly returned to Fanny's side.

"I bet on both of them," she said. "But I admit I put most of my funds on Lucy." She winced slightly as she glanced toward Fanny.

"I would have too," Fanny said with a laugh. "And

Lavinia wouldn't fault you for it. Why are you wagering?"

Sarah lifted a shoulder. "Unlike you, I have no marital prospects and haven't ever. It seems prudent to plan for my inevitable spinster future."

Fanny turned toward her friend. "It is not *inevitable*. There are plenty of gentlemen."

"I'm beginning to accept the likelihood, and, honestly, the freedom is rather enticing." She shot a look at Mr. Kinsley behind his desk. "It's too bad he's not on the market."

"How do you know he's not?"

Sarah tipped her head to the side and blinked at Fanny. "My parents would never allow me to marry a secretary."

Fanny couldn't help but think of her sister and West. His mother despised the fact that her son had married a commoner from the working class. "That's silly. What if you fell in love?"

Sarah laughed. "My parents don't care about that. I should say they hope that I fall in love, but it would have to be with an acceptable gentleman."

For the first time, Fanny wondered if her background would be a problem when it came to marriage. Her mind naturally went to David. Would he care? He didn't seem to, but then she had the advantage of now being connected to a duke.

The course was a U-shape, but with sharp corners instead of a curve, which would require expert turning. Fanny hoped Lavinia was prepared. The first race didn't feature Lavinia or Lucy, but it was exciting nonetheless. Both drivers raced curricles, and it was a very close finish.

Lavinia's race was next, and Sarah and Fanny clutched hands as Felix sounded the bell to start. Lavinia's opponent was driving a high-perch phaeton. At the first corner, one of the vehicle's wheels left the ground and the driver shrieked. Sarah's grip tightened on Fanny's hand as the woman worked to keep her horses from dashing off the course. Lavinia easily raced past her, and crossed the finish line well before the phaeton.

"She won!" Sarah hugged Fanny, and they laughed with glee.

The next race began, but they were focused on Lavinia, who had turned her curricle over to the groom so that she could join Beck. Lavinia grinned widely as they approached, and Beck's pride was evident.

"You did it!" Sarah exclaimed, rushing to hug her friend.

Lavinia adjusted her glasses as she stepped back, then hugged Fanny. "I was just telling Beck that I think I might like a phaeton instead. I rather enjoyed that."

"We'll discuss it," Beck said, his brow darkening. "I didn't enjoy watching the other driver's wheel leave the ground."

"Yes, well, I'll be better at it." She winked at him.

The third race concluded, but Fanny couldn't have said a thing about it. She turned to the start, where Lucy was poised in her *Daring* phaeton. "Lucy's ready."

"This should be lively!" Lavinia said.

It was a phaeton against a phaeton, though no one would characterize Lucy's vehicle as a regular version. Felix started the race, and Fanny held her breath as the two women sped toward the first turn.

The other driver got off to a faster start, but Lucy's turn was tighter. And her wheels stayed firmly on the ground. They ran close together, but at the second turn, Lucy ducked her head and turned sharply. This time, one wheel barely lifted from the ground. She didn't even flinch. She came out ahead and raced over the line in front.

Cheers filled the park, and Sarah squealed. "I won! I

mean, Lucy won!"

There were more hugs, and this time they all hurried to the finish line where the Earl of Dartford swept his wife from the phaeton and lifted her in a circle. "To the Duchess of Daring!"

Lucy laughed as he set her back to earth.

"Well done, ladies!" Felix's voice boomed through the horn. "We've just drawn the names for the men's races, and I've an announcement. To make things interesting, the men will take a passenger—a lady. If a lady would like to ride, she may offer a favor to the gentleman of her choice."

"This really is like a jousting tournament," Sarah said wryly.

Lavinia frowned. "We were not offered that enhancement." She strode toward Felix.

Beck chuckled. "Oh, he's poked the wrong bear." He stalked after her.

Fanny picked David out near the starting area. Should she offer him a favor? It seemed a public declaration of…something. And what was wrong with that?

Sarah moved closer to stand next to her. "You should do it."

Fanny turned her head. "Do what?"

Sarah rolled her eyes. "Offer him a favor. He'll accept it, of course."

Of course. "Will he?"

"Why do you doubt him? From everything you've said, it seems your relationship is progressing toward a natural, marital end."

Fanny supposed so, but she took nothing for granted. Not after what had happened to Ivy.

Sarah looped her arm through Fanny's. "Come on, then."

They walked toward the start, passing Lavinia, who was chastising Felix for not having the men offer favors to the ladies.

"I promise we'll do it next week. I hadn't thought of it yet." Felix held up his hands in surrender, and Beck laughed.

Anthony was nearby and also laughed. He looked at his sister. "Who are you offering a favor to, Sarah?"

"No one. And don't taunt me about it," she said sternly.

He blinked at her in mock innocence. "I would never dream of that."

"I'm sure you already have." Sarah sped up her pace, and Fanny rushed to keep up.

Several women had come to the starting area and were approaching the gentlemen, many of whom were married, and so it was just their wives making the offer.

Fanny took her arm from Sarah. "What should I give him?"

Sarah appraised her from head to toe, chewing her lip in thought. "A flower from your hat." She reached up and plucked a silk flower from the band of Fanny's bonnet. "Here."

A mix of anticipation and anxiety skittered along Fanny's nerves as she took the flower. She turned and found David, who stood alone. Gathering her courage, she strode toward him with purpose as she thought of what to say.

Arabella Stoke intercepted Fanny just before she reached David. "Good afternoon, Miss Snowden."

"Good afternoon, Miss Stoke." Fanny slowed her pace to be polite, but she was also afraid someone would beat her to David's side.

"I'm on my way to offer a favor," Miss Stoke said

brightly. "That's my earl."

The direction of her nod could not be disputed. Fanny stopped cold and turned her head toward the other woman. "St. Ives?"

Miss Stoke nodded.

She was going to marry *David*?

Fanny felt as though the ground beneath her was shaking and about to open up and swallow her in one piece. And for a moment, she wished it would. Then she looked at David and decided it should devour him instead.

"Are you going to offer one?" Miss Stoke asked, starting toward David once more.

Fanny fell in beside her, quickening her pace. "In fact, I am."

They arrived in front of him together, but it was Fanny who spoke first. She extended her hand, with the now-crumpled silk flower—she'd apparently crushed it in anger—toward him. "I'd like to offer you a favor, my lord, and so would Miss Stoke."

His eyes widened briefly, and his gaze moved from her to Miss Stoke.

Fanny dropped the flower into his palm, careful not to touch him and stepped aside.

Miss Stoke gave him a rose-colored ribbon, clearly taken from the sleeve of her gown. "Here is my favor."

Holding a favor in each hand, David looked between them, and Fanny nearly laughed at the conundrum clearly pronounced in his features. She would have felt sorry for him if she wasn't so angry.

Forcing a smile, she batted her eyelashes at him and asked, "Whom do you choose?"

Chapter Seven

‹·E·3·›

HELL AND THE DEVIL.

David couldn't seem to form words. Fanny's blue-green eyes sparked with indignation, which meant she had to know about Miss Stoke. But how could she? Unless Miss Stoke had said something? But what could that have been?

Miss Stoke, on the other hand, looked...confused. She wore a half frown as she glanced toward Fanny, then returned her attention to David.

"Well, my lord?" she prompted softly.

He had to make a decision. He wanted Fanny—of course. There was no decision to be made. Yet, his father's voice echoed in his brain, *"Promise me, David. It would mean everything to me…"*

That hadn't been a decision either. David had made the promise, willing to say or do anything to give his father comfort. Or keep him from dying. It was absurd to think that making a promise would save his life, but it was the only power he'd had in that moment when he'd felt utterly helpless.

He was saved by the arrival of Ware, who looked at the two favors in his hands. "Looks as though you need help."

David blinked at him, wondering what that could be but eager for it just the same. "I do, indeed."

"Another gentleman also had two favors. He chose a number between one and ten and whispered it in my ear. The women chose numbers, and the one closest to what he'd picked will be his passenger. Does that sound acceptable?" He looked from David to Fanny and Miss Stoke.

"It's acceptable to me," Fanny said, her voice smoldering. Oh yes, she *had* to know.

Miss Stoke nodded primly. "It is to me as well."

David tensed, hoping it would turn out the way he hoped...

Ware leaned his ear toward David. Right, he had to choose a number. David didn't even think before whispering next to Ware's head.

With a nod, Ware straightened. "Who extended their favor first?"

"I did," Fanny said.

"Then I shall allow Miss Stoke to choose first." Ware turned his head to her. "What number do you choose?"

"Five."

The tension in David tightened as he awaited Fanny's guess. Ware pivoted to her. "Miss Snowden?"

She didn't hesitate nor did she look at David. "Three." Her tone was bold and confident.

Because she was right.

"Brilliant!" Ware exclaimed. "You guessed it exactly." He turned a sympathetic eye to Miss Stoke. "My apologies, Miss Stoke. There's always next week! Provided St. Ives wins." He chuckled before taking himself off.

David handed the ribbon back to Miss Stoke. "I'm sorry too."

"It's all right," she said brightly. "I'll still cheer for you." She turned to look at Fanny. "Enjoy the race, Miss Snowden."

Fanny reached out and touched the other woman's hand. "I shall, and next week, it will be your turn. I only offered the favor because I wanted to race. I should have approached another gentleman."

"It's quite all right," Miss Stoke said. "I was a bit nervous to ride in the high-perch phaeton. This gives me time to work up my courage." She gave Fanny's hand a squeeze. "You must tell me all about it afterward."

"I'll do that." Fanny slid an accusatory glance toward David, and he suddenly wondered if he'd hoped for the right woman to ride with him. Fanny was going to give him an earful.

Which he deserved.

Miss Stoke wished him luck, then turned and went back to where most of the spectators were congregated, including her mother. David hated disappointing the young woman.

He plucked Fanny's flower from the palm of his hand and looked into her eyes. "Thank you for the favor. Allow me to escort you to my phaeton." He held out his arm.

She stared at it a moment, then lightly placed her hand on him, barely touching his sleeve as if it were made of something very toxic. "I understand congratulations are in order."

David suffered a shaft of sheer panic. What had Miss Stoke told her? "For what?"

"Miss Stoke told me you are to be married."

The hell she had. "We are not engaged."

"Perhaps not formally, but she told me it was forthcoming."

The racers were moving toward their vehicles, and since they were the second race, he started steering her to his phaeton. "She told you this just now?"

"Actually, she came to my meeting the other day about—" She shook her head. "Never mind what it was about. She came to my meeting, where I met her for the first time. She said she was going to become engaged to an earl. Then today she told me that earl is you." She fixed him with an irritated glower.

Hell and the devil.

He couldn't seem to stop thinking that. The curse was a litany in his head.

They'd reached the phaeton, and he pulled down the step and helped propel her up inside. He followed her and retracted the step before sitting beside her on the cushion.

David picked up the reins, allowing plenty of slack since they wouldn't be going anywhere yet. The first racers were just positioning themselves at the start. A hollow sensation in his chest seemed to expand inside him. "She expects I will marry her. I promised my father as much when he was dying." He heard the breath Fanny sucked in beside him and turned his head slightly. She looked up at him with a deep furrow in her brow. "He and her father were the best of friends and sought to unite our families. My father was so ill. I would have said anything." He *had* said anything.

"You're going to honor this promise," she said quietly

He couldn't tell if it was a question or not. "I'm not sure. I was… Until I met you." He shook his head. "That's not quite right. I planned to honor it even after I met you at Christmastide. But that's because I never thought to see you again. Then when I encountered you in London…" He smiled. "It seemed Fate wanted to give us a chance."

"You could also argue that Fate wants to give you and Miss Stoke a chance." Her tone had softened a bit, but she was still rigid beside him.

"Yes, you could. And therein lies my dilemma. I want to be with you, and yet I feel I owe it to my father to see if Miss Stoke and I would suit."

Fanny clasped her hands in her lap and looked down at them. "Do we even know if you and *I* would suit?"

The first race started, and cheers filled the air. But David was immune to the excitement. He was entirely focused on the woman beside him. "You guessed three."

She turned her head. "That's the number of times we've kissed."

"Exactly right," he whispered.

"You think because of that, we suit?"

He clutched the reins more securely and gave the horses the signal to move forward. "I think because of that, we share *something*. Don't you?"

She exhaled. "I did. I do." She pursed her lips and clenched her hands more tightly together. "But what of the promise you made to your father? If you don't give Miss Stoke a chance, you risk harboring a regret that could tear you up inside." She understood him so perfectly.

"How do you know me so well?"

"I don't. Not really. I just know that's how *I* would feel." She unclasped her hands and laid them flat atop her lap. "You didn't promise me anything."

No, he hadn't. Nevertheless, he felt as if he'd let her down. He drove the horses to the starting line and brought them to a stop just as the other racers finished.

"Oh goodness, we're next," she said, sounding nervous. She clutched the side of the phaeton with her left hand. "I won't fall out, will I?"

"Not unless you leap from the vehicle."

She whipped her head around in alarm. "Why would I do that?"

He chuckled. "You wouldn't. That's the point." He briefly touched the hand that remained in her lap. "I'll make you this promise: you won't fall."

Her eyes narrowed skeptically. "Don't make promises you can't keep. You know how clumsy I am."

"If you fall out, the blame will be entirely mine."

"As much as I'd like to blame you for something, I will hope that I remain firmly in this seat."

He stared into her upturned face. "Trust me, Fanny," he said softly. "I would never let anything happen to you."

Her eyes lost every bit of their spark. "You are not in a position to say such things."

The bell sounded.

She elbowed him in the arm. "Go!"

Christ, he'd been so wrapped up in her that he'd paid no attention, and now he was starting late.

Hell and the devil.

Bracing his feet, he picked up the whip and plied the reins, hoping the horses would perform as well as they had yesterday during his practice. With new horseflesh, it was hard to know what to expect.

His opponent was also in a high-perch phaeton, but if the start was any indication, his horses didn't look as fast as David's. They approached the first turn. David concentrated on making his arc without losing much speed. "Hold on."

He didn't spare the slightest glance for Fanny as he completed the turn just behind the other racer. David's focus was entirely on driving the horses toward the second and final turn. He wouldn't have time to overtake the other phaeton before the turn, but if he came through it tight and fast, he could make the pass.

They rounded the bend marked by a small tree, and he felt the phaeton lift just slightly. It was nothing to him, but he heard Fanny swear under her breath.

Grinning, he still didn't chance a look in her direction. The spring air rushed over him as excitement pulsed in his blood. He worked the reins hard, pushing the horses to overtake the other phaeton. They were so close, but so was the finish. He applied the whip, and the team soared past the other racer and hit the line first.

Exhilaration washed over him as he lifted his whip hand in victory. Laughing, he turned to look at Fanny. She looked a bit…green.

His joy faded. "Fanny, are you all right?"

"I think I may be sick."

David dropped the whip and jumped down as quickly as he could. He hadn't even bothered with the step but now pulled it down and helped her to descend. Her foot caught, and she fell forward.

Scrambling to clasp her to him, David lost his balance and went sprawling backward. She landed on top of him, knocking the air from his chest. She pushed at him, but he didn't want to let her go before making sure she was all right.

However, she was insistent, renewing her efforts to push away from him. "David, if you don't let me go, I'm going to cast up my accounts all over you."

"Ware, a hand, please!" He called out to the nearest person he knew.

Ware dashed over and helped Fanny up just as she heaved. A few people gasped as everyone nearby turned to gape at her bent form.

Miss Colton rushed to her side and spoke softly to her.

Fanny held up her hand and a moment later straightened, then smiled widely as if she were the one who'd just won the race. And she may very well have been given the cheers she received.

She laughed and pressed her hands to her cheeks. "That was a little faster than I'd anticipated!"

David went to her and bowed. "My apologies. I do hope you don't suffer any ill effects."

"From the race? No, I don't think I shall." Her meaning was clear—any ill effects she suffered would be because of *him*.

He hated this. He wanted to reassure her. But of what? "I hope to see you tonight at Almack's so you can obliterate my feet into the floor."

She delivered him a saucy stare. "I do not have a voucher to Almack's, but perhaps Miss Stoke does. Good-bye, my lord."

"Not good-bye," he said softly but with great urgency.

She said nothing before she turned and walked away with Miss Colton.

"Well done," Ware said. "You're in for next week." Then he took himself back to the platform, where he apologized for the delay.

Next week. When he wouldn't have Fanny as his passenger. Hell, he might never have Fanny next to him ever again.

That was a possibility he didn't want to consider. And yet he had no other choice.

Hell and the devil.

"I DON'T KNOW," Fanny said, surveying the large main room of the former warehouse. "Do you think this is too dreary?"

There were few windows and the light that made its way in was feeble and woefully inadequate. It would be expensive to keep illuminated, particularly in the winter months.

West stood in the corner, staring up at the ceiling. "Perhaps. A fresh coat of paint would go a long way, but the cost of candles would still be great," he said, echoing her thoughts. Then he frowned. "However, my primary concern is the water coming in here." He removed his glove and poked at the wood as Fanny made her way to the corner.

"Is it bad?" There were streaks down the plaster, discoloring the wall. "As you said, paint would improve it."

He flaked some of the paint and plaster off. "It's more than cosmetic. We'd have to repair this, and I'd wager the wood beneath is rotten."

Fanny exhaled. It was only the second potential property they'd visited today, and there would be others. The first had been too small, and this one was just too…depressing. Or did she think that because she was still upset about what had happened at the park the day before?

She'd told Sarah and later Ivy what had occurred with David and Miss Stoke. Then she'd endured an evening, which she'd spent at home with Ivy, imagining them dancing at Almack's. Miss Stoke would be graceful and elegant, and people would remark on what a marvelous couple they made.

"Fanny?" West's question drew her from the pit of her thoughts.

"Yes?"

He laughed softly. "I asked if you were ready to leave."

"I am, thank you." She turned and started across the creaking wood floor.

"You seem rather distracted," he said, walking alongside her. "Ivy said you might be."

Ivy had stayed home with Leah, who hadn't wanted to take her nap. They feared another tooth might be coming. "She told you about what happened?" Fanny asked. She expected Ivy would have since she and West told each other everything.

"About St. Ives courting Miss Stoke?"

It was a bit more than courting—he'd promised to marry her. However, Fanny didn't correct him. Courting was just as bad.

She could practically hear her mother's voice: *"You've no reason to be angry. He didn't promise you anything."* But he'd kissed her! And Mother would say that was her fault, not his.

"His father and her father wanted to unite their families. His lordship promised to marry her."

"Then why the devil was he calling on you?" West's question held a note of irritation, and while it made her feel good to have another ally, it wasn't as if he could do anything about it.

"If I knew that, I might not want to kick him in the—" She snapped her lips shut.

West laughed and patted her shoulder. "That's our girl. Don't think I will let this pass. I'll look for him at the club later."

They stepped out into the gray sunlight. The day was thick with clouds, but still remarkably bright. Fanny blinked after coming from the dim interior. "I feel much better being outside. That property won't suffice."

"I don't think so either." He guided her to his coach, which waited for them on the street.

"West, I'd rather you didn't speak to Dav—St. Ives about this business. He's free to do what he likes or feels he must."

Offering her his hand, West helped her up into the coach. "You are an understanding and generous young woman."

She settled herself on the seat. "What else should I be?"

He climbed in and sat down beside her. "Whatever you

like." He gave her a warm smile. "Truly, Fanny. Your sister and I only want you to be happy, and we'll do whatever we can to help you. You shall always have a home with us."

She knew that, just as she knew she was incredibly fortunate to enjoy a freedom most young women didn't have. She thought of Sarah, whose parents were eager to see her wed at the earliest possible moment. Fanny's parents were the same, but Fanny didn't have to rely on them for anything, so their preferences didn't matter even a whit. Especially not after the way they'd turned their backs on Ivy.

They drove home, and, after checking in on Ivy and Leah, Fanny decided to take a walk to the park. Her maid accompanied her, and the thick morning clouds burned mostly away as afternoon came upon them.

"I want to walk down to the water," Fanny said. Most people enjoyed Hyde Park at the height of the fashionable hour when the paths were clogged with Society, but Fanny liked having the space to herself. Or mostly, anyway. There were people about, but they weren't there for the purpose of being seen.

"Are you sure you want to risk it?" Barker asked with a wry smile.

Fanny grinned, almost always able to laugh at her clumsiness. "I am feeling particularly bold today."

"Well, I am feeling particularly warm," Barker said. "I hope there's a bench in the shade."

"There are several. We'll take a respite before we turn back."

The call of a bird drew Fanny's attention to a tree a few feet ahead along the path. She searched the foliage for the source but couldn't see it, nor was she certain what sort of bird made that call. She'd learned a few in the months since she'd taken to studying birds. Since she'd met David.

Would she continue to watch and learn about them now, or would they just remind her, frustratingly, of David? As they moved next to the tree, a chaffinch flew out from the branches, ascending above them.

They continued to the Serpentine, and Barker immediately found a bench set beneath the dappled shade of an oak tree. Fanny was about to sit beside her when she caught sight of a pair of birds on the water. They were elegant with a black tuft of feathers on top of their heads and bright amber coloring on the sides of their faces. The fronts of their long necks and their bellies were snowy white, while their back feathers were a mix of black and brown with hints of amber.

But it was their activity that caught Fanny's eye. They faced each other, their heads flicking from side to side, with a fan of feathers around their faces that reminded her of a lion's mane. Their feathered fans opened as their heads moved in what looked to be some sort of communication. She was absolutely fascinated and found herself pulled to the water's edge.

"Careful there."

The deep, masculine voice was familiar. She turned her head to see David standing a few feet to her left. "I'm not going to fall in again. Anyway, that was your fault."

"So it was." He bowed deeply, and she refused to be moved by his demeanor. Instead, she turned her attention back to the beautiful birds.

"Those are great crested grebes." He'd moved closer. She could see him from the corner of her eye but kept her attention on the birds. It wasn't difficult. Their dance, for that was what it looked like to her—if birds could dance—was utterly captivating.

"Have you any idea what they're doing?" she asked, thinking he must.

"That's their mating ritual. Do you see how they're moving closer and closer together?"

She did. "And why do they keep pecking at their feathers?" Every so often, they'd dip their heads back and flick their beaks into their back feathers before coming back up and resuming the headshaking from side to side.

"It's part of their dance."

She smiled now, since he'd used the word she'd been thinking. "I think they're better dancers than me."

He laughed. "They don't have to worry about intricate steps or patterns. Or feet."

She glanced at him, still smiling. "I don't know. That business out there looks rather complicated to me. For all we know, there's a sequence to those head flicks and beak dips."

"There could very well be. I haven't ever written down the specifics." He cocked his head to the side as he studied the birds. "I think I shall have to do that."

Suddenly, one of the grebes ducked its head beneath the water.

Fanny started. "Oh dear, what does that mean?"

"Just watch."

She heard the anticipation in his voice. A moment later, the bird resurfaced very close to the other one with a mouthful of greenery from the lake. Fanny brought her hand to her mouth and laughed. "Is that supposed to be a bouquet of flowers?"

"An apt description, I think." He pointed toward the water. "There goes the other one."

As he said that, the second bird ducked beneath the water but came back up more quickly. She—or he; why couldn't the female have gone first?—offered a beakful of watery foliage. The birds now touched at the neck and rose up out of the water, their breasts pushed out. They remained thus for several moments, seemingly basking in the joy of their mutual offerings.

"It's lovely," Fanny breathed.

"Not as lovely as you."

Fanny turned her head toward David, but he wasn't watching the birds. He was staring at her. She was instantly reminded that he'd promised to wed someone else and ought not be looking at her like that or saying such things to her.

She looked back to the water, but the show was over. The birds were swimming away—together. She turned from the lake. "Their dance is finished. And so is ours, I think."

"Fanny, I am so very sorry about yesterday."

She pivoted to face him. "Just about yesterday?"

"No, about all of it. I should have told you about Miss Stoke."

"Why? What you should have done was not kiss me or lead me to believe there might be a courtship. I thought we were well on our way."

"I thought so too." He took a step toward her. "When I met you at Christmastide, it was the first light I'd seen in the darkness after my father's death. I reveled in that encounter, even though it was brief. In fact, I relied on the memory of it for some time to lift my spirits. I never should have kissed you then, but the moment was so perfect, and it had just felt…right."

She'd felt exactly the same way. "I have never regretted it, and I still don't." Despite what she'd just said about what they shouldn't have done.

"Then when I met you again in London, I was thrilled to see you again and to know that you weren't actually a housemaid."

It would be easy to be drawn in by his heartfelt words—and she was certain he was being honest. But she couldn't do that. "And that is where I grow confused. You knew you'd made a promise to Miss Stoke, and yet you flirted with me, called on me, kissed me…" She pressed her lips together. She didn't want to become angry.

The edge of his mouth lifted. "I did all those things, and I can't apologize enough. It's not fair to you to say I was swept away, that you beguiled me completely. I should have ignored my burgeoning feelings—at least until I determined if Miss Stoke and I would suit."

She tried not to dwell on what he said about feelings. "Do you plan to find out?"

His face creased, and she detected anguish in the fine lines around his eyes and mouth. "I think I must."

"You did promise." And she knew how deeply he missed his father, how important he'd been. "Your father would want you to." How she wished she had that sort of relationship with a parent. She did, however, with another family member—Ivy. If Ivy had asked her to do something, she'd do it without hesitation.

Fanny took a step so that they nearly touched. "You should see if you will suit. Miss Stoke seems quite charming. Perhaps it will all work out."

His jaw tightened, and his gray eyes darkened to steel. "You are far too kind and understanding. Fanny, you are a singular woman." His voice was thick with some emotion she refused to ascertain.

"Family is important, especially the ties to those who love and support us as no one else ever could." She offered him a smile, though it had to have been tinged with the sadness she felt in her heart. "I came to care deeply for you, and I truly want you to find happiness."

"No more than I want that for you." He took his hat off and leaned slightly toward her. "And if Miss Stoke and I don't suit—"

She lightly touched his chest, then jerked her hand away. She couldn't touch him. Standing this close, she wanted to do that and more. It took great effort not to look at his mouth and wish it were against hers. "I won't wait for you, David."

"I wouldn't expect you to." He sounded sad. Resigned.

Good. She felt the same.

It was a thoroughly depressing moment. Right until a bird—fittingly—shat directly on David's head.

Chapter Eight
◆Ƹ•Ʒ◆

THOUGH DAVID HAD said he would make the effort to get to know Miss Stoke, he wasn't looking forward to it. Which wasn't at all fair to her. He had to at least *try*.

And so he found himself at the Findlay ball looking for her and trying not to think about his encounter with Fanny that afternoon. He smiled thinking of their laughter over the grebes' mating dance. But the smile faded as he recalled how it had ended—with them going their separate ways, toward different futures.

He caught sight of Miss Stoke standing with her mother and made his way in their direction. He didn't particularly want to dance, given his difficulty in mastering the steps, but since she enjoyed it, he'd ask.

She was delighted to see him and eager to dance the cotillion, at which he—mostly—succeeded. When the music finished, he offered his arm and escorted her from the floor. The touch of her hand on his sleeve didn't ignite anything within him, not like how his body came alive when Fanny did the same thing.

Instead of leading Miss Stoke back to her mother, he escorted her in the opposite direction. "Would you mind if we promenaded around the ballroom before I return you to your mother?"

"Not at all. I'd be delighted to spend more time with you." She sounded so pleased, so *eager*.

Which only made him feel like a dastardly prick. "Miss Stoke, I think it's only fair for me to tell you that I don't know if I can keep the promise my father made to yours."

"Oh." She sounded disappointed. "Is it something I've

done?" she asked, tipping her head up to look at him. She was quite petite compared to Fanny. Hell, would he always compare them?

"Of course not," he said. "We've barely spent time together."

Her features softened into a smile. "Yes, and we need to rectify that."

They could, but David suspected it wouldn't change his mind. Or his feelings. Particularly the ones he had for Fanny, not her.

She continued before he could speak again. "I do think it's good that we not rush into anything, but take our time to know each other—our minds and our hearts."

Time. He wasn't sure a lifetime would be enough—not to find love with her or to fall out of it with Fanny. Wait, did he love Fanny? He wasn't sure, but he knew that contemplating the future without her made him ache with emptiness.

Suddenly, he saw her. He could pick her red-gold hair and tall, willowy frame out of the thickest crowd. She stood near the wall with Miss Colton and another young woman. Fanny's head turned, and their eyes connected. The room grew quiet for that brief moment while he imagined it was just the two of them.

The press of Miss Stoke's hand on his arm pulled him from the reverie. He spoke without thinking. "I believe I have feelings for someone else."

Miss Stoke slowed, her hand digging into his sleeve. "Is it Miss Snowden?"

Had she just seen them looking at each other? David kept himself from glancing in Fanny's direction. "I would rather not say. I'm sure you understand."

"Not really." Her voice held a slight edge.

His gaze snapped to hers. The green irises of her eyes

darkened to the color of something buried deep in a thick forest.

"I understand you promised your father that you'd marry me," she said. "And now you're reneging on that vow."

The only way she could know that he'd promised his father was if his mother had told her. He was going to have a pointed conversation with her about not disclosing private information.

"I don't know what you heard, but whatever promises were made—or not—are between me and my family."

She visibly swallowed but didn't take her gaze from his. "I didn't mean to overstep. It's just—" Now her gaze wavered, moving briefly to the side before finding his once more. "Couldn't you at least *try* to get to know me?"

Bloody hell. She sounded so small and sad, and he felt like the biggest scoundrel. "Miss Stoke, it's nothing to do with you, truly. It's simply that I met someone else, and I am afraid I may not be able to put the feelings I have for her aside. That would not be fair to you."

"I think marriages have been made in the face of worse," she said quietly.

Perhaps, but that wasn't a marriage he wanted. "Let me escort you back to your mother. I am deeply sorry."

"I think you'll be sorrier than you could know," she said without heat. "I will hope you change your mind."

If she wanted to hold out hope for him, he likely couldn't dissuade her from it. She seemed rather...dogged in her determination that they be together.

They arrived at her mother, who smiled brightly upon seeing them. Then she saw her daughter's downcast expression, and her face puckered with concern. "Is everything all right?"

Miss Stoke took her hand from his arm. "Lord St. Ives

has decided not to pursue any sort of courtship."

David worked to keep his jaw from dropping. She wanted to have this conversation *here*?

Mrs. Stoke's mouth tightened. "I'm certain he'll change his mind. Talk to your mother, my lord. She'll convince you of the rightness of the union—you and Arabella are perfect for one another. Did you know that swans are her favorite animal? She's keen to learn all you have to teach her about fowl." Mrs. Stoke forced another smile, but her eyes, a green-gray, were hard as stone.

There was no point in further debate with either woman. Instead, he bowed to them. "Have a pleasant evening."

He turned, eager to quit the ballroom as quickly as possible. He saw Fanny again—near her sister this time, but didn't dare go to her. There would be time to tell her that he wished to court her, that he couldn't imagine a future without her.

Tomorrow.

On his way to the exit, a man fell into him, sending him off balance.

"You'll meet me at dawn, Royston!" a second man called to the man who was just straightening himself.

Both gentlemen were young bucks—one dark and one fair. The dark-haired one had issued the challenge. David recalled Ware speaking of this the other night at the club.

"Don't be ridiculous, Hornsby," the fair-haired gentleman said. His collar was impossibly high and stiff, his cravat the most intricately tied David had ever seen. "There's no need to risk your life over your sister's foolish infatuation. It's not my fault I don't find her attractive."

The ballroom fell almost completely silent as people gathered around the two men. A wide circle formed, and David hoped they wouldn't come to blows. Other than the pushing that had apparently occurred when Royston had crashed into him.

Hornsby sneered as he advanced on the taller man. "You dare insult her? And in front of an audience?"

Royston clucked his tongue, his eyes narrowing. "I'm not the one who instigated this scene."

"You started this when you were rude to my sister. You don't give a lady false hope and then turn your back on her."

David winced. He hadn't given Miss Stoke false hope— not directly, but wasn't he responsible just the same? Perhaps, but he was far more responsible when it came to Fanny and her disappointment. Which was why he would make it right.

Hornsby's lip curled. "Name your second."

"This isn't worth dueling over," Royston said.

"Your continued abuse is why the challenge is necessary. To say my sister isn't worth a defense of her character is beyond the pale."

Hornsby exhaled loudly. "I am not abusing your sister. You're the one causing humiliation with your public display."

Hornsby lunged forward, and a feminine voice called, "Stop!"

Without thinking, David clapped his hand around Hornsby's arm and kept him from launching into Royston. Hornsby whipped his head around, scowling at David.

"Careful, there," David said quietly. "Save it for the dueling field."

Hornsby shook him off, and two other gentlemen moved forward. They were Anthony and Ware. Anthony moved close to David while Ware inserted himself between Royston and Hornsby.

"This is not the place to have this…discussion. Step outside to make your arrangements." Ware spoke pleasantly, with an affable smile, as if he were inviting them to one of his entertainments.

Hornsby seemed to relax slightly while Royston sniffed.

"Outside?" Ware prodded.

Hornsby abruptly turned and marched from the ballroom. Ware inclined his head toward Anthony and David. Anthony nodded and started out after him.

David took their unspoken communication to mean they intended to ensure the two men didn't come to blows outside either. He planned to provide assistance, but before he could follow Ware, who gestured for Royston to precede him, he felt a hand on his arm.

Turning his head, he was surprised to see his mother's concerned face. Before he could assure her that he was fine, she pulled him to the side of the ballroom as conversation erupted around them.

Her dark brows pitched into a V, and she spoke in a low, furious tone. "What are you doing?"

"I was trying to prevent a disaster," he said, thinking it should have been obvious.

Confusion clouded her eyes briefly before she pursed her lips. "I'm speaking of Miss Stoke. You're not going to honor your promise?"

Irritation at her meddling crested within him. "A promise she never should have known about. You broke a family confidence."

His mother's eyes narrowed. "I didn't realize it was a confidence. It was an agreement your father made with her father, and you committed to it."

David gritted his teeth. "In private."

"Does that make it less binding? Were you being disingenuous with your father before he died?" The question stung with the force of her derision.

"I'm not going to discuss this with you here," he said quietly but firmly.

She inhaled, stretching her frame. "Then we'll discuss it later."

"No, we won't. This is none of your affair, and I won't tolerate you inserting yourself in my personal business."

Her eyes widened, then settled into a glare. "You won't *tolerate* me?"

"Not about this."

"I'm not going to sit quietly by and watch you lower yourself to court Miss Snowden," she hissed.

David gaped at her. "*Lower* myself? Her sister's a bloody duchess." He shook his head. "We're not discussing this here. Or anywhere. If you can't keep your opinions to yourself, I'll ask you to leave."

Anger blistered his insides as he spun from her and strode from the ballroom. By the time he got outside, Anthony and Ware were speaking with Royston in low tones.

Eager to focus on something other than his mother's horrid behavior, he asked where Hornsby had gone. "We convinced him to take himself off," Anthony said.

David looked between them, his gaze settling on Royston , who seemed a bit pale. "Did you also convince him that a duel is a terrible idea?"

"Not quite," Ware said. "However, I think he'll get there. I agreed to be Royston's second and will speak with Hornsby's second later. For now, we're going to take Royston to the club for a much-needed drink. Are you coming?"

"Absolutely." He was also in much need of a drink.

His mother's onslaught about Miss Stoke was troubling, but nothing he wouldn't overcome, even if he had to send the countess packing. He wasn't going to let her—or anyone else—come between him and Fanny.

◆ε•3◆

CONVERSATION IN THE ballroom climbed as the gentlemen left. Fanny and Sarah had watched the entire spectacle, moving out of the shadows of the corner to achieve a better vantage point. Fanny wondered how David had managed to be in the thick of it but, of course, would never have the chance to ask him.

"I'll get the full details of that from Anthony," Sarah said.

They hadn't been able to hear what had gone on, but it looked as if David, Anthony, and Ware had prevented the other two gentlemen from coming to blows.

Sarah looked at her with concern and picked up the discussion they'd been having when the excitement had started. "You're certain you don't wish to leave?"

"No, I refuse to be bothered by him dancing with Miss Stoke." Fanny said it to convince herself as much as Sarah. Because it did bother her. So much.

"You're far too kind," Sarah said softly, touching Fanny's arm briefly but with great warmth. "I wouldn't care about some promise he'd made, not when there was clearly something between the two of you."

"You say that now, but you'd do the same in my position. David's father meant a great deal to him, and promises made to those who are dying shouldn't be tossed aside." No matter how badly she wanted them to be.

"People shouldn't marry someone because someone else wants them to." It was hard to tell if Sarah was still speaking about David or herself.

"Is your mother pushing you toward someone in particular?" So far she hadn't, but Sarah's parents wanted her married. They had no interest in supporting her into spinsterhood.

"Not yet, but I fear it's coming." Sarah glanced around the ballroom. "Speaking of my mother, I see her threading her way in our direction." She exhaled in resignation.

Fanny clasped Sarah's hand for a quick moment. "Never fear, we can be spinsters together. We shall have the workhouse to keep us busy."

"Yes, about that," Sarah said. "I wanted to speak with you about an idea I had. It will have to wait, however." Her mother was upon them.

"My goodness, what an exciting evening!" Viscountess Colton said, smiling. "I am very much looking forward to Anthony's account of what happened and whether this duel is actually happening."

"Duel?" Fanny and Sarah said in unison.

"Oh, you probably couldn't hear what was going on. Mr. Hornsby challenged Mr. Royston to a duel. He alleged that Royston had insulted his sister."

"Is that true?" Sarah asked.

"I'm not entirely certain. It seems to be a simple issue of Royston not wanting to court Miss Hornsby and her feeling disappointed. That's the gossip anyway."

Fanny did *not* understand Society. "That hardly seems like something worth dueling over."

"Indeed," Sarah's mother agreed, turning to her daughter. "I came to fetch you, Sarah. I'm ready to go."

Sarah gave Fanny an apologetic wince. "I hate to leave you alone."

Lavinia wasn't at the ball, and Fanny hadn't seen their other friend, Jane, since earlier in the evening. Fanny gave her a reassuring smile. "Don't concern yourself. I'll find Ivy. I'm sure she's ready to depart too."

They said their good-nights, and as Fanny searched the ballroom for her sister, a woman in a rather plain white gown trimmed with lavender velvet approached her. There was something familiar about the set of her mouth and the shape of her eyes.

"Good evening, Miss Snowden. I am Lady St. Ives."

Of course. Fanny instantly recognized that she was David's mother and offered a curtsey. "Pleased to meet you, my lady." And a bit nervous. The countess's eyes carried a chill.

"I'd like to speak with you for a moment, if I may." Lady St. Ives strolled closer to the wall.

Fanny followed despite the sinking sensation carving through her stomach.

The countess offered a brief smile that didn't warm her demeanor in the slightest. "I think possessing appropriate expectations is incredibly important. Wouldn't you agree?"

"Yes," Fanny said slowly, not bothering to mask her unease.

Lady St. Ives clasped her hands in front of her waist. "Good. I don't wish to be indelicate, but I fear I must be straightforward. You must stay away from my son. He is promised to someone else, and his attention needs to be entirely devoted in that direction. Do you understand?"

Fanny's heart pounded a heavy rhythm. "I think so. I am assured that your son's...*attention* is not directed at me."

"That is relieving to hear. I should hate for anyone to learn of your sister's background." She clucked her tongue and dashed a look toward the middle of the ballroom. "Not even becoming a duchess can erase some things."

The woman's threat was unmistakable. Fanny fought to take a breath. Rage pooled in her belly and was quickly joined with fear. "Are you threatening me and my sister?"

The countess pierced her with a devastatingly icy stare. "I'm explaining how the world works, my dear. You are not fit to marry my son. How your sister managed to land a duke is a mystery, and yet I suppose one must consider *which* duke she married. It's not as if he had a good name to uphold. Not like my son." Her lips stretched into a mild grimace. "I'm sure you think me heartless, but I assure you this is for your own good."

Fanny clenched her hands into fists to still herself from shaking. "Why, because I would then be deprived of having you for a mother-in-law? On that score, I must agree. I pity whomever he takes for a wife."

Lady St. Ives's eyes widened as she sucked a breath through her flared nostrils. "You're as common as your sister."

A nasty smile curled Fanny's lip. "Of course I am. *We are sisters.*"

"Then I shall also assume you have behaved in a loose fashion. I can only hope you haven't done so with my son. Let me reiterate: you must stay away from him, or your sister's indiscretions will be made public."

The shaking in Fanny's body was impossible to quell. She felt her shoulder twitch and fought to speak without her voice quavering too. "I will also repeat that there is nothing between your son and me." *Not anymore…*

"Excellent." Lady St. Ives unclasped her hands and inclined her head. "Have a pleasant evening." Then she turned and left as if she hadn't just said the most horrible things Fanny had ever had to listen to.

There was no telling how long Fanny stood there, her

mind numb and her body slowly calming from the distress Lady St. Ives had wrought. She wished she'd asked the countess how she knew about Ivy, and *what*, specifically she knew. Was it that Ivy had been in a workhouse? That she'd borne a bastard? That she'd been ruined by Viscount Bosworth?

But she wouldn't have asked, especially not here. She hurriedly glanced around to see if anyone had overheard what *had* been said.

And then she saw Ivy. Her sister had approached without Fanny realizing. She was instantly taken aback by the look of anxiety in Ivy's gaze. "What's wrong?"

Had Lady St. Ives said something despite Fanny's assurances that there was nothing between her and David?

"Did you hear about the duel that was challenged earlier?" Ivy asked.

"Yes." Fanny relaxed slightly. "Why does that upset you?"

"It doesn't. But people are now talking about past duels, mostly the one fought by Lord Axbridge last year."

Lady Axbridge was a close friend of Ivy's. Her husband, the Marquess of Axbridge, had killed her former husband in a duel. That she'd married her husband's killer was still a bit of a scandal. Fanny had met them both, however, and could see that they were very much in love. "The gossip about them will die down at some point. It has to."

"One would think," Ivy said wryly. "However, that's not the only duel they're talking about. I heard some people discussing the challenge West issued."

Fanny's stomach clenched. "But that was so long ago."

"Some people never forget," Ivy said derisively. "I'd like to go home now."

"I would too." Fanny felt queasy and horrible. Between

Ivy's consternation and the horrid threat from Lady St. Ives, she felt as though she could toss up her accounts. Or hit something.

Or both.

They left the ball and didn't speak until they were in the coach, seated side by side on the velvet cushion. Ivy stroked a hand over her rounded belly, her brows gathered with concern. Fanny wanted to assuage her but had a hard time mustering any words of comfort.

"I want to go home," Ivy said. "To Stour's Edge. I'd planned to go next month as the pregnancy progressed, but I think I've lost my taste for Society. You're welcome to stay, if you wish."

There was no question. After what had happened with David yesterday and especially after tonight, Fanny was more than ready to abandon her first—and likely only—Season. "I'd rather come with you and Leah."

Ivy smiled. "Thank you. I'm sorry to take you away."

"I'm not," Fanny said, taking her sister's hand and squeezing it tightly. "I don't think London Society is for me."

"It isn't for me either," Ivy admitted. "But I endure it because of my dear friends, and for West."

"He'd abandon it too." Fanny was certain of it—he'd do anything for Ivy.

"If I asked, and I won't. I don't mind it in small doses—I prefer to just spend time with my friends. However, I did more this year because you're here." She winced, then waved her free hand. "Don't listen to me. I'm tired and cranky from the babe." She turned her head toward Fanny. "I'd do anything for you and that includes giving you as many Seasons as you'd like."

The love Fanny felt for her sister welled in her chest and threatened to spill from her eyes. "I'd do anything for

THE DUKE OF KISSES

you too." Including staying away from the man she'd fallen in love with—not that he wanted her anyway.

She also wouldn't ever tell Ivy what Lady St. Ives had said. She just hoped the countess would maintain her end of the bargain and keep her mouth shut.

"Can we leave tomorrow?" Fanny asked.

Ivy's eyes gleamed with appreciation. "Yes, let's."

Fanny nodded. She would miss her friends, but they would understand. She was ready to leave and find a future without judgment or pretense.

A future without David.

Chapter Nine

◆·℥·◈

IT WAS AFTER three in the afternoon before David was able to make his way to Berkeley Square. He'd been busy with other appointments and commitments and was finally free to do what had been at the forefront of his mind since last night: see Fanny and tell her he only wanted to court *her*.

He walked briskly up the steps to the front door of Clare House and was instantly greeted by the butler, who welcomed him inside.

"I'm afraid Miss Snowden is not present. Would you like to see His Grace?"

Disappointment pitched through David. Perhaps Clare could tell him when she would return. Or perhaps he could speak with Clare *until* she returned. "Yes, please."

"Very good. If you'll just wait in the sitting room." The butler gestured for David to enter a bright room decorated in golds and blues that looked out to the square. Once David was inside, the butler closed the door, leaving him alone.

David's gaze caught a pretty painting of a blue tit hanging on the wall. With its gold breast and blue wings and head, it perfectly complemented the room's décor. It was a stunning piece of art as well as an accurate depiction of the species.

The door opened, and Clare strode inside. "Good afternoon, St. Ives. I understand you came to see Fanny."

David turned, clicking his heels together. "I did, though I'm delighted to see you as well."

The duke flashed a smile, but his gaze was serious.

"Fanny and Ivy have returned to Stour's Edge."

They'd left town? The disappointment inside him spread, leaving a hollow expanse. Had he driven her away? "I came to tell her I wanted to court her." He realized he should have asked Clare's permission.

"You're too late, I'm afraid." Clare's tone was unsympathetic.

"Am I?" Just because she'd left London didn't mean she was lost to him—unless there was something he didn't know. "Is there someone else?"

Clare lifted a shoulder. "Not that I'm aware of. I am, however, aware that your attentions are directed to another young lady. Or did I misunderstand?"

"You did not. It is a complicated explanation, and one I'd rather not bother with, particularly since it is now moot. My attention will only be directed at Fan—Miss Snowden. If she will permit it." He winced. "Would it meet with your approval for me to court your sister-in-law?"

Narrowing his gaze at David, the duke scrutinized him for a moment. "I won't allow you to break her heart. I'd have to thrash you."

"Only after I thrashed myself," David said.

Clare straightened, exhaling. "Good. I understand you got in the way of things last night with Royston and Hornsby. I'd hate for you to be involved in another duel."

Was he threatening David? Yes, he rather thought he was. "That duel didn't happen. Hornsby came to his senses."

"Most men do."

David wondered if the duke was speaking of his own experience. He'd heard last night that the duke had challenged a viscount named Bothwick, who had dared insult Ivy. The duel hadn't occurred, however, and David was curious about what had happened. Despite that, he had no intention of asking.

"May I call on her at Stour's Edge, then?" David asked deferentially.

"I might suggest writing to her first, but I have no objection—provided you keep your word to me."

David had been about to say he was a man of honor, that he always kept his word. Except he hadn't. Not to his father. The anguish inside him drove him to say, "If I break her heart, you have my permission to thrash me, destroy me, utterly ruin me."

"We've an agreement, then." Clare nodded, and his demeanor lightened. "You can't be planning to leave London now? You just took your seat in the Lords."

In truth, he shouldn't leave until the Season was over. Or at least nearly over. "I won't go—not yet. I will, however, write to her. Thank you for the suggestion. And your permission."

"Just remember that Fanny has a father," Clare said. "If you desire to move past courtship, you'd best speak with him—John Snowden in Pickering, Yorkshire."

"I will do that, thank you." David made to leave, but Clare pivoted, which halted David's progress.

Clare pinned him with a steady stare. "Ivy and I care for Fanny very much. It seems she may care for you—I would hope that the depth of her feelings would be reciprocated."

"I believe they are." David could only hope that she would return his affection. "And maybe more so," he added softly.

"Excellent." Clare grinned. "See you later, then."

David inclined his head and left, feeling a bit less enthusiastic than when he'd arrived. He hated that she'd left town and hoped it wasn't his fault. He'd write to her immediately and eagerly await her response.

As soon as he returned home, his mother intercepted him before he could reach his study. "David, might I have a word?"

He could well imagine what she wished to speak with him about. He'd successfully avoided her all day. And while he'd prefer to continue doing so, he acknowledged that he couldn't put her off indefinitely. "If you plan to discuss Miss Stoke, I recommend you don't bother. My decision is firm."

He continued his path to his study, unsurprised that she followed behind him.

"You barely gave her a chance," his mother said.

David went to his desk and turned to face her. He lowered himself to perch on the edge and regarded her with a restless glower. "It isn't about her. I'm sure she's lovely. However, I met someone before I had the chance to make Miss Stoke's acquaintance. Fate delivered me a different path, and I'm going to take it."

"Fate also stole your father." Her voice was dark and bitter, like the coffee he drank on cold mornings. "Fate is cruel and chaotic. You must make your own choices."

He gave her a wry stare. "That's precisely what I'm doing."

She exhaled in exasperation. "You can't mean to choose Miss Snowden."

"I do, and I don't care what you have to say about the matter."

"She comes from a working-class family, and her sister was ruined by a viscount."

David rose from the desk and angrily stalked toward his mother. "Do not slander her."

The countess lifted her chin. "It's true. Lord Bothwick ruined her more than a decade ago. He even got her with child."

The denial died on his tongue. This was more than reason for Clare to have challenged the man to a duel. "None of that matters," David said, thinking he might want to challenge Bothwick too.

His mother's gaze flared with outrage. "Of course it matters! You can't marry someone like that. As if that isn't bad enough, she is a *Snowden*."

David blinked at her, perplexed. "What the hell is that supposed to signify?"

Taking a deep breath, she went to the window and looked outside briefly before turning back to face him. "You know of the footman who abducted your aunt."

Ice crystallized along his spine. Though they hadn't spoken of her often—it had been too painful for David's father and Uncle Walter—David knew of the story about his Aunt Catherine. She'd gone missing with a footman and had later been brought home dead along with a babe. "What does that have to do with Miss Snowden?"

"The footman was her relation."

The footman who'd supposedly killed his aunt after getting her with child. His father had carried the grief all through his life, as had Walter. Even now, the subject of his sister sent him into the blackest of moods.

David couldn't imagine someone like the murderous footman being related to Fanny. "How can you possibly know that?"

"The same way I know about her sister's indiscretion. Lady Bothwick—the dowager viscountess—is a friend of mine. The Duchess of Clare was born Mary Snowden, and her great-uncle was the footman at Huntwell who killed your aunt."

David felt unsteady, as if the floor had caved in beneath him. "You're certain?"

"Of course I am. You couldn't possibly betray our family by marrying her. It's bad enough you won't honor the promise you made to your father, but to wed someone from *that* family?" She shuddered. "It's perhaps best he is dead so that he wouldn't have to suffer such heartache."

David sank back onto the desk, his body folding under the weight of this terrible revelation. None of this was Fanny's fault. She'd had nothing to do with any of it. Nor had David. Still, his mother's words about honor and his father burned his heart and mind.

The touch of his mother's hand on his arm startled him. He twitched, and she pulled away.

"I'm sorry about this, David, truly. But surely you understand how a future with Miss Snowden is simply impossible."

He didn't believe that. He couldn't. The thought of never seeing her again, of not pursuing what he believed they could share filled him with a sharp pain. Was it worse than the regret and sorrow he felt for betraying his father?

His mother left without saying another word. She'd barely gone before Graham came inside and closed the door behind him. He walked silently to the sideboard. The sound of liquid splashing into a glass reached David's ears.

A moment later, Graham pressed a tumbler into his hand. "Drink."

David did as his secretary—no, his friend—instructed. Then he looked at Graham. "You heard?"

Graham grimaced. "The lot of it. What a bloody mess."

"I don't know what to do." He knew what he *wanted* to do.

"What had you planned—before you walked in here with your mother?"

David's chest tightened. "I was going to write to her. To Fanny. I was going to ask if I could court her."

"Marry her, you mean. Because courtship leads to that. There's no going back." Graham's tone was stern yet caring at the same time. "At least not without considerable difficulty."

David shot him a skeptical look. "How did you become the marital expert?"

He gasped in mock affront. "Don't you dare cast me in that role. I'm acting as your counselor. My father said I may need to do that from time to time."

"I can't help thinking what my father would say if he were alive. He'd be horrified to hear I wanted to marry a Snowden."

"Do you really think so?" Graham cocked his head to the side. "Is there no chance he'd understand that she isn't to blame for her relation's crimes? The man I knew possessed a kind nature."

That was true, but Graham hadn't seen everything. "He rarely spoke of his sister, but when he did, his fury simmered just beneath the surface. More than once, he said he'd wanted to kill the man."

And now, as David recalled his father's threats, the name of the footman came back to him: Snowden. He felt as though he were being ripped in two.

His mother was right. Fate was incredibly cruel to have put Fanny in his path only to have her be from the one family he could never join with his.

"You don't have to make any decisions right now," Graham said. "But perhaps you should avoid Miss Snowden for the time being—until you work things out in your mind."

"I don't have to. She's gone."

Graham arched a brow in question.

"I just paid a call to Clare House. The Duke said she's returned to the country with her sister. I don't need to avoid her. I could simply never contact her again and let the entire…matter between us fade into the past." God, that sounded awful, to relegate the feelings he had for her to some small moment in time that had come and gone like a migration.

"Perhaps that's for the best." Graham winced, then took a drink of his whisky.

David did the same, only he swallowed every drop. "I think more drinking is for the best." He tracked across the study to the sideboard and refilled his glass.

He had time to work things out in his mind—and he would. But what was he to do about his heart?

❧•3•❧

FIVE MORE DAYS.

Fanny could endure five more days at her parents' house. She owed it to her brother John to see him wed. Plus, he was marrying Mercy, the younger sister of Fanny's oldest and dearest friend, Patience Jeffers. Rather, Patience Smithson now.

Ivy had not accompanied Fanny. She was within the last several weeks of her pregnancy and had no desire to travel. Furthermore, she had no interest in visiting her estranged parents for more than a few hours at a time, and Fanny couldn't blame her.

The room Fanny had once shared with Ivy—when she'd been Mary—seemed small and sparse when compared with the elegance of both Stour's Edge and Clare House. Fanny's bed, in which she and Ivy had both squeezed, took up a large portion of the space, while a tall, slim dresser occupied one corner, an ancient, rickety armoire stood in another, and a compact writing desk sat beneath the window.

She'd come upstairs to fetch her bonnet for a walk but found herself drawn to the desk. More accurately, to the pair of letters tucked into the top drawer. She pulled them out but didn't open the parchment. It was enough to look at his handwriting, and she'd read them so many times to have memorized their contents.

David had sent the first one a week after she'd left London. In it, he'd apologized for his behavior and said he'd called on her at Clare House. He'd asked if he was the reason she'd left London. Then he'd asked to visit her at Stour's Edge at the end of the Season. Which would be soon as June had just begun.

She wasn't sure if she ought to expect him or not since she hadn't responded. Not to that letter, nor to the second one he'd sent a fortnight later.

He'd asked if she'd received his first correspondence. Then he'd asked if she'd decided not to answer. He'd said if he didn't get a response to that letter, he'd leave her alone.

She hadn't yet written to him and wasn't sure she would. It seemed he wasn't courting Miss Stoke. There hadn't been any news of a courtship or a marriage, much to her relief.

Not that any of that mattered. His mother's threats weighed heavy on her mind whenever she thought of David. So she tried very hard not to.

Shoving the letters back in the desk, she slammed the drawer closed. She turned and fetched a bonnet from a hook on the wall and strode from the room, eager to escape the confines of the house and enjoy the late-spring day.

She'd grab her sketchbook from the sitting room and

see if she could improve upon her drawing of the common pochard ducks she'd seen yesterday at the pond. Setting her bonnet atop her head as she descended the stairs, she heard her mother's voice from the back of the house.

"I've told you a thousand times to leave your boots outside, Jacob!"

Fanny ducked into the sitting room, hoping she'd be able to escape before drawing her mother's notice. She sounded particularly testy today.

The table where Fanny had left the book and pencil earlier was now empty. Which meant her mother had moved it. Fanny turned and surveyed the immaculately kept room. Her mother preferred tidy, open spaces, which meant there was a minimum of clutter. It also meant monochromatic color schemes. The entire sitting room was decorated in a single shade of yellow. It wasn't even a particularly cheery yellow. It was faded and dingy and, due to her mother's thriftiness, would never be replaced.

The sketchbook was nowhere to be seen. Resigned to leaving without it, Fanny turned to make her way out. Her mother stood in the doorway, hands on her hips.

"Are you looking for that drawing book?"

"Yes." Fanny hoped she hadn't burned it.

Her mother adjusted her apron. "That's the second time you've left it in here."

And the last. "My apologies."

"It's no surprise to me that Mary allows you to be careless with your things. She coddles you, as far as I can tell." Mother's gaze swept over Fanny's walking dress. She'd already made a fuss over Fanny's new, expensive clothing, as well as Fanny having a maid, which she'd also done when Fanny had come home in March for the birth of Patience's babe.

Fanny ignored her mother's gibe. She adopted her most polite and deferential tone. "Where might I find it now?"

"I gave it to Jacob."

Jacob was her other brother. Two years older than her, he'd been a lifelong nemesis, joining with their brother John to torment Fanny. John had seemed to grow out of his ill behavior, but Jacob was still as obnoxious as ever. And now Fanny had to get her sketchbook back from him? She wouldn't even bother trying.

As if conjured by their conversation, Jacob strolled by the open door. Tall, with a chest the size of a keg, he was an imposing figure. He waved at Fanny as he made his way to the stairs.

Mother didn't even turn to look at him, her attention focused entirely on Fanny. "Where are you going?"

"Just out for a walk," Fanny said brightly.

Her mother frowned. "Don't be gone too long. Mr. Duckworth will be paying a visit later."

Fanny stifled a groan. "I hope he isn't coming to see me." He'd tried to visit in March too, but Fanny had spent most of her time with Patience.

"Of course he is." Her mother looked at her as if she were daft. "He considers it a boon that you've returned from London without a husband." She shook her head. "I can't understand how that's possible. The entire reason to have a Season is to marry, and you didn't even stay for the whole thing. I daresay your coming home to be with Patience ruined your options."

"It didn't, actually," Fanny said flatly. She hadn't told her mother a thing about London, only that she and Mary—Ivy—had left due to Ivy's pregnancy.

"Well, now that you're home, you will likely see that Mr. Duckworth is an excellent choice. His house is quite large and well-appointed, and you won't want for anything." Her gaze dipped again to Fanny's costume. "Though you won't need to dress like that here."

It wasn't even a fancy dress! But it had come from London and was made of fine fabric and was the latest style. Fanny suspected the real reason her mother didn't like her clothing was because Ivy and West had paid for it. She made no secret that she didn't regret turning her eldest child out. It baffled Fanny that she wouldn't let the past go, nor would she be happy for Ivy.

Unable to hold her tongue, Fanny blurted, "What is it you have against Ivy? And West, for that matter?"

Mother stepped into the room with a deep breath. "Her name is Mary in this house. She was always a foolish chit, hoping to marry above her station. She thought to trap Bothwick with her machinations, but men like him are not to be trusted."

"And men like Mr. Duckworth are?" Fanny didn't understand what her mother had against titled men in particular.

"Far more than men like His Grace. Men like him are arrogant and privileged. They think they're better than everyone else." She said this with such vitriol that Fanny was taken aback.

Lavinia and Sarah came to Fanny's mind. They weren't any of those things. And neither was David. "I met many nice people from titled families. They aren't all like that."

"Of course they are. They are above us mortals—above the law, even. Don't you remember Uncle George?"

Fanny tried to recall... And then suddenly did. "You mean my great-uncle?"

"Yes. He was a footman in a great house. They accused him of something terrible, and he disappeared, never to be seen or heard from again." Her lip curled. "Your grandfather was devastated, as was your father."

She'd never known the story, just that her great-uncle had disappeared. Then her parents had invariably lowered their voices to angry whispers. "You think they did something to Uncle George?"

"I know they did. He and the earl's daughter fell in love and eloped."

"They did?" Her footman great-uncle had run off with the daughter of an earl? "That sounds so romantic."

Her mother's eyes turned the color of the pond in winter. "It was *foolish*. The earl and his family hated your Uncle George. He never should have run off with the girl, regardless of how they felt about one another." Her shoulders twitched as she scoffed. "They defied her family—they defied *reason*."

It still sounded romantic to Fanny. "What happened?"

"Uncle George wrote to your grandfather about their marriage, but when we never heard from him again, your grandfather became worried. He wrote to the earl to ask after Uncle George and his wife, but his letters were ignored. Then he went to speak with the earl, who told him George's wife had died and George had left the country. Your grandfather didn't believe him. George wouldn't have left England without telling his brother. So your grandfather went to the magistrate. But he refused to look into the matter." She sniffed in indignation. "They won't interfere when a powerful, wealthy family is involved."

This was why her parents hated nobility. It was probably best she didn't have a future with David. Her parents would have loathed the union as much as they loathed Ivy's. Not that she and David would have ended up married. The space between them had never felt more vast. He was an earl, and she was the daughter of a cabinetmaker and the grand-niece of a footman who'd been a victim of power and privilege.

"I'll just go for my walk," Fanny said, starting toward the door. As she came abreast of her mother, the older woman touched her arm, startling Fanny with the contact.

"Don't forget to come back in time to see Mr. Duckworth. Your father will be furious if you don't."

Fanny didn't particularly care how her father felt, but also acknowledged it was easier to just meet the man. She certainly wasn't going to agree to anything else. "I will."

Mother dropped her hand. "If you want your sketchbook, I left it in the kitchen."

"You didn't give it to Jacob?"

"I thought about it, but no. Please keep it in your room. You know how I like the house to look."

"Yes, Mother." Fanny went to the door.

"And Fanny?"

She turned and blinked.

"I am happy to have you home. I missed you while you were gone."

Fanny appreciated the sentiment. She knew her mother—and her father—loved her. It had just become difficult to remember that knowing all she did now about how they'd treated Ivy. "Thank you."

"Just remember where you came from and what's really important. There's nothing wrong with a simple, meaningful life. You don't need a title or expensive clothing or to go to London to be happy."

No, she didn't. She just wanted to feel like she belonged.

Fanny walked to the back of the house into the kitchen where the cook was preparing dinner for later. Hard of hearing, she merely nodded at Fanny, who smiled in return.

The sketchbook sat at the edge of a worktable near the pantry. Fanny plucked it up and hurried outside into the kitchen garden.

A soft breeze stirred the ribbons of her bonnet, reminding her that she hadn't tied them. She didn't bother now either but continued on her way out of the garden toward a path that would follow the cow enclosure until it veered through a thicket.

Her thoughts were filled with her mother's harsh words as well as her endorsement of Mr. Duckworth. She and her father would do their best to work a match between Fanny and the man she'd already said she didn't wish to marry.

Ten minutes later, she made her way down a gently rolling hill, which reminded her of the first time she'd met David. When she'd slipped on the snow and tumbled over herself into an embarrassing heap.

She passed through a narrow gap in the hedgerow and came upon the pond, her small, private space partly nestled beneath the shade of a massive willow tree. It had been Ivy's space too. She used to bring Fanny here when she was very young and read her stories. They would dip their toes into the water and chase butterflies.

The pair of ducks she'd seen yesterday were nowhere in sight, but in their place was a pintail duck guiding her ducklings. Smiling, Fanny walked to the edge of the pond. "Well, aren't you the sweetest things?"

"Pardon me if I take issue with that."

Fanny swung around at the sound of the familiar voice. Standing near a tree was the man she couldn't marry.

Chapter Ten

❧

"IN MY OPINION, *you're* the sweetest thing." David couldn't believe his good fortune. He'd been on his way to see Fanny, and here she was.

"Are you really there?" she asked. Her voice carried to him across the water.

The pale green ribbons of her bonnet hung loose and dangled against the floral print of her walking dress. A matching ribbon was drawn beneath her breasts, accentuating her curves. Her gown was white with small blue flowers edged with leaves that coordinated with the ribbon. The color scheme perfectly matched her eyes, and he drank the entirety in like a man stranded in the desert.

"Yes." He moved forward, but the pond was between them. He began to skirt the edge.

"Careful you don't fall in," she said.

"Shouldn't I be cautioning you?"

"Probably."

He didn't stop until he was a few feet away from her. "Is that a drawing book?"

She glanced down to the item in her hand. "Yes. There was a pair of common pochards here yesterday."

"And you were sketching them? May I see?"

A pretty blush bloomed in her cheeks. "It isn't finished."

He shrugged. "I don't mind."

She held the book up and flipped it open. "Here." She turned it in her hands and showed him the half-drawn sketch.

He peered at the pencil drawing and smiled. "You're

quite good."

She closed the book with a laugh. "Now you're just being polite."

"Polite would be saying it's a nice picture."

Her eyes narrowed skeptically, but she didn't respond.

"Will you draw the pintail and her babies today?"

"I was considering it," she said. "Until I saw you. David—Lord St. Ives—what on earth are you doing here?"

He took a step toward her. "I saw a golden eagle and couldn't help but follow it. They're quite rare."

"You followed a golden eagle from London?"

"From the road." He gestured toward the west. "It's maybe a ten-minute walk that way."

"I know where the road is," she said. "I live near here."

He blinked, taking pleasure in pretending this was a chance meeting. Which it was. Partly. "Do you?"

She flattened her lips. "If you expect me to believe that you don't know that, I will know you are being more than polite. You're being downright condescending."

He was instantly contrite. "Fanny, I was only teasing, never condescending. And please don't call me Lord St. Ives. I couldn't bear it."

"I can't very well call you David." There was an edge to her voice, and he wondered if she'd even received his letters. She hadn't responded, and he'd been afraid she might not welcome him.

"I wrote to you," he said softly. "Did you get my letters?"

"I did." She turned from him and appeared to study the ducks, who had swum to the other side of the pond. Her demeanor seemed to indicate that his fears were accurate.

He stepped toward her again. "I came a long way to talk to you."

She didn't turn. "You said in your last letter that if I didn't respond, you'd leave me alone."

"Turns out that's far easier said than done. But if you want that, I'll go."

She looked toward him, her aqua eyes unfathomable. "I don't know what I want. I know I wanted you, but I think that moment has passed."

"Was it really just a moment?" he asked. "I am not going to marry Miss Stoke. How could I consider anyone when the only woman who occupies my mind is you?"

"Please don't say anything more." Her voice was tight, and he caught a glimpse of anguish in her eyes before she turned her head. "There are...reasons we can't be together."

He'd been about to go to her, had hoped to touch her. But her words stopped him cold. Yes, there were reasons—according to his mother. Was Fanny aware of them too?

"Your mother—"

"You mustn't listen to her," David said. He erased the distance between them and clasped her waist, turning her to face him. "None of what matters to her matters to me. I don't care that your family and my family despise each other. I refuse to allow something that occurred before we were even born dictate our happiness."

She stared up at him then blinked. "It was *your* family that employed my great-uncle and accused him of kidnapping and murder."

He couldn't tell if she was asking him a question or not. It hadn't sounded like a question, but her expression seemed to indicate surprise. "You didn't know? What other reasons could there be to keep us apart?"

She shook her head and glanced toward the pintails. "Your promise to your father, for one. Can you really turn your back on that pledge?" When her gaze met his once more, her uncertainty was plain.

He put his other hand on her waist and longed to pull her against him, to reassure her that he was choosing her. "I miss my father every day. And I loved him so very much. It pains me to break that promise, but I made it in a time of grief and anguish. He would have wanted me to be happy. And you, Fanny, you will make me happy. As much as I loved him, I vow to love you even more."

"You love me?"

He wanted to erase the doubt lingering in her eyes. "More than I can say."

She dropped her sketchbook, and her arms came up to encircle his neck just before she pressed her mouth to his. He'd waited so long for this kiss. Months. Weeks. A lifetime.

He tilted his head and pulled her to his chest, desperate to feel her heat and desire. Her lips slid along his, tantalizing his senses. Then he felt her tongue, and he opened to meet her, surrendering himself to delicious abandon.

Their secluded location meant he didn't have to worry about someone stumbling upon them. Unless… He pulled back. "How far away is your house?"

She tugged at his neck, urging him to continue the kiss. "Far enough."

That was all he needed to hear. He splayed his hands along her lower back, caressing her curves and relishing the feel of her body pressed to his. Need pulsed through him. It would be very easy to take things much too far. He nibbled her lower lip and pulled his mouth from hers.

Her eyes were dark with desire, her lips reddened and parted as she drew in rapid breaths. "How can you love me?"

His mouth curved into a smile. "If I knew that, I'd be a far wiser man than I am."

"And why did you stop kissing me?" She looked supremely put out.

"Because I don't want to overstep. Not until we're married. Will your parents accept me, or will they be as opposed to our marriage as my mother and uncle?"

She jerked back from him. "Marriage? I'm fairly certain they won't allow it."

He frowned. "I came to ask your father for your hand—provided you wanted it. Of course, I must ask you properly."

"No, don't." She shook her head, edging away from him until he dropped his hands from her waist. "I can't marry you."

⬦ε·3⬦

HIS EYES WIDENED and then his jaw clenched. "This business between our families doesn't matter. It has nothing to do with us."

"No, but it would be difficult." And it wasn't the only thing. How could she tell him that his mother had threatened her?

"We can overcome difficult," he said. "I am breaking a promise I made to my father, and I would do it a thousand times to be with you."

His words filled her with joy and hope, but also grounded her with worry. "How can you be so certain?"

"Because I am. I told you I loved you."

She'd thought she was falling in love with him, but had then spent the last several weeks banishing him from her mind. And yet seeing him today brought all the emotion she'd tried to bury rushing back over her. He was a song in her heart and a bird taking flight.

"I love you too," she said softly.

His brow gathered into a tight pleat. "Then why won't you marry me?"

She wanted to tell him, but the words just wouldn't come.

"Tell me, Fanny. You owe me that."

She *owed* him? Her eyes narrowed as irritation sprouted in her chest. "I am not beholden to you for anything."

He exhaled, his features relaxing briefly. "No, you're not. But if I love you and you love me, you can't just tell me we can't be married and not give an explanation." His gaze hardened with determination. "I'm not going to give up easily. Not when I know you love me."

How could she walk away from that? "It's more than our shared family history. When I mentioned your mother earlier, I was referring to a conversation we had before I left London."

His face paled. "Is that why you left so abruptly? What did she say to you?"

"It was after that man—I don't remember his name—challenged Mr. Royston to a duel. You'd left the ball, and she came to introduce herself. She brought up…things from my sister's past. Things people don't know." Fanny bent to pick up her sketchbook and turned toward the pond. "The mention of a duel had people talking. About West."

"I heard about that. He called a man out for insulting your sister." He took a step toward her. "Fanny, I don't care that your father is a cabinetmaker."

She glanced at him but returned her focus to the water. It was easier not to look at him. "That's not the real reason he insulted Ivy. They met here in Yorkshire more than a decade ago. Ivy fell in love with him, and he asked her to marry him. She…gave herself to him, thinking they would be wed. She's the first one to tell you it was foolish, but I daresay I understand how one might be carried away." She cast him another sidelong glance as heat crept up her neck.

"He got her with child and refused to marry her. When my parents found out, they banished her. She ended up in a workhouse where she birthed the babe, but it didn't survive. A kind patroness took pity on her and found her work as a companion. Eventually, she ended up working for Lady Dunn." She turned to face him then, her insides a tumult of anguish and anger for what had happened to Ivy. Yes, she'd made a mistake, but who among them hadn't? Ivy had more than paid for trusting the wrong man.

"I would want to kill Bothwick too," David said softly, his voice a dangerous thread.

Fanny appreciated his loyalty to her sister. "Apparently, his mother, Lady Bothwick, is a friend of your mother's. If I marry you, your mother will tell everyone Ivy's secret. I can't let that happen, David. I will do anything to protect my sister—even walk away from you."

His stare was dark but compassionate. "Which is what you did."

She nodded. A moment passed, and she watched his expression alter.

His lip curled, and his eyes were a thunderstorm. "I won't let her say a word."

"How can you stop her?"

"No one will believe it." He sounded certain, and Fanny wished she shared his confidence. "Your sister is a duchess."

"And your mother is a countess," she said. "Ivy is already looked at with derision by some because of our family, because my father is in trade. It may not matter to you, but it matters to others."

"Why should we care what others think?"

"Perhaps we shouldn't, but I won't put Ivy through that sort of notoriety, nor will I subject her children to it. They're too young to know anything now—and one isn't even yet born—but the past would follow them." Fanny clutched her book to her chest. "Furthermore, West's behavior before he married Ivy was less than esteemed by those who think themselves superior. People won't think twice about denigrating his wife."

"My mother will keep quiet. I'll make sure of it." His eyes were cool, his tone firm.

His assurance gave her no comfort. Maybe it was because she couldn't forget the nastiness of his mother's demeanor. She'd been so cavalier and disparaging. She searched his face, needing a definitive answer. "How? She was rather adamant I leave you alone. She thinks I'm utterly beneath you, David. How are we to have a marriage when your mother thinks that?"

She recalled that her mother despised Ivy's husband, and it didn't matter. Except Ivy didn't have a relationship with her mother. David did. "Are you and your mother close?" Fanny asked.

He looked past her, perhaps at the mother pintail duck. "Not as close as I was to my father, but I thought we were, yes." His gaze found hers again. "However, since my father died, things have been strained. It was such a shock for both of us. This promise I made to my father seems to be very important to her."

Fanny hadn't experienced loss like that and struggled to understand. She wanted to be compassionate. "Perhaps keeping that promise somehow keeps your father more alive—at least in her mind."

"You're very wise, Fanny. Wiser than I am." He glanced back toward the pond. "She can be…difficult, but I know she only wants what's best for me. I'll convince her that you're what's best for me."

"No one can ever know—about Ivy," Fanny said. "I don't even want Ivy to know that your mother is aware of her background."

"I completely understand. Will you trust me to protect her?"

If it were just her, Fanny would have no hesitation, but Ivy had already been through so much. Fanny couldn't ever expose her to more pain. "I would trust you with my life, but this is Ivy's, not mine."

His answering stare was heartfelt and sincere. "Your family is my family."

Again, the joy his words gave her were tempered with worry. "I think my father and your uncle might have something to say about that."

He grimaced. "Then we won't give them the opportunity. Perhaps we should leave for Gretna Green straightaway." He glanced toward the road.

"You want to elope right now?"

He lifted a shoulder. "Why not?"

She thought of what awaited her at home—Mr. Duckworth and a weighty dose of pressure to marry him. Suddenly, dashing off to Scotland seemed a brilliant idea. But then what? Then they'd have to deal with the consequences, and what if his mother exposed Ivy anyway? Fanny wanted to believe the woman wouldn't do such a thing to her daughter-in-law's family, but the countess's contempt was emblazoned in her mind. There was also the matter of why she'd returned to Yorkshire in the first place. "My brother is getting married day after tomorrow."

"You don't want to share the same wedding date?"

She couldn't help but laugh, and he smiled in return. "That's not the issue, and you well know it. I came here to see him wed. He's marrying the younger sister of my oldest and dearest friend."

"Fanny, I shall say it again, you've the kindest, most generous heart of anyone I've ever known."

"It's not just the wedding. I'm still nervous about your mother." She worried her lower lip as she stared up at him. "You can promise me the moon, but you can't control her."

His eyes glinted like candlelight on polished silver. "I can if I cut her off. She won't want to lose the income I provide her or give up living in one of my houses."

"You would do that to your own mother?" she asked.

"To protect my wife and her sister, yes."

Fanny's heart swelled. She went to him and cupped his face in her hands. "I love you so very much."

"Not as much as I love you."

"Shall we argue about it?" she teased.

"I'd much rather kiss you."

"Of course you would. You're the Duke of Kisses." She grinned just before she stood on her toes, and his lips swept over hers.

Heat and desire rushed over her. She dropped her sketchbook again and threw her arms around his neck. To know he loved her and that they would be together filled her with joy. He'd been a dream she'd never imagined would come true. And yet how could it not? He felt so perfect against her, so *right*.

The first kiss was long and lush, their tongues exploring, while the next ones were shorter as their hands began taking over the exploration. He stroked her back, her hip, and then up the side of her rib cage until he cupped her breast.

She gasped into his mouth, eager for more. There was a tightness in her belly—and lower—that she longed to feel release.

His shaft was hard against her, just as he'd said it would be that day he'd kissed her in the garden at Clare House. She knew enough about sex to understand what it was and where it would go. What she didn't know was how it would feel.

And how she wanted to.

She pushed into him, wanting his touch and wanting to touch him too. Dragging her hands down his chest, she thrust them under his coat to find his heat. But it wasn't enough. She wanted more.

She dug her fingers into his shoulders, dislodging the coat.

He groaned just before breaking the kiss. "Fanny. I want—"

"What I want. We're to be married, David. Why must we wait to lie together?"

He kissed her again, hard and fast. "You're sorely tempting me."

She looked around, her gaze landing on the willow tree. "Come with me." She took his hand and started to lead him to the other end of the pond.

"Wait, your book." He leaned down to pick it up before following in her wake. "Where are we going?"

"This is my private place." She threw him a smile over her shoulder.

She pulled him under the canopy of the willow, the branches draping down around them making it seem as if they'd walked into their own secluded sanctuary. Turning, she took her sketchbook from his hand and set it near the base of the tree. Then she removed her bonnet and placed it on top of the book.

She faced him and reached behind herself to grope for the laces of her gown. Unfortunately, she couldn't find them. For the most part, her London wardrobe required Barker's assistance, and Barker was, thankfully, back at the house.

His brows pitched low, and he regarded her with deep suspicion. "Fanny, what are you doing?"

"Seducing you."

Chapter Eleven

❦❧

"SEDUCING ME?" DAVID looked so confounded, she nearly laughed. But this was a serious moment, and she wanted him to know *she* was serious.

She moved toward him. "I want to be with you."

He glanced around before settling his surprised gaze on her. "Here?"

"Can you think of a better place? Whenever I am outside, I think of you and how we met. Birdsong is music, as is the rustle of the trees and the swish of the wind."

"When you put it like that, no, I *can't* think of a better place." He reached for her hand. She quickly removed her gloves, tossing them toward her bonnet, but they fell short. When David didn't immediately remove his, she took his hand and tugged the glove off.

Then she laid her palm over his, her fingers to his wrist, and lightly pressed her flesh against his. "This is better."

He ran his thumb along the side of her hand. "You deserve more than this when we're together for the first time."

She shook her head. "No, I deserve you."

"I'm not entirely sure the same can be said of me," he said wryly. "But I will spend my life trying to." He pulled his hand from beneath hers and tore his other glove away, flinging it aside. His hat followed.

Then he cupped her head, driving his fingers into the base of her hair and stroking his thumbs along her jawbones. "God, you're beautiful." He kissed her again, with sweet ferocity, his tongue driving into her mouth, claiming her.

She put her hands beneath his coat once more, and this time when she brought her hands up to his shoulders, he helped her to shrug it away from his body, pulling his touch from her just long enough for the garment to drop to the ground.

The loss of his coat was glorious, but she wanted more of him. She worked at the buttons of his waistcoat, pushing it open when they were free. He threw that aside too, and she went to work on his cravat, loosening the knot with ease and then pulling it free.

All the while, he kissed her, exploring and devouring, then moving his lips along her jaw and down her neck. Her hands found the open neck of his shirt, and she ran her fingers along his heated flesh, gasping at the contact.

He pulled away from her briefly as he guided her to the ground. "You must tell me to stop at any moment. Promise me, Fanny."

She stared into his eyes, never more sure of anything. "I won't. Touch me, David. Love me."

His lips claimed hers as they reached the ground, her sitting and him kneeling beside her. He kissed along her jaw once more and moved around to her back, his mouth trailing fire along her skin. His fingers found the laces of her gown, and she felt the bodice loosen. Meanwhile, his tongue traced a wicked pattern on her nape and down to the top of her dress.

She shivered, her body pulsing with need. Turning her head, he kissed her, their tongues meeting in a rapturous dance of desire.

He moved away from her briefly, and when he returned, he folded his coat and set it behind her before gently guiding her backward.

"You made me a pillow," she said, laughing softly.

"It's the least I can do."

"The *least* you can do is satisfy this ache inside me. Please tell me you're going to do that."

"I should like to, but perhaps you should be more specific." His brow furrowed. "What sort of ache?"

She wasn't sure if he was teasing her. "Shouldn't you know? I hate thinking of you with other women, but I am not so naïve to think you're a...virgin. Surely you know how to induce pleasure."

"Well, I don't want to speak of my past experience— ever. But I will say that I know...enough. However, every woman is different." He winced. "Forget I said that. All that matters is you, and you must tell me what you want and if I'm getting it right. Tell me where you ache." He lay down beside her and propped his head on his hand so he could look at her.

Heat burned her cheeks, but not as much as it burned between her thighs. She couldn't start with that, however. She wasn't sure she could start with anything. "You really want me to say it?"

He leaned down and licked the outer edge of her ear before whispering, "Talking during sex is incredibly arousing."

"Is it?" The question erupted from her mouth as a pitiful squeak.

His tongue continued its exploration, and the need inside her blossomed into stark desire. Or maybe even lust, as base as that sounded. Of course it was base. This was absolutely primal, and she wanted every bit of it.

"When you touched my breast...before...that was nice."

"Just nice?" His fingertips traced along her throat, making circles as he moved lower. Her bodice was loose enough that he easily slid his hand beneath her clothing.

"It made me feel…wild. Passionate. I wanted you to touch it more."

"How?" His lips and tongue kissed along her throat, sucking her flesh and sending shafts of heat directly to her sex.

"Harder. Without clothing." She swore. "My corset is going to be in the way."

"Turn." He guided her to roll to her side, exposing her back to him once more. He loosened her gown even more, then pushed it down over her shoulders to her elbows. Then he loosened her corset and turned her back toward him. He tugged her sleeves down her arms until the gown was free from her torso.

She held her breath as his hand came up and slipped under her gaping corset and the chemise she wore beneath. He cupped her naked breast, then closed his fingers over the nipple. "Is this better?" he asked.

"Oh *yes*." She closed her eyes and arched up from the ground, seeking more of his touch. He squeezed lightly, and she moaned, the seductive sound foreign to her ears.

She felt her garments tugged lower and then a wet sensation on her nipple. Opening her eyes, she saw his head bent over her. His tongue teased her flesh just before his mouth closed over the tip, and he sucked. Gently at first, then harder. Each sensation was new and spectacular, and she felt as though she might combust into a roaring flame.

Grasping his head, she tangled her fingers in his dark hair. He increased his speed and pressure, taunting her with his tongue and lips and even a graze of his teeth. There was a pause, and she opened her eyes.

He looked up at her, his eyes gleaming in the filtered light making its way through the willow branches. "Where else?"

There was no hesitation this time. She was too far gone to do anything but beg for release. "Between my legs," she whispered.

Her gown began a slow rise over her calf and then her knee before sliding over her thigh. Cool air bathed her heated flesh.

His gaze never left hers as he settled the gown at her hips, exposing her. She felt reckless and shameless, and she didn't care a whit. Nothing about this was wrong or bad. She loved him and he loved her, and nothing in her life had felt so perfect.

When his fingers stroked along her sex, she stopped thinking. Sensation took over, and she closed her eyes once more, instinctively opening her legs to his touch.

He teased her flesh with light brushes of his fingertips. "Is this where it aches, my love?" His voice was soft and urgent against her ear before he nibbled at the lobe, once again driving passion straight through her like an arrow finding its target.

"Yes." Her breath came in short rasps as her heart thumped with desire. "More, please."

"What about here?" He touched a spot at the top of her sex, rubbing and pressing. Lights danced behind her closed eyes, and the ache intensified. She was racing toward something.

"It's like the phaeton race. There's a finish line, isn't there?"

"Most definitely. Would you like me to take you there?"

"Yes, please."

"Will you let me do it with my mouth?"

Her eyes flew open, and she stared into his eyes. "You would do that?"

"Eagerly." His stare was dark and provocative, his lips parted as he moved down her body. "Bend your legs." He guided her to bend at the knees, and he settled himself between her thighs.

At first, he just continued to touch her, his fingers pressing on that delicious spot. "What is that?" she asked.

"Your clitoris. It's very sensitive, as you've realized." He stroked along her folds, his touch lightly probing.

She moaned, opening her legs even more. "Please, David." She wanted to go faster. She wanted to reach the finish.

What had been slow and languorous suddenly became swift and desperate. His lips moved across her clitoris as his finger slid into her sheath. Her hips moved up off the ground, partly in surprise but mostly with need. This was what she wanted.

He stroked into her, filling her and enticing her—satisfaction seemed so near and then so far away. His hand left her, and he clasped her thighs, guiding them to his shoulders as his mouth opened over her sex. It was like when he kissed her, his lips and tongue licking and sucking, driving her to want more.

The pressure she felt built tighter and hotter, the excitement roiling as the finish came into view. She could sense it was close, her body quivering as his tongue delved deep inside her. He held her fast as her hips bucked up. She couldn't seem to stop from moving. She needed to feel him, to welcome him, to own him.

One hand left her thigh, and then something—his thumb, maybe—pressed her clitoris. He moved her flesh, working her into a frenzy that was already upon her. She cried out as the pressure broke free at last.

Then his mouth was gone from her as he continued to work her flesh with his fingers. After a moment, she opened her eyes to see him position himself between her legs.

His gaze found hers. "Do you want me to stop?"

She couldn't quite make sense of his question. Why would he stop when he'd already given her what she wanted? She glanced down and saw that his hands were on his fall, and she felt stupid. Or at lease naïve. Of course they weren't finished.

"I didn't realize there was more to do than just you putting your…penis inside me."

"Or cock, if you prefer. I tend to like that word, being a bird man." He winked at her. "We can stop if you want to."

She shook her head. "I don't want to. I want to feel you. It may be a month or more before we're married. I'd rather not wait that long. It feels as though we've waited long enough." He'd occupied her mind for so much of the past six months.

"I'll go slow," he said, unbuttoning his fall.

She clasped his hips, pulling him against her. "You'd better not. I've decided I like fast."

He groaned, and she felt his cock nudging against her opening. "Fanny, you are going to ensure this is faster than it should ever be. A man prides himself on lasting a long time."

"Does he?"

"To prolong the pleasure."

"I think pleasure should be measured by intensity, not time. Wouldn't it be better to do this ten times than just once for the same amount of time?"

He laughed. "Yes, but, ah, men's equipment doesn't exactly work that way. If I'm ever able to do this ten times in a row, I fear I may end up dead."

"Why would you say such a thing?"

He slid into her slowly, and she felt a moment's pain to go with the uncomfortable pressure of having him invade her flesh. "The intensity you so aptly mentioned. Coming ten times might kill me, especially since I think this may be the most intense orgasm of my life."

The pain was lessening, and Fanny liked how the conversation was keeping it from bothering her. "Is that what just happened to me? An orgasm?"

"Yes." His voice was strained. "Christ, Fanny, I really hope time isn't an issue, because I may come if you move. *Please* don't move."

"And coming is another way of saying orgasm? How fascinating."

"Is this a lecture?" he asked, sounding a bit incredulous.

She curled her hand around his nape and drew his head down. "It's an education, and I am exceedingly glad to have you as my tutor."

He pushed a bit farther, filling and stretching her. She gasped, and he asked if she was all right.

"Just accommodating. This is…different." The discomfort was all but gone. "I'm waiting for that desperate sensation to return." She looked up at him with worry. "Unless… Am I only to have that one orgasm?"

"Not if I can bloody help it. Though I understand the first time can be less satisfying." He kissed her, his lips lingering against hers. "Let's see if we can get you there again." He slipped his hand between them and found her clitoris again. He circled her flesh, sparking that now-familiar desire.

"Yes, that's it," she breathed as arousal flared through her. Having him inside her elicited a new and delicious sensation. But there was something missing. She wanted to move. "Can I really not move?"

He took his hand from between them and planted it next to her head. "You can. You should. That's what we do. Allow me to demonstrate." He nearly withdrew from her, then pressed forward. He repeated the motion again and again.

"That's quite nice."

He nipped her neck. "There you go with 'nice' again."

"It's lovely. Wonderful."

He moved a bit faster, driving into her with more force. She sucked in a sharp breath. "Oh, now that's *spectacular*. Do it again."

He did, his hips snapping against hers. The next time, she moved with him. "Divine," she said as the pressure built inside her once more.

"Wrap your legs around my waist."

Her gown was bunched between them, but she lifted her legs and moaned as the movement fit them more snugly together. "Oh!"

"Hold on to me, Fanny." He claimed her mouth and kissed her with a fierce passion that was mirrored in the movement of his hips and the stroke of his cock.

She closed her eyes and clasped him tightly, gripping his back and accidentally caressing his backside. He groaned again, and she decided it had been a good accident. But how she wished he was naked so she could feel all of him. Some day soon, she would. For now, she would lose herself in this glorious moment.

He moved faster still, carrying her upward, and she truly felt like a bird taking off in flight. Once more, his hand brushed her clitoris, pushing her toward that looming finish. It seemed a bit farther to reach this time, but at last, the world broke open, and light and heat rushed over her.

Removing his hand, he gathered her close and drove into her several more times before crying out. She stroked his head and kissed his cheek, his neck, before falling back and resting in sweet oblivion.

Some moments later, he'd slowed and began to withdraw from her. "You're leaving me?" she asked.

"I must." He kissed her forehead. "We can't stroll around joined as we are."

She giggled as he sat back from her.

He reached for her skirts with a wince. "I don't have anything to help you clean up."

She sat up, and he rushed to help her. "That's what a petticoat is for, silly." She'd just be sure to launder it herself.

They took care of tidying themselves, and then he helped her up so he could lace up her garments.

"Fanny!"

They both froze and time seemed to stop. Fanny recognized the voice—it was her brother Jacob.

She turned her head. "Hurry. That's my brother. I'm supposed to be home." She'd completely forgotten about Mr. Duckworth's visit.

David made quick work of the laces, and she stepped away from him. "I'll come with you."

She shook her head. "Absolutely not. I can't have my parents knowing I was alone with you. It will be Ivy all over again." She winced, realizing this *was* Ivy all over again. She'd given herself to a man—with a title—on the promise of marriage. "You're not going to abandon me, are you?"

He picked up her gloves and bonnet and set the latter atop her head with infinite care. "Never."

"Fanny!" The voice was much closer. He was almost to the pond.

"I have to go," she whispered fiercely.

"I'll call on you tomorrow, then," he said.

Fanny looked through the branches of the willow and saw her brother come through the hedgerow. She was out of time. Pulling her gloves on, she dashed from the canopy and ran to meet Jacob.

He frowned down at her, his green-brown eyes cutting over her. "You look like you rolled around in the grass. Did you fall asleep?"

"Yes." She seized on the excellent excuse.

He glanced toward the willow, and she prayed he couldn't see David. Hopefully, David had hidden himself or left the area entirely.

"You're late," Jacob snapped. "Mother is livid."

"When isn't she?" Fanny muttered.

"Isn't that the truth?"

Fanny shot her gaze to Jacob, surprised at his response. He merely lifted a shoulder. "She's been especially difficult since you left," Jacob said. "I'm counting the days until I can leave."

She started through the hedgerow, eager to leave the pond. "To do what?"

"No idea. If you think of something, let me know."

Jacob had learned cabinetry from their father, but he'd never seemed as passionate about it as John. Jacob seemed to prefer looking after the animals and caring for the crops they grew.

"You should be a farmer," she said, an idea forming in her mind.

"Are you going to get Mary to set me up the way she has you?" he asked sharply.

Fanny flinched. "I didn't realize you might want that. I could talk to her, if you want me to."

"Don't do me any favors."

"Why not? You're my brother. And you're *Ivy's* brother too."

Jacob shot her an uncertain stare that quickly turned into a scowl. "I don't want anything from her or her fancy husband."

Fanny exhaled. "Now you sound like Mother and Father. Don't let them color your mind. Ivy and West are good and kind, and they'd help family."

"You likely won't have a chance to talk to them anyway. Father's keen to marry you off to Duckworth."

"Well, *I'm* not keen to marry him."

"Fanny, when are you going to realize you don't have a lot of choice in this world?" He actually sounded a bit sad.

"Oh, but I do, Jacob," she said softly. "I do." And tomorrow, David would come and formally present that choice. He'd ask for her hand, and her parents would be furious—both because she wouldn't be marrying Mr. Duckworth and would instead marry into the family that was perhaps responsible for the disappearance of her father's beloved uncle.

As they neared the house, she realized she'd forgotten her sketchbook. Ah well, David could bring it to her tomorrow—she'd just have to make sure her mother didn't notice that he had it.

Right now, however, she had to make sure *no one* noticed she'd just had a tryst beneath a willow tree.

⚜

THE FOLLOWING MORNING, David wrestled with his feelings of excitement and joy over his future with Fanny and his disappointment and anger toward his mother and her meddling. He was eager to set her straight and ensure she understood that he was marrying Fanny whether she liked it or not.

Though they weren't in London, he determined it was still too early to call on the Snowdens. Perhaps he should have a glass of brandy to bolster his nerves. If they were any more determined to keep him and Fanny from marrying as his mother was, he'd need it.

David picked up Fanny's sketchbook. She'd left it beneath the willow yesterday. In it, he'd written a note to her along with a drawing of the golden eagle that had inadvertently led him to her. The species would forevermore be his favorite bird.

He'd been tempted to draw a picture of Fanny instead. Her on the ground with her eyes half-closed and her lips parted in seductive invitation. And he *would* draw that— someday. When she could pose before him.

His body stirred with arousal. He grabbed his hat and headed for the door, intent on a vigorous walk to cool his ardor and organize his thoughts before calling on the Snowdens.

He opened the door and stopped short. Standing in the corridor was Fanny. She was the picture of fresh beauty— her red-gold curls peeking from beneath the crown of her straw bonnet. A bright blue ribbon was tied beneath her chin, matching the pin-width stripes on her day dress. Beyond her stood another woman. She was a good ten or so years older than Fanny and garbed in a more somber costume, indicating she was probably her maid.

"Fanny." He belatedly bowed. "I wasn't expecting to see you until later."

"You said you were going to call on me." She winced. "I don't think that's a good idea." She turned to the other woman. "Barker, would you mind waiting here for a moment while I go in and speak with his lordship? We'll leave the door open."

The maid nodded, but there was a glint to her gaze and a slight tilt to her mouth that betrayed some measure of amusement.

David stepped back and allowed Fanny to enter. Her

gaze dipped to his hand. "Oh, you have my sketchbook, thank goodness."

"I was just going to take it on a walk with me in case I came across some aviary wonder."

She smiled. "I have no doubt you would." She looked around the small, well-appointed chamber, and her gaze fell on the four-poster bed.

He set the book on the table near the fireplace where a few coals smoldered, and moved closer to her. "You shouldn't look at the bed unless you want to use it," he said softly.

Her eyes shot to his. "With the door open?"

"Probably a bad idea."

"Most definitely, but now that you've mentioned it, I shall be loath to forget the suggestion..." she murmured, her eyes bright with desire.

The arousal he'd felt earlier stoked into something hotter, and he had to work to tamp it down. "I should be sorry I brought it up."

"But you're not." She smiled again. "How I adore you."

"And I you."

The happiness faded from her expression. "As I said before, you can't call on me today. My parents will never approve our marriage."

"We don't need their approval," he said. "You're of age. We can wed whenever we choose."

"Precisely. So why bother telling them at all?"

"Because they're your parents?" he asked.

"And they despise your family. Furthermore, they despise titles of any kind—because of your family." Her eyes narrowed in disgust. "My sister married a bloody duke, but in their eyes, you'd think she'd wed a murderer."

"They sound unpleasant." And that sounded like an

understatement.

"The entire situation is unpleasant. If your family hadn't been so angry that their daughter had fallen in love with the footman, perhaps my great-uncle would still be here."

"Fallen in love? Is that what they told you?" David recalled his father's anguish over his sister being kidnapped by the footman who'd brought her body home a year later.

Suspicion lined her features. "What did your family tell you?"

"That your great-uncle kidnapped my Aunt Catherine. My family searched but wasn't able to find them. A year later, he brought her body home. She'd died in childbirth."

Fanny sucked in a breath, her eyes darkening with sorrow. "I'm so sorry. However, my Great-uncle George loved her. They'd defied her father—and propriety—just to be together. It sounds terribly romantic."

"It would if it were true."

Emotion blazed in her eyes. "Why wouldn't it be?"

"Because your great-uncle lied. It's very possible he fell in love with my aunt. By my father's and uncle's accounts, she was a beautiful and kindhearted young woman, if a bit shy. She hadn't yet had a Season due to her reticence, but she looked forward to it. Why would a woman with aspirations for a Season run off with a footman?"

Fanny crossed her arms as her brows formed a V on her forehead. "Because she was in love with him. I had aspirations for a Season, but then I met you, and now I don't give a flying fig. *You* had plans to marry your father's best friend's daughter, but that didn't happen either. Sometimes, life doesn't go the way we intend."

He didn't want to argue with her or to be angry. "This isn't our fight," he said, taking a step toward her.

She uncrossed her arms, and her features relaxed slightly. "No, it isn't. We can never know what really happened. I prefer to think they were in love, don't you?" She looked up at him, and she was so earnest, so heartfelt in her query, that he couldn't help but agree.

"Why wouldn't I want love to be the reason?" He curled his arm around her waist and drew her against him. "Love is *my* reason."

She rested her hand on his shoulder. "It's mine too."

He dipped his head and kissed her. She tasted sweet and fresh, like his favorite summer day outside. Reluctantly, he stepped back. "Unless you want to end up on that bed, we'd best put some distance between us."

She nodded, her eyes glazed with desire.

"So if I'm not to call on your parents, what is your plan?" he asked. It was an important question, plus it took his mind off the distracting pulse of his cock.

"The wedding is tomorrow. I can leave after that."

"You'll go back to Stour's Edge?"

She nodded again. "You could follow me. Then we can share our plans with West and Ivy."

"Where shall we be married?"

"St. Peter and St. Paul's in Clare."

"That's a beautiful church," he said, smiling. "We'll have the banns read as soon as we arrive."

She frowned, her features darkening. "We can't do that."

Alarm rushed through him. "Why not?"

"Because the banns will also need to be read here, and my parents will likely try to say there is an impediment."

"But there isn't." At least none that he was aware of.

"Of course not. They'll likely say I'm promised to Mr. Duckworth." She wrinkled her nose in distaste.

"The hell they will. I'm obtaining a license the minute

we get to Clare. We'll wed as soon as possible."

Her gaze warmed as she smiled. "We're really going to be married." Her voice carried a hint of awe as well as uncertainty.

He took her hands and lifted one to his mouth to press a kiss on the back of her glove. "Nothing will stop us."

She squeezed his hands before letting him go. "Until tomorrow."

"When the future shall be ours."

She picked up her sketchbook and blew him a kiss before departing the room. The air lost all vitality, and David couldn't help but glance toward the bed and think of opportunities lost.

Tomorrow suddenly felt like a lifetime.

No, tomorrow was the start of it.

Chapter Twelve

❦

DINNER AT THE Snowden house was to be a family affair to celebrate John's wedding the following day. The kitchen was abuzz with preparations for the wedding breakfast, which would take place immediately following tomorrow morning's ceremony at the parish church in Pickering.

Fanny gathered with her family in the dining room, where her father offered a toast. "To John. May you and Mercy enjoy a long and happy marriage." He bestowed a proud, paternal smile on his second eldest before taking a sip of wine.

Everyone lifted their glasses to John before drinking. As Mother, seated at the opposite end of the table from Father, set her wine down, she said, "It's so nice to finally be celebrating a wedding." She cast a glance toward Fanny that was laced with disappointment.

Fanny bit her tongue lest she tell them they could have celebrated Ivy's if they hadn't been so horrid. But then if they hadn't thrown Ivy out ten years ago, her life would have been vastly different. Indeed, *she* may have found herself married to Mr. Duckworth.

Her conversation with David floated through her mind—things often didn't go as planned and sometimes, maybe oftentimes, that was for the best.

"Perhaps there will be another wedding soon," John said, looking toward Fanny.

For a brief moment, she wondered how John could possibly know she would be marrying David within the month. But of course he couldn't. The only person who knew was Barker, and she wouldn't tell.

"Very soon, if only she would accept Mr. Duckworth," Mother said. "You had a nice visit yesterday, didn't you?"

Fanny had arrived to find Mr. Duckworth in the sitting room, tapping his foot impatiently. He'd stared derisively at her rumpled clothing and asked if she'd tumbled out of a tree.

She'd laughed and given the excuse Jacob had offered—that she'd fallen asleep by accident. She'd then sought to bore him with talk of birds, but he'd maneuvered the discussion in the direction of mating habits in an effort to be flirtatious.

Fanny had pleaded the need to tidy herself up, which had thankfully drawn the visit to a close. "Yes, it was fine," Fanny answered.

"She doesn't fancy him," Jacob said, once again surprising Fanny. Why was he being so...helpful?

"She could if she wanted to," Father grumbled before taking a bite of boiled beef. His gaze fixed on her while he chewed. Once he swallowed, he asked, "Why were you in town this morning? Henry said he saw you and your maid near the Black Rabbit."

Blast. She'd looked around to see if anyone might have noted her presence, but she'd somehow missed her father's assistant. If she'd encountered anyone, she'd been prepared with an answer to just such a question. "I was looking for property for a workhouse. I am working with a group of patronesses to fund a workhouse for young women and orphans who need to learn a skill. It will better prepare them for a life of meaningful and gratifying employment, which will improve their livelihoods."

Her mother and father gaped at her while John continued attacking his plate of food. Jacob, who sat beside her said, "That sounds very useful. Do you truly know people who can make such a thing happen?"

She nodded, ignoring her parents' reactions. "I do—through Ivy."

"*Fanny.*" Her father's sharp voice cut through the tense air.

"I can't very well call her Mary," she said, indignant. "She is Ivy now. And why should you care anyway? It's not as if you want to recognize her as a member of this family. Never mind that she's a duchess with considerable standing in Society."

"Watch your tongue, gel," her father rumbled, his graying brows gathering above his wide-set eyes. "Don't make me change my mind about letting you go back to her house."

"I'm old enough to make my own decisions," she muttered, poking at her food.

"Bad ones," Mother said. "This workhouse nonsense is a terrible idea. You'll encourage young women in ways they ought not be encouraged."

Fanny blinked at her mother as anger boiled within her. "And how should young women with no means to care for themselves be encouraged? Should we put them into a workhouse where they can't hope for a better life, for freedom or independence?"

"Fanny, you've always had lofty ideas," John said, laughing. He seemed oblivious to the aura of stress hovering around the table. "Spending time in London with Mary and her duke hasn't helped."

Stifling a groan of frustration, Fanny speared a piece of potato and shoved it between her lips.

"Pickering doesn't need a workhouse," her father said. "No one wants that here."

Fanny stared at him. "You can't see the good it would do?"

"I can see it would be a blight on our town.

"If she's thinking of starting a workhouse here, that must mean she wants to come home for good," John said. He looked over at Fanny with an encouraging smile. "Perhaps she's considering Mr. Duckworth after all."

She worked to keep her ire in check. "I'm not."

Mother sniffed. "She's too good for us now, John. She's got her sights set on a title, no doubt."

As the youngest, Fanny had always felt a bit picked on by everyone else, with the exception of Ivy, of course, and of her father, who had doted on her when she was a child. That had faded after Ivy had left home. It was as if he'd turned his back on both his daughters. And her brothers had always teased her and made her feel rather alone. Turning to her mother hadn't helped. She'd simply put Fanny to work and told her not to wallow in self-pity. Consequently, Fanny had spent a great deal of time at Patience's house. It was too bad she couldn't escape there now, but Patience shared a small cottage with her husband and baby. While Fanny would always be welcome at Patience's parents' house, they were busy preparing to marry off their last child tomorrow. Fanny couldn't possibly intrude.

"I can't imagine what a peer would see in our Fanny," Father said, talking as if she weren't sitting immediately to his left. "But then I've no idea what one would have seen in Mary either, particularly given her demeanor."

"What do you mean? That's precisely what one saw in her," Mother said. "For all we know, she seduced the poor man."

Fanny looked between her parents as rage poured through her. Could they speak of their daughters this way? And right in front of one of them?

"He seemed rather besotted when he visited with her,"

Jacob said.

"Because she's a seductress." Father lifted his gaze heavenward. "God bless her soul."

Fanny dropped her fork and abruptly stood. "I can't sit here and listen to this any longer. Ivy made a mistake and trusted the wrong man, and instead of supporting her, you turned your backs on your own flesh and blood. God should bless *your* souls, but I fear he may not."

Her mother gasped, and her father pounded his hand on the table. "Sit down!"

"No. I'm leaving." She glanced at John, who stared up at her, his arm arrested in mid-motion on the way to spooning peas into his mouth. "I'll attend your wedding tomorrow, but then I shall leave, and I won't return. I'm to marry the Earl of St. Ives, which I didn't wish to tell you because I knew you'd be angry. But I no longer care how you feel. Indeed, I wonder why I ever did." She dropped her napkin onto her chair and marched from the dining room.

Her heart pounded as she dashed up the stairs. She startled Barker, who was just coming from Fanny's room. "What's the matter?" the maid asked, looking concerned.

Fanny went into the bedchamber. "We need to leave."

"Now?" Barker asked. "I was just going down to dinner."

Wincing, Fanny turned to face her. "Yes, now. I'm sorry. We'll go into town and find something to eat at the Black Rabbit." She hoped they had a room for her. If not, she could stay with David, as scandalous as that would be.

"Help me pack, please. I can't stay here another moment."

Barker touched her hand and gave her a reassuring smile. "I understand. I've heard how your parents are, particularly your mother."

"They were being just awful about Ivy." Fanny shook her head, wishing she could banish this evening from her mind. "It doesn't matter. I don't ever need to return."

She'd felt a duty to be a good sister and come for John's wedding. She didn't feel that duty anymore. In fact, if it weren't for seeing Patience tomorrow and being there for Mercy, she wouldn't even bother attending the wedding.

Barker pulled the trunk from beneath the bed. "Then let's be on our way."

DAVID TURNED THE page of his well-worn copy of *History of British Birds* as a knock sounded on his door. At dinner earlier, the innkeeper had said he would bring up a glass of port, much to David's appreciation.

He set the book on the bedside table and stood up from the four-poster where he'd been reclining. He'd discarded his coat and cravat, but didn't bother donning them for the innkeeper.

Only it wasn't the innkeeper.

"Good evening, my lord!" It was one of the other guests, a Mrs. Oglethorpe. Widowed, she was traveling back to York after visiting her sister on the coast. She was a few years older than David, with bright blonde hair and a quick laugh. She'd provided amusing companionship at dinner along with four other guests.

"I do hope I'm not intruding." Her gaze dipped to where his shirt was open at the neck. "Mr. Lyle has offered us port and sherry downstairs. He was going to bring your port up, but I thought you'd much prefer to join us. We're going to play cards."

Port and cards did sound intriguing. It was that or

spend the evening counting the moments until he would see Fanny tomorrow. "Let me dress properly, and I'll be right down."

Mrs. Oglethorpe shot another glance toward the triangle of flesh he displayed. "If you must," she murmured before flashing him a brilliant smile. "See you downstairs!"

He closed the door and quickly put himself to rights, then joined the guests gathered in the common room. Aside from Mrs. Oglethorpe, there were two brothers—the Misters Keeling—and a married couple, Mr. and Mrs. Tabor, and Mrs. Tabor's sister, Miss Vaughn.

"Ah, here's Lord St. Ives," Mrs. Oglethorpe said. Her smile dripped into a frown. "We are just one woman shy of equal numbers. What a shame."

"Was there to be dancing?" David asked, thinking he maybe ought to have stayed upstairs.

"No, but that's a splendid idea," she said. "I just like to have even numbers—it's a silly thing my brain focuses upon."

"What card game are we to play?" David approached the long dining table, where bottles of port and sherry stood near the center. He poured himself a glass of port before taking a seat.

"Loo," Mrs. Tabor, a dark-haired woman near David's age, answered.

"We're playing for pennies," Mr. Tabor said.

"I tried to make things more interesting," Mrs. Oglethorpe said with resignation. "However, no one wanted to increase the wagering."

"Would you like to deal, my lord?" one of the Misters Keeling asked David.

"No, you go ahead." David sipped his port and dug out some pennies from his coat pocket.

As Mr. Keeling shuffled the cards, the door to the exterior opened. Everyone turned their attention to the new arrival, except David.

"Pardon me, is the innkeeper about?"

The sound of the familiar feminine voice drew David out of his chair. Fanny's eyes registered recognition as she stepped into the common room, followed by her maid.

"Fan—Miss Snowden." David bowed, catching himself before he betrayed their intimacy.

Her cheeks were flushed, and she seemed rather harried, which filled him with concern. "I'm in need of a room for the evening."

Hell and the devil. What had happened with her bloody parents? David wished they weren't standing in the midst of so many strangers.

"I'll fetch him," Mr. Tabor said, rising.

"I don't think there are any more rooms available," Mrs. Oglethorpe said. She smiled at Fanny. "But you're welcome to stay with me."

All David could think was that he wanted Fanny with him. Yesterday had been a tantalizing glimpse of what it would mean to have her as his wife, and he was eager for their future to arrive.

Fanny shot a look toward David before smiling weakly at the widow. "Thank you."

The innkeeper, Mr. Lyle, came into the common room, his gaze lighting on Fanny. "Good evening. Miss Snowden, isn't it? Your father made that table for me." He gestured toward where everyone sat.

"I'm in need of a room for this evening, Mr. Lyle."

Lyle frowned. "I'm afraid I'm full for the night," he said with regret. "You could try the Raven at the other end of town, but that's…" He shook his head. "No, I can't let you go there. We'll find room. There's a small chamber in the attic. It's more of a storage closet, really, and we'll have to make up a pallet on the floor, but it's only for one night."

"My maid is with me too," Fanny said, gesturing to the woman behind her.

"She can stay with me," Mrs. Oglethorpe repeated. "And we can make the pallet in my room for her maid."

"That's very kind of you," Fanny said, again darting a glance toward David.

If he was interpreting her correctly, she was expressing her disappointment at not being able to speak with him. Or at least signaling that she wanted to. Good, he wanted to know what in the devil she was doing here.

"Do you have a coach?" the innkeeper asked.

"Yes, my coachman and footman have taken it to the mews."

The innkeeper nodded. "I'll instruct them to take your baggage to Mrs. Oglethorpe's room, and I'll set up your maid's pallet. Would you care to come along, and I'll show you upstairs?"

"Let her stay and have a drink," Mrs. Oglethorpe said. "You're awfully pale, dear. Sit with us for a spell and play loo."

"I don't know how to play loo," Fanny said. "But I daresay a glass of port would be welcome."

The maid whispered in Fanny's ear, and Fanny nodded. "My maid will go up with you, Mr. Lyle," Fanny said.

Lyle gestured for the maid to precede him, and they disappeared up the stairs.

David held a chair for Fanny and, as she sat down, whispered, "Are you all right?"

She nodded at him. "I'll explain later."

The promise of later sped his heart rate, but he wondered how in the hell she would manage that when she was lodging with Mrs. Oglethorpe. He poured Fanny a glass of port and handed it to her, allowing his bare fingers to graze her gloved ones. It was an enticing taste, but not nearly enough to sate his hunger.

"What brings you to the Black Rabbit so late in the evening, Miss Snowden?" Mrs. Oglethorpe asked.

"I'm just visiting," she answered vaguely, raising her glass to her mouth.

David couldn't help but look at her lips. How he longed to be that glass of port...

"On your way somewhere?" Mrs. Oglethorpe asked.

"Yes, back to Suffolk."

Mr. Tabor looked at David. "You're from near Suffolk, aren't you, my lord?" They'd discussed it at dinner.

"Yes." He offered nothing else.

"And you are acquainted with Miss Snowden," Mrs. Oglethorpe observed.

Because he'd called her by name when she'd entered. He'd been too surprised to see her here.

"I think I saw her here earlier," Miss Vaughan said.

"We met yesterday," Fanny said. "We're both bird enthusiasts, and I loaned him a book, which I picked up earlier today."

A neat and excellent explanation. David lifted his glass ever so slightly in her direction before taking a drink.

"Well, shall we play loo, then?" asked the Mr. Keeling who was in possession of the cards.

Mrs. Oglethorpe winked at Fanny across the table. "You can watch and learn, dear."

Fanny watched and learned all too well, winning several pots, much to her delight. The cloud of distress cloaking her when she entered had completely dissipated by the time they broke up the game to seek their beds.

Mrs. Oglethorpe led Fanny up the stairs to her room,

which was next to David's. "We're just ahead there, dear," she said, pointing toward the door and allowing Fanny to go in front of her.

The widow paused at David's door, waiting for him to stop. "I'd hoped to visit you later, but with my guest, that may not be possible." She sighed. "Ah well, I will try." She flashed a smile at him and didn't wait to hear whether he would welcome her visit or not.

Bloody hell.

He caught Fanny's eye for a moment before Mrs. Oglethorpe ushered her into the chamber. The door snapped closed, and David went into his room teeming with frustration and anxiety. Would Fanny show up at his door later? Or would Mrs. Oglethorpe? Or would neither?

He stripped down to his shirt and breeches and lay down on the bed. His attempts to read *British History of Birds* were a complete failure. His mind kept wandering next door as he tried to puzzle out why Fanny had shown up here tonight.

Something had to have gone very wrong with her family. She'd been concerned about causing trouble with them, which was why she'd asked him not to call. What sort of parents allowed their daughter to leave their house after dinner?

It was a silly question. She'd traveled here from Suffolk with a maid, a footman, and a coachman. She could certainly travel to an inn to spend the night.

His thoughts were interrupted by a soft rap on the door. He bolted upright and sent a silent prayer as to who it might be.

Slipping from the bed, he padded to the door and took a deep breath before cracking it open. "Thank God."

He grabbed Fanny's hand and pulled her inside. As soon as the door was closed, he turned and was instantly greeted by Fanny throwing her arms around his neck and pressing her lips to his. Surprised, he pulled her close and poured all his pent-up desire into the kiss. It was several long moments before he pulled away.

"What happened to Mrs. Oglethorpe?" he asked, glancing toward her room.

"She finally fell asleep. Why did you say 'thank God' when I arrived?"

"Because Mrs. Oglethorpe said she would come to my room if she could get away. I was terrified you were going to be her."

Fanny giggled. "Terrified?"

"Distraught, to say the least." He took in her dressing gown and bare feet and tried not to think of how close she was to being naked. "Why are you here and not at your parents' house?"

"Can we sit?"

His room was rather small, and there was just one chair at the table. Mr. Lyle had wanted to give him larger accommodation because he was an earl, but David had insisted he take the smallest room since he was by himself.

"You can take the chair," he offered.

She went to the bed instead and indicated he should join her by patting the space beside her. He wasn't sure how wise it was to even sit beside her there, but was powerless to resist.

"I'm afraid I lost my temper with my parents. They were talking about Ivy in the most horrid way." She turned her body toward him, lifting one leg slightly onto the bed as she shifted position.

"What do you mean you lost your temper?"

"I told them I was marrying you." Her nose wrinkled. "They were not pleased."

"Did they toss you out?" David tamped down a burst of anger at the idea of her parents treating her so badly.

"No, I left. I couldn't bear to stay under their roof another moment. I would miss the wedding tomorrow, but I want to see my friend Patience before I leave."

"I'll go with you," he said, hating the anguish her parents had clearly caused. He touched her hair, which was braided and hung over her shoulder. Trailing his hand down the winding strands, he caressed the curling ends, letting them tickle his fingertips. "You don't have to face them alone."

She turned her head and kissed his wrist. "Thank you." Her gaze found his. "I plan to leave directly after the ceremony."

"We shouldn't travel together, but I will follow you."

"I was thinking… Can't we pretend to be husband and wife? You couldn't be you, of course. Not an earl, I mean."

He laughed. "You are incomparable. How would we explain two coaches?"

"One is for our luggage?" She grinned up at him, and he surrendered to the delicious pull of her allure.

He gripped her braid and tugged gently as he cupped the other side of her neck and drew her close. He seared his lips along hers, but only for a moment before he slipped his tongue inside. She tasted of port and vibrance, and she smelled of lilies of the valley. It was a heady combination, not that he needed anything to push him to the edge of desire.

Their kisses spilled over as they sought to explore each other. The first time her tongue traced along his jawline, he let out a soft moan. Her boldness was intoxicating.

He drew his hand down her collarbone and along the swell of her breast. She inhaled sharply and arched toward him. It was all the encouragement he needed. He dipped his hand beneath her dressing gown. The thin cotton of her night rail was all that separated him from the sweet silk of her bare flesh.

"Should I go back to my room?" The question was a bare whisper.

He kissed along her neck and untied the front of her dressing down—in front of her breasts and at her waist. "If you wish."

"I don't wish, but what if Mrs. Oglethorpe wakes up?"

"I doubt she will, but if she does, you can say you went downstairs for…something. Or maybe you went for a walk in your sleep."

"Or maybe I was jealous of her planning to visit you and wanted to claim you for myself."

He lifted his head to look at her. "You didn't know she wanted to visit me."

"No, but I would have been jealous if I had."

"Why? I would have turned her away. You've no need to feel jealous of any woman."

Her eyes narrowed seductively. "Protective, then." She shrugged the dressing gown from her shoulders, and the outline of her breasts as well as her nipples was clearly visible. "You're mine."

No words had ever stirred his desire more completely. With a growl, he laid her back on the bed and cupped her breasts. He dipped his head and took her nipple into his mouth, suckling her through the fabric and wetting it completely.

She gasped and thrust her hands into his hair, holding him against her. "Oh, David."

He blew on the fabric as her nipple tightened, then held her more securely, enslaving her to his mouth. She arched up off the bed, her body begging for more as her heart beat a rapid rhythm beneath her breast.

"Take it off," she urged. "I want to feel you against me."

He stopped himself from ripping the garment in two, instead whisking it up over her hips. The dressing gown became tangled up with the night rail, making him groan in frustration. She took over and removed both garments entirely, then tossed them to the floor.

Her body lay naked before him—long limbs, curved hips, a delectable dip at her navel, and the pale globes of her breasts tipped with pink roses. He ran his thumbs over those flowers, stirring them into rigid peaks. Then he tugged them, eliciting the most delicious cry from her mouth. He pitched forward and devoured the sound with his mouth and tongue.

She clasped his neck, kissing him with wild fervor. She pulled at the collar of his shirt, then moved her hands down until she found the hem. Warm fingertips grazed along his abdomen as she stroked his flesh. He tore his lips from hers and kissed a path to her breasts, laving first one and then the other, drawing moans and cries from her mouth.

Her fingernails dug into his shoulders, and he realized she'd pushed his shirt up to his neck. He tugged it the rest of the way off, and she pulled him down on top of her so that her bare breasts pressed against his naked chest.

"I've wanted to feel this for so long." She kissed his neck, his jaw, his mouth. Her hands plucked at the waistband of his breeches. "Can you take these off too?"

He pushed away from her and stripped them from his body as quickly as possible. Her gaze settled on his cock as he moved between her legs. "May I touch it?" she asked.

"Please." He watched as she lifted from the bed and

reached for him. Her fingertips grazed the tip, and blood instantly rushed to the head. Heat danced across his flesh and pooled in his gut.

"It's wet," she said, smoothing the moisture over him with her thumb.

"That's a sign of what's to come."

"I'm wet too, I think."

"God, Fanny, don't ever stop talking to me like that."

Her lips curved into a seductive smile. "Do you want to know how I know?"

Hell, yes. "Tell me."

"Last night, I dreamed of you, and I woke up feeling feverish. Hungry. Desperate for you. I burned. Here." She moved her hand from his cock to between her legs. "I pressed on that spot—my clitoris. It felt...good. Then I slipped my finger inside, like you did."

"That's how you know."

"Yes." She shocked him by doing what she'd just described.

He'd never seen a woman touch herself like that, let alone the woman who would be his wife.

"Don't stop," he rasped.

She didn't, her finger stroking slowly in and out. He took her hand and moved her focus back to her clitoris, then entered her with his finger. Together, they worked, their breaths becoming louder and faster.

"Oh God, David. I'm going to come."

"Did you come last night?" He had to know.

"Yes, but it wasn't quite the same."

He thrust two fingers into her and felt her muscles clench. Then he pulled away to guide his cock to her sheath, sliding in as her muscles began to spasm. She cried out and clasped his backside, digging her fingers into his flesh as she pulled him into her.

He drove deep, and her legs came up around him. He'd wanted to go slow, to be controlled, but she'd cast him to the edge of oblivion with her erotic demonstration. He was mindless with need, overcome with lust.

She moved her hips to meet his thrusts, and her mouth found his, her tongue seeking his as they fought the rising tide together. Her climax barely finished—or so he thought—before she seemed to climb again, her channel tightening around him.

Surrendering to the darkness, he moved hard and fast, pushing her to the same edge upon which he barely balanced. And then he was lost.

Blood rushed to his cock as his release enveloped him, body and soul. He cast his head back and cried her name. He pumped into her as his body slowed. Her legs quivered around him, and he leaned down to kiss her again, his lips gently caressing hers.

A few, languorous moments later, he rolled to his side, his heartbeat still fast, his breathing still erratic. He inhaled deeply, thinking he'd never felt so good in his life.

Fanny curled into him, her hand splaying across his chest. "I should go before Mrs. Oglethorpe realizes I'm gone."

"Stay—for a bit. I won't let you fall asleep."

She pushed on his chest and rose up onto her elbow.

He stared up into her eyes, stirringly luminescent in the flicker of the candlelight. "You are incredibly beautiful." Her hair had come mostly loose from the braid, and he unraveled it the rest of the way, his fingers gliding through the silken red-gold strands.

She arched a brow at him. "How are you going to keep me from falling asleep?"

He chuckled. "Give me a moment, and I'll show you."

Her fingers trailed a circle over his chest. "You really

don't mind coming with me to the wedding tomorrow?"

"Not at all. It will be a lovely precursor to our own wedding."

She smiled, but it faded into a pout. "That's weeks from now. Are you certain we can't pretend to be married as we travel south? Just for a few days? We can be Mr. and Mrs. Bird."

He laughed, then pulled her down for a swift but heated kiss. "I adore your mind."

"I adore many parts of you." Her hand trailed over his nipple and then moved down along his abdomen.

He groaned. "My moment is nearly expired."

She nodded. "Tell me, can I put my mouth on you the way you did with me?"

A frantic need pulsed through him, and he didn't need a second, let alone a moment to recover. "Yes."

She rotated her body and threw her leg over his as she slid down his side. "You'll have to tell me what to do."

"Fanny, something tells me you will do just fine all on your own."

Unsurprisingly, she did.

Chapter Thirteen

❦

IN THE END, Fanny and David had decided it would be best if David didn't attend the wedding. He did, however, plan to wait for her outside the church so that they could leave directly.

And so he could talk to her father. David had been adamant that he would tell the man it was time to bury the past.

Fanny was nervous throughout the ceremony, but moved to joy as she watched Mercy marry her brother John, at last making Fanny and Patience sisters, at least through marriage.

After the wedding, the guests mingled in the vestibule, but Fanny steered clear of her parents. That didn't stop them from glowering at her across the gathering of people, and her anxiety shot right back up.

She was so intent on avoiding them that she nearly walked straight into Mr. Duckworth. In his middle thirties, he was a man of average height and thinning blond hair. He bore the florid features of a man inclined to drink, as well as a burgeoning waistline that also proclaimed that habit.

"Good morning, Miss Snowden. You look unbearably lovely this morning."

Unbearably? She forced a smile. "Good morning, Mr. Duckworth. Thank you for coming to John's wedding."

"It puts me in the mood to take a wife again." He chuckled, his sherry-colored eyes sparkling with mirth. "I should be very honored if you would assume that role."

Was that supposed to be a proposal? Fanny wasn't

entirely certain, nor did she particularly want to address it as such. "Yes, well, I am leaving for Suffolk immediately."

He frowned. "So soon? I'd heard you planned to start a workhouse here. Jacob mentioned it to me earlier this morning."

He had? That was incredibly surprising. Her gaze traveled across the room to where he stood near their parents. He looked very handsome in his wedding finery, and Fanny wondered how long it would be before he took a wife. And would she want to come back to celebrate with him? She might—he seemed to have changed quite a bit, and yet she wasn't sure she wanted to put herself in her parents' orbit again.

But she wouldn't have to. She could travel here with her husband, and they'd stay at the inn, to which she'd become quite partial.

"You're smiling," Mr. Duckworth noted. "Are you thinking of the workhouse? It's a splendid idea, I must say. I'd be delighted to help you with its implementation."

She blinked at him. In the years she'd known him, he'd never indicated a desire to help anyone. Then again, they'd never discussed it. "That's very kind of you. I doubt I'll be starting a workhouse here. We'll found one in London and see how it goes."

"Bah, you don't need to return to London. Marry me, and if you like, we can found one in York."

He was simply not going to give up. "Except all the other patronesses are in London," she said sweetly.

"You don't need them, Miss Snowden," he said. "My income is rather large. I just can't let you leave without pressing my suit. I would be a devoted husband and father."

He already had two children, and since she'd never heard him speak of them, she rather doubted the latter. In any case, she'd had enough of his "suit." "Mr. Duckworth, while I appreciate your kind…proposal, I am already betrothed to the Earl of St. Ives. We're to be married within the month."

His pale brows knitted, causing his entire face to look as though it was puckered. "I heard about that nonsense too. You can't think he'll really marry you."

Nonsense? Just what had her family told him? She sent a scowl in their direction. "Of course he will marry me. Please excuse me."

She turned and madly searched for a safe haven. Spotting Patience cradling her daughter near the door, Fanny stalked in that direction, eager to be away from Mr. Duckworth.

Patience's eyes lit as she approached. A petite slip of a woman, Patience never failed to make Fanny feel like a giant. As Fanny had grown taller and Patience remained small, they'd laughed at how odd they looked together.

"You look upset," Patience said, her features darkening as Fanny came to her side.

"Just annoyed."

"Because of Duckworth?" Patience swayed gently, and Fanny could see that the baby was sleeping.

"He's rather persistent in his desire that we wed. He even pretended to want to help with my workhouse." Fanny had told Patience of her idea earlier during her visit.

Patience snorted. "So charming. I hope you told him you were already betrothed." Patience had been thrilled to hear the news earlier that morning when Fanny had arrived at the church before the wedding.

"I did, but he said David wouldn't ever marry me, and you can guess where he heard that."

Patience was aware of the Snowdens' dislike of titled

gentlemen and of the fact that they didn't care for Ivy's duke. She found all of it absolutely maddening as well as absurd. "I'm so sorry, Fanny. I'm sad that you're leaving so soon, but I do understand why. I'm just glad I got to see you again and that you were able to spend some time with Frances." She smiled down at her daughter, whom she'd named after her dearest friend.

Tears stung Fanny's eyes as she realized she didn't know when she would see Patience next. But wait, of course she did. "Patience, you must come to Suffolk for my wedding. Promise me you will. I will pay for everything, if you need me to." Fanny winced inwardly, hating how that sounded, but desperate for her friend to come.

"I wouldn't miss it." Patience's eyes shone as she beamed at Fanny. "Now, go on your way before we both turn into watering pots."

Fanny bent and kissed Frances's cheek, then did the same to her mother. Moving quickly, she exited the church, where she met John and Mercy, who were speaking with guests as they departed. She darted a glance toward David's coach across the street but didn't see him.

"Are you really not coming to the breakfast?" John asked, drawing her attention. He was tall and fair-haired like their father, before the elder John's hair had turned mostly white.

"No," she said. "I'm eager to start my journey south. Mother and Father wouldn't want me there anyway."

He exhaled. "No, they likely would not. I'm sorry to see you leave like this, Fanny. I do hope your earl will marry you."

"You don't believe he will either?" She let out a rather unladylike snort.

Mercy elbowed her new husband in the ribs. "Of

course her earl will marry her. Don't be a dolt like your father."

Fanny had to stifle a smile at her friend and ally. Feeling slightly better, she turned to her brother. "I wish you every happiness, John." She gave him a brief hug, then hugged Mercy.

As she pivoted toward her coach, which was parked in front of David's, she wondered if he had perhaps changed his mind about speaking to her father. That might be for the best, she decided.

Alas, David had not changed his mind.

He approached her parents, who stood on the path leading to the street through the churchyard, his face intent. Fanny hurried to join them, hoping things could stay somewhat civil.

David offered a gallant bow that made Fanny's heart sing. If this went poorly, it wouldn't be because of him. "Good morning, Mr. and Mrs. Snowden. I'm St. Ives."

Her father sneered. "The jackanapes who plans to run off with my daughter."

Fanny moved to stand next to David. "He's not a jackanapes, Father."

"Nor am I running off with Fanny," David said calmly. "We are to be wed in Clare. We'd hoped to obtain your blessing."

Fanny's mother reached for her and clutched her hand in a rather painful grip. "You can't marry him. His family likely had your great-uncle killed." She dashed a furtive glance toward David.

"We did no such thing." David's evenness was beginning to fray as his voice rose slightly. He sent a dark stare toward Fanny's father. "Your uncle kidnapped my aunt."

Fanny's father leaned forward with a menacing glower.

"He did no such thing. They were in love. He wrote a letter to my father saying so."

David's gaze flickered with surprise. "Where is this proof?"

"Long since lost." Fanny's father shifted his weight. "That doesn't make it any less true."

"Forgive me if I don't believe you," David said, his lip curling.

Fanny wanted to side with David—the man she loved. But it was entirely possible the story her father told was true. She moved slightly, angling herself between them. "There's no way to know what happened. We can all agree on one thing: it was a tragedy. Would it be better to move forward with a joyous occasion such as our wedding?" She wasn't sure why she was even trying to make amends with her parents when they were so intent on being disagreeable.

Her father turned on her, his eyes blazing. "It would not be a joyous occasion, you ridiculous chit. It would be a betrayal—as bad as anything your sister has done, if not worse."

"What did you just call her?" David's question was deathly quiet, but the violent surge in his gaze made Fanny's neck prickle.

"Whatever I want." Her father barely spared him a glance.

David's arm shot out fast, his hand gripping her father's elbow. "Apologize to her. I won't allow you to speak to my future wife in such a manner."

Her father wrenched his arm away. "I'll speak to her however I damned well please."

And then he pulled his other arm back and sent his fist into David's face.

THE BLOW DROVE David backward, but he kept himself from losing balance. However, before he could adopt at least a defensive position, the man came at him again.

Unfortunately, Fanny had inserted herself between them.

Snowden's closed hand connected with Fanny's cheek, sending her reeling into David's arms.

The sound of Mrs. Snowden's gasp was nearly drowned out by the noises coming from the people still collected outside the church.

David cradled Fanny against him. "Are you all right?"

She blinked, her expression one of shock as a bright red spot spread over her cheek where her father had struck her. "Did he just hit me?" She sounded dazed, and perhaps she was.

Raw fury spiked through David, and all he wanted to do was beat her father into the ground.

"Your Lordship, let me." The soft sound of Fanny's maid's voice broke into his angry haze. He turned his head and saw the woman, her chest heaving as if she'd run to the scene, which she likely had.

Turning Fanny over to the woman's care, he turned his attention to Snowden, advancing quickly and driving his right fist into the man's chin and then his left into his eye. Snowden staggered back but didn't fall. Good, David didn't want this over quickly. He wanted the man to *hurt*.

"I didn't mean to hit her," Snowden said, spitting blood from his mouth. "I meant to hit you." He lunged forward, his arms coming around David's middle as he sought to wrestle him to the ground.

Clasping his hands, David brought them down on Snowden's back. The older man grunted but didn't let go.

He squeezed his grip around David and tried to pull him sideways to put him off balance.

It worked.

David pitched over and hit the ground with a thud, his right arm taking the brunt of the fall. He brought his hands up and put them around Snowden's neck, not to choke him, but to push him away.

However, the effort ended up doing the former, and very quickly, Snowden's face turned a bright shade of crimson.

And then other hands were suddenly on them. Two men had joined the fray, one pulling at David's arms while the other pulled at Snowden.

As the older man's grip loosened and fell away, David also let go. He sucked in air as his heart hammered in his heaving chest.

The man holding him tried to help him rise, but David shook him off. He stood of his own accord and shook his shoulders out. "You're a despicable father," David spat.

Snowden stood with the assistance of the other man, who, judging from his looks, was also a Snowden, likely one of Fanny's brothers. "Your family are murderers. I'll do whatever I must to keep my daughter from marrying you."

David longed to hit the man again. "You can't. She is of age, and she can do what she likes. If you come within ten feet of her again, I'll kill you."

Snowden wagged his finger and shouted for all the dozens of spectators to hear, "See? Murderers, the lot of you!"

Growling, David started forward again, but two things stopped him: the man who'd tried to help him up— another Snowden—and the sight of a third man trying to tend to Fanny. She slapped his hand away as he tried to put it around her and take her from the maid.

Pivoting, David started toward the mystery third man instead. "Take your hands off my betrothed."

The man snapped his shocked gaze to David. "I'm only trying to help her, which is more than I can say for you." He sniffed.

It was all David could do not to punch this man too. Instead, he moved past the cretin and took Fanny into his arms. "Are you all right?" he asked again.

She nodded, looking less stunned than she had a few moments before. "Please, can we go?"

He touched her reddened cheek and tamped down his fury. "I'm sorry this happened."

She glanced around at the crowd and flinched, then turned her attention to the man who'd pulled David from Snowden. "I'm sorry, John. This shouldn't have happened on your wedding day."

John said nothing, just grimaced as he moved to stand next to a young woman who had to be his bride. She looked at Fanny with sympathy as her husband put his arm around her.

"Can we please go?" Fanny whispered as she burrowed into David's side.

"Yes." He turned to the maid and noticed that Fanny's footman had also come. He was a young lad, but his expression was dark and focused on Snowden, which pleased David. "Will you both see Fanny to her coach?"

The maid nodded and came forward, but Fanny pulled at David's coat. "I'm not leaving without you."

"Of course not," David said. "Just give me one moment." He squeezed her hand before giving her back to the maid and spinning around to address Fanny's family.

"You'll have nothing to do with Fanny from here on,"

he said, his gaze roving over the three men as well as her mother. "You've behaved abominably where it comes to her and her sister. Fanny has done nothing to warrant your treatment except fall in love with me. I love her beyond words, and I would hope that would be enough to satisfy you."

He spun on his heel and walked down the path, joining Fanny on the way toward the coaches.

She tucked her arm over his. "Thank you. I can see that took considerable restraint. I didn't realize you were a violent person."

"Typically, I am not. However, if you want to see me enraged, you need only strike my beloved." He looked down at her with fierce devotion. "Your father was right about one thing—I'd commit murder to protect you."

"I'm beginning to see how love can make someone do terrible things," she said quietly as they reached the street. "Perhaps my great-uncle *did* kidnap your aunt."

Though that was what David had heard and believed for so long, he wasn't entirely sure it was true. What if there had been a letter? Why would Snowden lie about such a thing?

Because he was a nasty prick. That much David *did* believe.

They crossed the street to Fanny's coach, where her coachman rushed to open the door. David took her hand to help her up inside. "I plan to conduct an investigation when I return to Huntwell. No matter what we find, Fanny, we will still be married. *We* can still be happy."

She didn't quite smile, but her gaze was warm with love as she looked up at him. "I know we can. From the moment we met, I felt as though we were meant to be together. With whatever happened between our families in the past, perhaps it's Fate's way of making things right again."

"What a lovely sentiment." David glanced back toward the congregation, which included Fanny's parents, still gathered on the path. How had such a kind and wonderful woman come from such horrid people?

Fanny turned to Barker. "I'd like to ride with David for a while. Can you please ride in his coach?"

The maid blinked in surprise but nodded. "I shouldn't, but I know you're shaken."

"Thank you."

David helped Fanny into the coach and climbed in beside her. She removed her bonnet and tossed it on the opposite seat. He drew her tight against him, pressing a kiss to her forehead. "This is rather scandalous."

"No more so than fighting with my father in a churchyard on my brother's wedding day."

David would have laughed if his anger wasn't still so close to the surface. "Try to put it from your mind."

"I'm afraid it will be a long time before I can do that." She fell quiet, her head resting on his shoulder.

David's anger gradually receded into a hopeless despair. The Snowdens' reactions and behavior had been appalling enough. What could he expect from his own family?

He was almost afraid to find out.

Chapter Fourteen

◆ʒ•ʒ◆

THE FIVE-DAY journey south started tense and gradually became relaxed, for which Fanny was extremely grateful. She wished the scene in Pickering had never happened, but didn't blame David at all. She'd put herself in his position and knew that if someone had hit him, she'd want to hurt that person too.

Love, she decided, was an all-encompassing and fiercely primal emotion.

As the coach pulled into the drive at Stour's Edge, Fanny looked over at David. "I'm glad you decided to come straight here instead of going home first."

They'd all but cast propriety to the wind during the trip, though Barker had tried to play the role of overprotective chaperone. After a few days, she'd surrendered and had taken to riding in David's coach by herself so that Fanny and David were alone—at least during the day. She'd insisted on sleeping in Fanny's room at night, but Fanny had been able to sneak away on two separate nights. If Barker was aware of her leaving, she had decided not to say so.

The coach rumbled to a stop in front of the house, and the footman rushed to open the door. He helped Fanny down, and her legs both protested the movement and appreciated the ability to stretch.

When David descended, Fanny took his arm, and they walked together into the house, the door held open by the butler, Munro. "I've sent a footman to summon Her Grace," he said. "Would you care to wait in the library?"

"Yes, thank you," Fanny said, guiding David into the

massive room adorned with elaborately carved wood and an impressive collection of books the likes of which Fanny had never seen before coming to Stour's Edge. She took her arm from David's.

"This is quite a library," he said, wandering toward a bookshelf.

"It's where I came to learn about birds after meeting you. I've grouped all the ornithology texts over in that corner." She gestured toward the cozy nook where she'd also moved her favorite chair.

"You're home!" Ivy swept into the room and immediately embraced Fanny in a tight hug—as tight as her rather large belly would allow. She apologized for prodding Fanny with it. "I'm so much bigger than I was with Leah. West is convinced this one's a boy." She frowned at Fanny. "What happened to your face?"

Fanny lifted a hand to her cheek. It had bruised where her father had struck her, but the discoloration had faded to a faint yellow. It was, however, still noticeable. "Oh, it's nothing."

Ivy didn't look convinced as she glanced over her shoulder at her husband, who'd followed her into the library.

He welcomed Fanny, then his gaze traveled to David, who'd moved to stand just behind her. "You've brought a guest, I see."

David reached forward to shake West's hand, then bowed to Ivy. "I've come to ask your permission to marry Fanny."

"*My* permission?" Ivy asked.

David looked toward West. "And yours. It seemed most appropriate."

Ivy frowned then looked to Fanny. "What happened with Mother and Father?"

Fanny looked at her sister sadly. "It was an absolute disaster."

"Let us sit," West said. "Or at least let your sister sit." He guided everyone toward the seating area near the fireplace, where smoldering embers provided a minimum of heat.

Ivy took a place on the settee and indicated that Fanny should join her. "Tell me everything. How was the wedding?"

West sat on the other side of Ivy on the settee while David took a chair near Fanny.

"The wedding was fine," Fanny said. "Mercy was beautiful. John seems very happy."

Ivy smiled. She didn't harbor any ill feelings toward her brothers. "That's nice to hear. How was Jacob?"

"Odd, if you must know. He was...nice."

Ivy blinked. "He was always nice to me when we were younger, but I was older than him, so I think he felt he had to be. I'm glad to hear he's finally treating you better."

"Compared to Mother and Father, he was positively charming."

Ivy adjusted her skirt around her belly. "How was it a disaster?"

"After the wedding, David came to the church to meet Mother and Father."

"I'd hoped to gain their blessing, but they weren't amenable." His face darkened to a scowl, and she reached over to briefly clasp his hand.

"Oh dear, what happened?"

"Father hit him."

"And then he hit her," David said before she could.

"Good Christ!" West exclaimed. "Tell me you thrashed him to within an inch of his life. Give or take an inch."

"I would have, but her brothers pulled us apart."

"If you decided we should try again, let me know," West said, his gaze icy with fury. He took Ivy's hand and held it on the settee between them.

Fanny noted that West had said "we" should try again. Their families might be at war, but at least they had Ivy and West.

Ivy lightly touched Fanny's cheek. "It's not nothing," she said softly, her gaze full of concern. "What was their opposition to the union, just the fact that he's an earl?" Her eyes turned sad, and Fanny's heart pulled. "I'm so sorry I ruined things for you with my poor decision."

Fanny shook her head. "It isn't your fault. Their attitude has nothing to do with Bothwick." Her lip curled as she said the name, and Fanny noticed West tense. He traced his thumb over the back of Ivy's hand. "Well, maybe not nothing, but it's not the sole or primary reason. Do you remember Great-uncle George?"

"I never met him. Did he show up after disappearing for so long?"

"No, he's still gone or missing or whatever he is. He was a footman at Huntwell." She sent a nervous glance toward David. Preferring to focus on their happiness, they'd decided not to discuss the past until they arrived home.

"What a bloody coincidence," West said.

"Indeed," was all David replied.

That left Fanny to finish the story. "Mother and Father insist that he ran off with David's aunt because they were in love. However, David's family believes she was kidnapped."

Ivy's eyes widened, and West blew out a whistle.

"That isn't the worst of it," David said, his voice a bit tight. "Snowden returned with my aunt a year after they disappeared—she'd delivered a stillborn babe and was dead."

Lifting her hand to her mouth, Ivy gasped. "I'm so sorry, St. Ives."

David inclined his head in appreciation. "Please, you must call me David since we're to be family. If you give your permission, that is."

"Yes, I give my permission. I've known that Fanny was in love with you for some time. I just wasn't sure you'd find your way to each other, and now to hear this…I'm shocked. My parents always spoke of George's disappearance with sorrow and anger." She looked at Fanny with grave concern, her gaze clouded. "So not only is David titled, he's from the family behind their hatred of titles."

"Exactly so," Fanny said with a nod. "It was all they could do not to marry me off to Duckworth while I was there. He did his best—which was beyond pathetic, really—to try to woo me." When David had learned he was the man who'd attempted to comfort her after the fight in the churchyard, he'd regretted not hitting him too.

"I see," Ivy said softly. "Unsurprising."

The butler chose that moment to enter with a tray of refreshments. There was lemonade, cakes, and even two glasses of whisky.

Ivy immediately dove for a cake, then offered a weak smile. "I can't seem to eat enough lately."

West's eyes twinkled. "My boy is rather demanding."

Ivy rolled her eyes at him before nibbling her cake. She studied David while she chewed, then asked, "How will your family react to you marrying my sister?"

Fanny and David exchanged a quick glance. She'd told him she would never tell Ivy what his mother had threatened. Fanny didn't want her sister even knowing that someone else knew the truth about her past. David had sworn to keep his mother quiet and completely understood Fanny's need to protect her sister.

"They will not be thrilled," he said with a mixture of sarcasm and concern. "But they will accept Fanny or find themselves looking for somewhere else to reside." As it was, he wasn't entirely sure what the living arrangements would be after they wed. He'd explained that his uncle currently lived in the dower house, but that his mother would move there now that he was betrothed. Where his uncle would live was currently unknown.

"In the meantime," David continued, "I want to try to determine what happened with my aunt and your great-uncle thirty years ago. Your father said his uncle had written a letter to his father saying he and my aunt were in love. Unfortunately, that letter is lost."

"I do hope they were in love and that her death was a tragic accident," Ivy said. "I know how births can go wrong."

She glanced over at West, who took her hand and pressed a kiss to the back. His eyes met hers, and the love between them was palpable. They hadn't lost a child, but Ivy's first daughter had come early and been stillborn at the workhouse. That West shared in her loss filled Fanny with awe. She looked over at David, certain she'd found someone who would do the same for her.

"Fanny hopes the same thing," David said, his eyes meeting hers. "But we may never know."

"If I can provide assistance in any way, I hope you'll let me know," West said, reaching for a cake. "Do you plan to speak to your uncle?"

"I'm not sure that would be wise." David gave his head a shake. "Uncle Walter is particularly sensitive about the topic. He doesn't ever wish to discuss it and grows quite agitated when it's mentioned."

Fanny pressed her lips together. "Are you certain he'll come to accept me?" She'd worried about his family throughout the journey.

David looked at her with defiance and love. "He doesn't have any other choice. You and I have nothing to do with what happened thirty years ago. And I rather like your logic—that Fate has brought us together to heal the wounds of the past."

Ivy picked up another cake. "I like that too."

David finished his glass of whisky, then announced that he would take his leave.

"Take one of my horses," West offered. "You'll never make it before dark in your coach." That was probably true.

"Thank you," David said, rising.

West stood with him. "I'll take you to the stable."

Fanny rose, and David took her in his arms for a fleeting kiss, his lips just barely grazing hers. "I'll see you soon," he said. "Tomorrow."

"I hate that you'll be away from me," she whispered.

"Not for long. I'll obtain the license tomorrow, and then we'll be wed whenever you like."

She nodded. "I'll talk to Ivy about that right now. Please be safe."

"Nothing will keep me from you, Fanny. Don't ever doubt that." He smiled down at her before kissing her again. Then he turned and joined West, who was waiting near the door.

When they were gone, she sat down with a weary, lonely sigh.

"I've never seen you so happy," Ivy said, finishing a third cake.

"Quite ridiculously so." Fanny grinned as she turned to

face her sister. She gave her a quick, sudden hug. "I just needed to do that. It's been a very trying week."

"It sounds like it. I'm so sorry you had to face our parents alone."

"I'm so sorry they're our parents. When I think of what they did to you, I really hate them."

"I know, but you mustn't harbor animosity in your heart. Let me do that." Her lips curled into a devilish smile that made Fanny laugh.

"You've more than earned that right."

"Was Jacob really pleasant to you?" Ivy asked, clearly circumspect.

"Yes. In fact, he was the only one who was supportive of my workhouse idea."

Her eyes practically fell from their sockets. "You told them about that? I can well imagine what they might have said. Goodness, Fanny, were you *trying* to annoy them?"

"Perhaps I was. As I said, I can barely think of them without growing angry. I suppose I might make a point of pricking their tempers. Not that it's difficult."

Ivy nodded in agreement. "Well, I'm glad you're here. Let us talk about your wedding instead."

"Yes, let's!" Fanny was eager to make plans. "We'd like to marry at the parish church in Clare."

"That's where West and I were married."

"I wish I had been there," Fanny said wistfully. She hated that she'd missed so much time with Ivy.

"I do too. I should have come for you sooner. I was just so afraid to go back there."

Fanny took her hand. "Which is completely understandable. They treated me far better, and now I'm afraid to return!"

"No, you aren't afraid," Ivy said softly. "You're far stronger and braver than I."

"That's absolutely false. You're the strongest person I know. To have overcome what you did and look at you now… A duchess."

"It's certainly not what I expected. And I did try to dissuade West."

"So you've told me." Fanny laughed "I can barely imagine it, though. You're clearly meant to be together. Just like me and David."

Ivy tipped her head to the side. "Is that what you think?"

"Oh, I know it's true. I never told you this—and you mustn't be angry—but I met David at Christmastide. Do you remember the day I went for a walk and came back all dirty because I'd slipped in the snow?"

"Yes, I remember that day. You were gone a very long time. Because you met David?"

Fanny nodded. "I was lost." Her tone was sheepish, and she felt heat climb into her face. "David helped me find my way back. And then we pretended there was mistletoe."

Ivy picked up her glass of lemonade. "I see." She took a sip, then set it back on the table before the settee. "So when you met him in London, you already knew each other."

"Yes, but I thought he was a steward. And he thought I was a housemaid." She held her hand to her mouth to keep her laughter in check.

Ivy was also amused, her lips curving up. "Why did you tell him you were a housemaid?"

"He didn't believe I lived at Stour's Edge. And then I thought it would be rather scandalous for me—Fanny Snowden—to be alone with him, so I said I was a housemaid."

"Clever. Well done of you," Ivy said. "And why was he

a steward?"

"For much the same reason. That and he'd only recently become the earl after his father had died, and he said he didn't feel much like an earl yet. He and his father were rather close."

"That sounds nice. West loved his father very much too." Ivy patted her hand. "I'm glad you told me this. I did wonder that you were maybe rushing into something or that David was maybe not good enough for you." Now it was her turn to look sheepish. "I'm afraid I was worried you might repeat my mistakes." She held up her hand. "And don't tell me if you have with regard to sex. If you and David have already done that, it's not my place to advise you. I'm just glad you're getting married soon. And how soon is soon?"

Fanny suspected her cheeks were probably crimson. "He's going to purchase the license tomorrow. Then I suppose we just pick a day and arrange it with the rector. Thank you. For everything."

"I'm so glad you're happy and that you'll be living nearby."

Fanny was glad for that too. She just hoped things would go well when David arrived at Huntwell. If they didn't… Well, she didn't really want to think about that.

"You look concerned all of a sudden," Ivy said.

"I'm just thinking about David and hoping his mother and uncle aren't too upset. He just lost his father last fall. I'd hate for him to lose them too."

"He'll do whatever he must for you, Fanny. Just like you're willing to turn your back on our parents in the name of love—for me and for David. If they'll accept you and let love conquer the hate, they'll be happy too."

Fanny hoped her sister was right.

✦·ε·3·✦

DESPITE RIDING INSTEAD of taking his coach, David still arrived at Huntwell after dark. Thankfully the moon was nearly full to illuminate his way.

Arnold, his butler, greeted him at the door. "Good evening, my lord. We weren't expecting you." He looked past David toward the drive, where a groom was taking West's horse to the stable.

"I didn't send word ahead," David said. "My apologies. Are my mother and uncle here?"

"Your mother is. Mr. Langley is at the dower house."

David had expected that, and in truth, preferred to have a conversation with his mother first. He wasn't entirely sure how to deliver the news of his betrothal to Uncle Walter given how he reacted whenever Aunt Catherine came up.

"Is she in the drawing room by chance?" David asked, knowing that was where she typically spent her evenings following dinner.

"Yes sir. I'll let Gibbs know you're here." Gibbs, his valet, had been a bit put out when David had left him here instead of taking him to Yorkshire.

"Thank you." David made his way to the drawing room at the rear of the house and found his mother sitting in front of a low fire intent on her embroidery. She was working on a piece in a stand positioned before her. A bright lantern burned on the table to her right illuminating her work.

She looked up as he entered. "David, what a surprise." Her gaze dipped over his travel-worn costume. "Did you just arrive?"

"I did." He went to the sideboard and poured a glass of port. "Would you care for sherry?"

"A refill would not come amiss."

He looked over and saw she had an empty glass on the table next to the lantern. He took the bottle and filled the glass, then returned the sherry to the sideboard.

Picking up his port, he sat in a chair angled beside her settee. "I have news to share."

"Where did you go? You didn't say, and your staff wouldn't tell us either."

He decided to just tell her without preamble. "I was in Yorkshire with Miss Snowden. She has agreed to become my wife."

The countess had just taken a drink of sherry and began to sputter. David reached to take the glass from her fingers before she inadvertently splashed it on her embroidery.

When she regained her composure, she gaped at him. "After everything I told you, you're going to marry her anyway?"

He set her glass on a table between his chair and her settee. "I love her. Shouldn't I marry the woman I love?"

She stared at him a long moment, her lips pursing. "Why do you have to love *her*?"

He started to relax, feeling as if he were finally making progress. "I don't think we get to choose whom we fall in love with." He sipped his port.

"Nonsense. You have a brain, and you have choice. You could have chosen Miss Stoke. You *should* have chosen Miss Stoke." On second thought, his mother was being incredibly obstinate.

"Why are you so hell-bent on Miss Stoke?" David tried to keep his voice from rising and failed.

"Because your father wanted you to marry her. And you promised. Your word to him should mean something! He deserves to be respected." Her voice had risen too, and her cheeks flushed a dark pink.

David took a deep breath. "I don't want to fight with you about this. I am marrying Fanny, and you can either support our union or live far away from us and stay out of our lives. Which would you prefer?"

She clenched her jaw. "Your uncle will never understand or forgive you for this. Snowden kidnapped his sister and all but killed her. For all we know, he *did* kill her. We have no idea what happened."

David worked to keep his ire in check. "If Snowden had killed her, why would he bring her back here to be buried? Wouldn't he have run far away for fear of imprisonment? The same goes for kidnapping her. If he did that, why bring her back here and face all of you?"

"He was a fool. He didn't want to be charged with murdering her, so he brought her back and claimed they ran off together because they were in love."

"That just doesn't make sense, Mother."

She glared at him. "It makes perfect sense."

He set his port down next to her sherry and scrubbed a hand over his face. "I don't suppose you know what happened to Snowden? His family believes we are responsible for his disappearance."

"Bah, that's balderdash. Snowden ran off after he brought Catherine back. Walter says he went to America to escape the magistrate."

"Uncle Walter talked to you about this?"

She shrugged. "A bit."

David found that highly curious but supposed they might have discussed it at some point in the last thirty years. "I will speak with him about this."

"He won't be happy. You're betraying your family. You may even find a few of the older retainers haven't forgotten."

On the ride from Stour's Edge, David had wondered if there were still retainers on the estate from that time. He was suddenly itching to interview whomever he could. If he could put this matter behind them once and for all, it would be best for everyone.

David picked up his glass of port and stood. "Uncle Walter will need to find a way to accept it—as will you. And you won't breathe a word about the Duchess of Clare—Fanny told me of your outrageous threats. I'm ashamed of you, Mother, and I won't hesitate to cut you off without a farthing if you disclose secrets that are best left buried. I won't allow you to hurt my wife or her family." He took a healthy drink of the port and set the glass back on the sideboard on his way out.

He immediately went in search of Arnold and found him downstairs, speaking with the housekeeper. Arnold was in his forties and had come to Huntwell as a footman about fifteen years ago.

David looked toward Mrs. Reid. "Pardon me for interrupting, Arnold, may I have a word?"

"Of course, my lord." Arnold inclined his head.

"May we go to your office?" David asked.

"Certainly." Arnold indicated for David to precede him to the office. "How can I help?" He closed the door and faced David.

"I'd like to know which retainers were employed at Huntwell thirty years ago."

"I've a ledger." He went to his desk and opened a drawer from which he removed a bound volume. "This goes back some fifty years." He handed it to David.

Taking the book, David sat down in a chair situated at a small table in the corner. He opened the ledger on the table and scanned for entries in the 1780s.

"I seem to recall that a couple of the grooms were here

at that time, including Scully," Arnold said.

That was the head groom. David's eyes landed on the man's name. He'd started here as a groom in 1790. Two entries before that was George Snowden, who'd also been hired as a groom in 1789. "Excellent, thank you." David located a third groom who'd started two years later.

Going back a bit further, David recognized another name. He looked up at Arnold. "I didn't realize Mrs. Johnson had been here that long. Why isn't she the head cook?"

"She's never wanted to be," Arnold said. "She's quite content to be the primary assistant."

Nodding, David went back to the ledger but didn't recognize anyone else. Ah well, this gave him three people to interview at least. He closed the book and handed it back to Arnold. "Thank you."

"My pleasure. May I ask what this is about and if I can be of further assistance?"

"I'm investigating something that happened about thirty years ago. I'd like to speak with those three retainers as soon as possible."

"Is this concerning Lady Catherine?"

Apparently, Arnold had heard of the tragedy. "You're aware of what happened?"

"I've heard recollections from the retainers who were here at the time, some of whom are no longer in your employ." His face creased briefly with concern, a rare display of emotion from the typically stoic man. "It affected many people, particularly because it involved one of us." He glanced away.

"Do you have any sense as to what sort of man Snowden was?" David realized he was asking for rumor, but wanted to know what the staff had said about him.

"He was supposedly a friendly sort—always quick with

a joke. People liked working with him. They were shocked when he disappeared with her ladyship."

"They may have been in love." David realized he was starting to share Fanny and Ivy's hope—that his aunt and the footman *had* been in love. "Did anyone mention that?"

Arnold shook his head. "Not that I heard."

Disappointment curdled in David's chest. "Thank you, Arnold. I'll just go speak with Mrs. Johnson."

He left the butler's office and made his way to the kitchen. As soon as he entered, he heard a gasp. When he turned his head, his gaze fell on a young scullery maid who was sweeping the floor. Her eyes were wide at seeing him, and it took her a moment to duck into a curtsey. "Beggin' yer pardon, my lord."

David gave her a warm smile. "Don't concern yourself, please. I'm in search of Mrs. Johnson. Can you point me to her location?"

"She's in the larder." The maid tossed a glance toward the opposite corner of the kitchen.

"Thank you." David inclined his head, then crossed the room to the larder.

Mrs. Johnson, a round-faced—and round-middled— woman turned from the shelves. She wiped her hands on her apron. "Good evening, Your Lordship." She eyed him with a bit of apprehension.

David sought to put her at ease. "Good evening, Mrs. Johnson. I'm sorry to disturb you. I wanted to ask you a few questions about my Aunt Catherine and the footman called Snowden."

The woman's eyes widened briefly. Her answer was slow and measured. "That was a long time ago."

"Yes, but I'm hoping you'll recall some details. As you can imagine, that event caused a great deal of distress for

THE DUKE OF KISSES 225

my family—and for the Snowdens. As it happens, I am to marry a Snowden in a few weeks."

"Indeed? Well, that is happy news."

"It doesn't bother you that I am marrying someone from that family?"

She looked mildly horrified. "I wouldn't presume to judge."

"What I mean to ask is, do you harbor any ill will? Because of what happened?"

"I try to keep my nose out of the family's business."

He understood that. "Of course, but I would greatly appreciate your help in determining what actually happened. My family believes Snowden kidnapped my aunt. However, the Snowdens are certain the two were in love. Do you by chance know which was true?"

She exhaled and looked at the flickering candle she'd set on the shelf to her right. "I don't." She didn't meet his gaze, and he wondered if she was telling the truth.

"Did you know Snowden? I'd like to have an idea of what sort of man he was. Arnold heard he was well liked."

She shot him an uneasy glance. "He was, my lord. But I didn't know him well. I was a young scullery maid back then. I just focused on my work, like I do now."

"Mrs. Johnson, I am quite happy with your work, so you need have no worry that anything you say will affect your employment. If you can think of anything that might help me understand what happened with my aunt and Snowden, I'd be much appreciative. I want my new countess to feel welcome here."

"Oh, she will be." Mrs. Johnson looked at him now, and her gaze was fierce. "Snowden was a good man—to all of us anyway. To think that his relative will now be lady of the house would make him happy, I think."

"Do you have any idea where he is?" David asked

softly.

She looked down and shook her head sadly. When she lifted her gaze to his, he knew she was being honest. "I do not. But I hope that he's happy. It's so sad what happened to Lady Catherine." Her voice had grown small.

Though she hadn't said so, David was certain the woman had liked Snowden and believed that he and Aunt Catherine had wanted to be together—or that at least he hadn't kidnapped her. Why would she want a kidnapper to be happy?

"Thank you, Mrs. Johnson. I do appreciate your honesty and recollection. If you think of anything else about that time, I'd love to hear it."

She nodded. "Congratulations to you and your bride, my lord. We'll cook up quite a celebratory feast."

He smiled. "We shall look forward to it."

He turned and left the larder and made his way through the kitchen on his way back upstairs. Though he was tempted to go to the stables and speak with Scully and the other groom, he was bone tired after the day's travel. Tomorrow would come soon enough.

After he interviewed the others, he'd have to talk to Uncle Walter. David only hoped his uncle could understand. And forgive.

Chapter Fifteen

❦

AFTER SLEEPING RATHER late, Fanny was eager to see David. Unfortunately, he was fifteen miles away at Huntwell. Unless he was in Clare purchasing their marriage license. Surely he would come visit.

Certain this was the case, she went downstairs to wait for him in West's library where she would peruse her favorite book about birds in anticipation of sharing it with him.

Before she could get to the library, however, the butler intercepted her. "Miss Snowden, a note arrived for you." He handed her the folded parchment.

Fanny opened it and quickly read the contents.

My dearest,
If you can get away to meet me alone, I will be at the hunting
lodge all day. I hope to see you.
Yours,
David

Smiling, she held the paper to her chest. This was even better than coming here. He'd told her about the lodge as they'd traveled from Yorkshire. It sat on three hundred acres that adjoined Stour's Edge and was approximately two miles northwest of the house.

She'd ride out immediately. Dashing upstairs, she changed into her riding habit and informed Barker where she was going.

"You're going to take a groom, I hope." Barker gave her a pointed look, then rolled her eyes. "Never mind. I daresay you won't want a groom hovering about. Do be careful."

Fanny suppressed a smile. "I will. Thank you, Barker."

"Yes, well, don't tell anyone that I've utterly failed as a chaperone."

Fanny hurried to the stables, where a groom readied the mount West had given her last summer. She'd spent a great deal of time learning to ride more proficiently and getting to know the sweet mare.

After declining the offer of a groom—she said she was only going for a short ride around the house—she set out for the hunting lodge. She realized this was perhaps the only time they could meet like this. She couldn't keep riding off alone for a few hours at a time. She and David would have to devise some other plan. Perhaps he could come stay at Stour's Edge for a few days at a time. She missed him so.

When the hunting lodge came into sight, she rode a bit faster. His horse grazed in front of the small, two-story timber structure. It had a steeply pitched roof and a single chimney.

She dismounted and set her horse to graze with his. Surprised that he hadn't come out to meet her, she went to the door. Should she knock? Should she just walk in?

He *was* expecting her…

She unlatched the door and pushed it open. The ground floor was a large, rectangular room with a fireplace in the back left corner. A cozy seating area was arranged around a small blaze of a fire. To her right was a dining table, and a staircase marched up the far left wall.

But the room was empty.

"David?" she called. There was a doorway to the left of the center on the back wall. Perhaps David was in there. Or, maybe he was upstairs, where there was likely a bedroom.

Excitement stirred in her belly when she thought of him lying in wait for her in bed…

She moved toward the stairs, only to stop at the sound of an unfamiliar voice.

"Good afternoon, Miss Snowden! I'm so glad you've arrived."

She slowly turned as her excitement changed to apprehension. The man looked familiar. Had she seen him with David in London? He certainly resembled David.

"I'm Mr. Langley," he said, smiling warmly. "David's uncle. I'm pleased to finally make your acquaintance. I sent the note for you to come here—I wanted it to be a surprise."

What the devil was going on? "So David isn't here?" she asked, not bothering to keep the disappointment from her voice.

"Oh no. He's at Huntwell. This is my lodge, where I like to paint. I thought I would paint your portrait for a wedding gift for my nephew."

Fanny relaxed. "What a lovely idea. How long will that take? I came without a groom, so if I don't return relatively soon, I'll be missed."

His lips spread in a wide smile. "Oh, well, we wouldn't want that. I've got everything set up in the kitchen. The windows and the light are best there." He gestured for her to go through the doorway to the back.

She went into the kitchen, which was quite cheery. The fireplace from the front room also opened into this one. A cozy settle sat nearby, and on the back wall, there was a bank of three windows, which let in the afternoon sunlight. A stool along with a small canvas and his paints were set up in front of the windows.

"If you would just sit on the stool," he said, still smiling. There was something slightly unsettling about his ebullience. His eyes were gray like David's, but the similarity ended there. His gaze was cold and flat, making his smile and happy tone seem…hollow.

She shook her head as she positioned herself on the stool. She was being fanciful. This was an odd arrangement, to be sure—why hadn't he explained his intent in the note?

"Just angle yourself toward the window there. Look up, like you're studying the birds. I'll put one in the sky. David will like that."

Yes, he would. The sentiment made her relax. "What a thoughtful gift."

"Beautiful." He picked up a brush from the small table next to his easel. "Shall we begin?"

❦❦❦

DAVID'S CHEST SWELLED with anticipation as he rode up the drive to Stour's Edge. He'd planned to ride to Clare first to purchase their marriage license, but had found himself stopping here first.

He was anxious to share what he'd learned with Fanny, Ivy, and West. He'd spoken with Scully and the other groom, and they'd been far more forthcoming than Mrs. Johnson.

Scully had known Snowden fairly well. They'd worked in the stable together until Snowden had been given a position as a footman. He'd had aspirations to be a valet or a butler and had worked his way up to underbutler. He was rather handsome, and Scully recalled that the female retainers were always eager for his attention. He'd carried on with several of them over the years, but that had stopped in 1789, when Scully said Snowden had fallen in love.

When David had asked the identity of Snowden's love, Scully had become a bit reticent. He'd said that Snowden would never say. David prodded further, asking if Scully had been able to discern the woman's identity on his own. He was fairly certain it had been Lady Catherine but had never asked Snowden about it—if the man had wanted to keep things private, who was Scully to stick his nose in things?

Then Lady Catherine had gone missing, and Scully had kept his mouth shut out of fear of being fired or worse, of abetting something criminal. The groom, who was now Scully's right hand in the stable, had corroborated the entire story, except to say that Snowden hadn't been *that* handsome.

"Did she reciprocate Snowden's feelings?" David had asked.

Scully and the groom had exchanged looks. "I've never told anyone this—and his lordship, your grandfather, did ask, but I was too afraid to answer honestly." He winced, the lines around his eyes increasing. "I saw them kissing in the stable once. They didn't know I saw them, and I didn't say anything. It wasn't any of our business." He looked at the groom, who barely nodded but kept his head down.

David had needed to confirm what he now believed, along with Fanny and Ivy, to be true. "I'm sorry to ask, but I'd like to be certain. My aunt was a willing participant in this activity?"

Scully had nodded. "As far as I could tell."

"Do you recall what happened when he returned with my aunt?" David had tensed as he awaited Scully's response.

"He said she'd died giving birth to their child. The family was devastated, of course. I didn't see Snowden. He was barely at Huntwell a day."

"Do you know where he went?"

Scully had shaken his head. "We all knew better than to speak of him to the family, but I did hear that he'd left England. I assumed he went back to Scotland."

David supposed that was possible. Unfortunately, it seemed they would never know for certain. What they did know, however, was that his aunt and Fanny's great-uncle *had* been in love. He'd been so eager to tell Fanny that he'd asked Scully to saddle his horse immediately.

As he approached the pale stone façade of Stour's Edge, he saw an unfamiliar coach parked in the drive. He hoped he wasn't interrupting anything, but decided it didn't matter if he were.

A groom took his horse, and he made his way to the door, which was opened by a footman—not the butler he'd met the day before. He welcomed David into the hall. "Good afternoon, my lord."

David's attention was immediately drawn to the pair of men standing off to the side. His defenses immediately rose, along with his ire.

"What the bloody hell are you doing here?" West thundered as he came into the hall with Ivy at his side. West's gaze tripped over David. "I didn't realize you were here too. Is this a coincidence?"

"Yes," David answered. He faced Fanny's father and brother. "I thought I told you not to come anywhere near Fanny."

Her father's eyes narrowed with naked malice. "I'll go where I please."

David advanced on him. "Not where you aren't invited."

The other man—not John but Fanny's other brother, Jacob, stepped part way in front of his father. "Can we please keep this somewhat civil? We came for a reason."

"Out with it, then," West said sharply. "I don't want you here any longer than it takes you to deliver whatever message you thought it important to deliver personally."

"Where's Fanny?" Snowden asked.

Ivy turned her head toward the butler in wordless question. The butler departed the hall, seemingly in search of Fanny.

David didn't want the man here any more than West did. "You needn't wait for Fanny. In fact, I insist you don't. She doesn't need to see you at all."

Snowden's gaze cut over David with disdain. "You'd like that, wouldn't you?"

David clenched his teeth and spoke through them. "Exceedingly."

Slipping his hand into his coat pocket, Snowden withdrew a yellowed piece of paper. "I found the letter from my uncle." He unfolded the parchment and held it out to David. "Read it for yourself."

David took the paper and scanned it quickly. George Snowden had been deeply in love with Aunt Catherine, and if his words were to be believed, she'd felt the same way about him. He said they'd eloped to Scotland, where he'd found work at a coaching inn. The tone of the letter was happy, but with a darker tone when Snowden said he couldn't ever return, for fear of facing Catherine's family. She was terrified they would force her to return to Huntwell and abandon the man she loved. It was both lovely and tragic since David knew how their love story had ended.

"Don't you dare tell me Uncle George wrote lies," Snowden growled.

"I won't do that," David said quietly, handing the paper to Ivy for her and West to read. "I've interviewed some of my retainers, and I'd already concluded that they likely ran off together."

Snowden stared at David, appearing absolutely nonplussed. "You have?"

David took a deep breath. "The time has come for this feud, or whatever it is, to end. Our families will be united—in joy, I might add—whether you like it or not."

Munro reappeared in the hall. "It seems Miss Snowden is not at home. Her maid says she went for a ride."

West turned to the footman who'd let David in. "Please run to the stable and see if she's returned. If not, find out where she's gone and how long ago she left."

The footman dashed off leaving them to smolder in uncomfortable silence. At length, Snowden cleared his throat. "I still want to know what happened to my uncle. Do any of your retainers know that?"

"They did not, and I dearly wish that wasn't the case. Like you, I would like to understand what happened." It didn't sit well with David. While he couldn't see his grandfather, father, or uncle doing anything untoward, he also now knew that love could drive someone to commit terrible acts.

The footman finally returned, a bit breathless as he rushed into the hall. He turned his attention to West. "She's been gone nearly an hour, Your Grace. She did not take a groom."

"She didn't?" Ivy's brow creased. "Perhaps Barker knows where she's gone." As she started toward the stairs, West stopped her.

"Ivy, let Munro go and fetch the maid."

The butler took himself off once more, and it was only a few moments before he came back with Barker in tow.

The second her gaze fell on David, her eyes widened and her jaw dropped. "What are you doing here, my lord?"

David's heart stuttered, then began to pound. "Why shouldn't I be?"

"Miss Snowden went to meet you. Did she not show up?" The maid's face turned the color of ash.

David felt as though the world around him were falling down. He struggled to keep his wits about him as well as his composure. "Where did she go?"

"She said it was a hunting lodge on some property that borders the estate. I knew she was going alone. I'm so sorry, my lord." She turned to Ivy and West. "Your Graces." Her features crumpled.

"Why was she meeting me at the lodge?" David asked, his body humming with fear. He just knew something was dreadfully wrong.

"She received a note from you."

David looked at West, whose grim face reflected his own sense of foreboding. "I sent no such note."

"Let's go." West was already moving toward the door.

"Please hurry," Ivy said. "Dammit, I wish I could go with you."

"We're coming," Jacob said, following behind them.

David didn't care who came or if they kept up. He ran to the stable as if his life depended on it.

And, truly, it did.

Chapter Sixteen

⊶⊱⊰⊷

"Just tilt your head back a little. Show me a bit more neck. There you are."

Fanny's neck was beginning to hurt from sitting in this position for so long. It had to be going on an hour since she sat down. "I need a respite," she said, standing up.

"No, no, I'm making excellent progress. Please sit." He waved his brush at her. "I only need a few more minutes before I'll be finished."

Finished? Fanny was fairly certain paintings took several sittings and countless hours. "How can that be?" She moved her head from side to side in an effort to ease her aching muscles. "I think we need to be done for today. I should get back to Stour's Edge." She started forward, curious to look at the canvas and see just how far he'd gotten.

His brows darted low over his eyes. "No, you mustn't. Sit down. Please."

"Mr. Langley, please understand. I'm tired, and I wish to go." She kept moving toward the canvas, and he leapt up, startling her with the quickness of his movement. She caught sight of what he'd painted, and terror seized her heart.

It was, in fact, nearly finished, but it wasn't any sort of painting she'd ever seen. It was of a body lying in a pool of what must be blood, the woman's neck sliced across into a gaping wound. The woman's features were muddied—indeed, everything about her was somewhat indistinct. Except for her hair, which was the exact color of Fanny's, and the dress, which was a dark blue like

Fanny's riding habit.

Gasping, she tried to run past him back to the front of the house, but he grabbed her arm and pulled her back. He lifted his right hand, and she realized, too late, that he'd exchanged his paintbrush for a knife. Panic leapt up her throat.

His lips drew back to reveal his teeth. "I'm going to carve you up just like your filthy uncle."

Dear God, what had he done to Great-uncle George? She somehow managed to find her voice. "You killed him?"

"After he brought my poor sister back." Mr. Langley's eyes were wild, his lips parted as he breathed heavily. "He'd killed her. It wasn't bad enough that he'd ruined her. He killed her too." Tears ran down his cheeks even as his grip on Fanny's forearm tightened to an excruciating degree.

"Please let me go," she begged. "I had nothing to do with my great-uncle."

"I can't let you marry David. It would be a blight on our family to allow it. Why couldn't you have listened to Anne and just left him alone?"

Anne… Was that David's mother? And Mr. Langley somehow knew that she'd threatened Fanny? Had they plotted this together? Did David's mother know his uncle wanted to kill her? Her fear melded with anguish and desperation.

"You don't have to do this," she said, trying in vain to escape his grasp.

"It's already done, dear." He brought the knife down.

Screaming, Fanny reached for the palette with her free hand. She threw it in his face, splashing paint all over him.

His hold loosened, and she nearly pulled free, but he jerked her back towards him, bringing her face terribly close to his. His lips curled, revealing his teeth again in a ferocious sneer. He brought the knife down as Fanny reached toward the painting table, her fingers searching for any weapon she could find.

The movement brought her out of the direct path of the knife, but it sliced across her right shoulder. Her hand closed around a bottle. She picked it up and turned, smashing it against his head with all her might. The glass shattered, and she kept a hold of the neck, which now had a jagged edge. He staggered back, at last letting her go.

She turned to run, but he grabbed at her dress from behind, sending her tumbling to the floor. The impact sent pain radiating through her shoulder.

She managed to turn over as he lunged toward her. She slid to the right and sliced the broken bottle at his neck. The horrid feeling of the glass slicing through his flesh made her drop the bottle. He pitched forward, and she rolled away from his flailing body.

Without a backward glance, she scrambled to her feet and ran for the door to the front room. She felt as though she were running in place, but somehow got the door open and stumbled outside into the bright sunlight.

The horses were nowhere to be seen, and she practically fell down the steps in her haste. Her vision was hazy, and nausea rose in her belly. Doubling over, she violently cast up her accounts.

She didn't dare stay here. Forcing herself to move, she ran toward the copse of trees. But she was disoriented and so very sick. As she reached the trees, she tripped, sprawling face-first onto the ground. Pain shot through her as nausea threatened once more.

She had to get up, had to *move*. But she couldn't. Blackness rose and swallowed her whole.

THE TREES AND fields went by David in a blur. He didn't pay attention to whether West or the Snowdens kept up with him. He had one goal: to reach Fanny.

He had no idea what was going on, but whoever had pretended to be him couldn't mean well. Unfortunately, David could only think of a few people that would lure her to the hunting lodge…and that broke his heart.

Urging his horse faster, he finally crested the knoll that would lead him down to the lodge. Smoke curled above the trees. Whoever was there had built a fire. Good, maybe it was something innocent.

Just before he reached the clearing where the lodge was nestled, he found two horses, one of which he recognized as his uncle's. His gut tightened, and he rode straight for the lodge.

His horse barely came to a stop before he slid from its back. Fear pulsed through him as he tore into the lodge. "Fanny!" He raced for the kitchen and stopped at the sight of blood covering the floor just over the threshold.

But it wasn't her, thank God. His uncle lay facedown in a crimson pool. David didn't have to check to see if he was dead. No one could survive losing that much blood. Sadness and horror raced up his spine but couldn't overcome the fear he still had for Fanny. If Uncle Walter was dead, what might have happened to her?

"Fanny!" He dashed into the storeroom, but it was empty. Retracing his steps, he rushed back to the front room just as West came in the door.

"Is she here?"

"Not that I can see. My uncle is in the kitchen. He's dead." David said this without emotion as he ran up the stairs. He quickly looked through the two bedrooms and washroom. Each chamber was just as empty as the one before, and David shouted in frustration.

He started back down the stairs, his legs shaking.

West stood near the door to the kitchen, his features somber. "His throat was cut with a broken bottle."

David stared at him, feeling utterly hopeless. "Where is she?" His voice was a thready croak as a knot of tears and anguish gathered in his throat.

"What's going on?" David's mother walked in the front door and looked between David and West. "What are you doing here?"

"What are *you* doing here?" David couldn't have kept the menace from his voice if he tried, which he didn't.

"I came to see Walter."

West turned, positioning himself as a barrier in front of the doorway to the kitchen.

The movement drew her attention, and she craned her neck to see around him. She squinted, and when David heard her inhale, he knew she saw the blood.

"What's that in there?" Her voice had risen to an unnaturally high pitch, indicating she'd probably caught at least a glimpse of the scene in the kitchen.

"Uncle Walter is dead," David said flatly. He was past caring how anyone felt when he was going mad with fear.

She lifted her hand to her mouth as tears flooded her eyes and tracked down her cheeks. Dashing forward, she tried to get past West, who initially blocked her path.

"Let her go," David said.

His mother went into the kitchen, and David followed her, with West on her heels. David watched, feeling strangely detached, as she fell to her knees in the puddle of blood and touched Walter's gray face.

West had turned him over, and now David saw the jagged hole in his neck as well as the broken glass beside him. After seeing him lying there, David hadn't really looked at anything else. Now he saw the canvas.

It was a woman, prone and bloody, and while her features were indistinguishable, she was clearly Fanny. Because of the hair.

Walter had been an avid painter, using the lodge as a studio as well as having one at the dower house. Ice pricked along David's spine as he turned to his mother. "What did he do?" His tone was low and lethal.

She looked up at him and wiped the back of her hand across her wet cheek. "What do you mean? He's the one who's dead."

"And why do you care so much?" David suddenly saw something very clearly. She often came here with Walter when he painted. "How long have you and Walter been carrying on? Was it before Father died?"

Her face lost all color, and David already had his answer. "I loved your father," she whispered.

David wasn't sure he believed her, but now he saw guilt in so many things she did and said, namely her insistence that *he* keep *his* promise to her father. How easy for her when she'd broken her promise to be faithful to him. "Did you love Walter too?"

She turned her head away from David, and he saw her shoulders shake.

"St. Ives? Fanny?" The sound of Snowden's voice carried from the front of the house.

West turned and left the kitchen.

Fanny.

David had to find her. Where could she be? He pivoted and took in the painting scene. There was a stool near the window, where a model might sit. But the painting was not of a woman sitting. It didn't make any sort of sense. And yet he knew Fanny had been summoned here, and it was her image on that canvas. Unfortunately, he couldn't interrogate the one person who might know where she was.

Despair curled through him. He unlatched the back door and strode outside. A cloud had moved over the sun, plunging the day into shadow, as if the heavens would share in his anguish.

"She's here!"

David heard the call and ran to the sound. He raced around the house toward the copse of trees on the west side.

Jacob came from the trees, his arms carrying a figure in a dark blue riding habit.

Fanny.

Racing to the man's side, he took her from him without asking. Her eyes were closed, and blood stained her front, completely discoloring the white blouse beneath the jacket.

David carried her inside to the settee near the fireplace.

West joined him. "Where did you find her?"

"In the trees," Jacob answered from somewhere to David's right.

Snowden came around the backside of the settee. "What's happened to her?" He sounded stricken, and David wanted to scream at him. He didn't deserve to feel as upset as David did. But then David doubted he ever really could.

David dropped to his knees and smoothed Fanny's hair back from her scratched and dirty face. "Fanny, wake up, please, my love." He ran his hand down her cheek and felt the pulse in her neck then opened the buttons of her jacket to investigate the source of the blood.

Her chest rose and fell with her breaths, but he was still more scared than he'd ever been in his life. Watching his father grow sicker and die and been awful, but this pain was beyond anything he could imagine.

As he eased her jacket aside, her eyelids fluttered and opened. Her eyes were unfocused as she looked past him. She blinked again and again before seeing him. "David?"

"I'm here, love." Relief—however temporary it might be—poured through him.

"Where are we?" She looked around, and then fear took over her expression. "Are we back in the lodge?" She tried to sit up, her eyes wild.

"She's a murderer!" David's mother cried as she came toward the settee.

Snowden grabbed her and pushed her into the wall. "Don't you dare touch my daughter."

West moved between them, putting his back to the countess, and shoved at Snowden. "Back off!"

Fanny flinched and brought her hand to her shoulder. She quickly jerked her hand back. "What's wrong with me?" She looked at the blood staining her palm and then lifted her frightened gaze to David's.

"We'll fix it, love," he promised, tearing his cravat from his neck and wadding the linen in his palm to press it gently against the wound.

"He stabbed me." She stared up at him, dazed. "Your uncle. He wanted to kill me, just like he said he killed my Great-uncle George." She began to sob. David cradled his free arm around her.

"I knew it!" Snowden crowed. "I knew you bloody well killed him."

David's mother shook her head frantically. "No. Walter took him to the coast and put him on a ship to America."

"You believed that?" Snowden sneered.

The countess opened her mouth but said nothing. She turned her head, presenting a stoic profile as she clenched her jaw.

Fanny's sobs subsided, and David pressed a kiss to her forehead. He looked toward West. "She needs a doctor."

"I can ride to get one, but do you want me to leave?"

"I'll do whatever he needs," Jacob said. His gaze was fixed intently on his sister, and worry was etched into every line of his face.

David's mother stepped toward West, her features harsh. "When you go to town, fetch the magistrate too. So he can arrest her for murder."

She pointed at Fanny, and that was when David completely lost control.

Chapter Seventeen

❦

FANNY SLUMPED AS David raced around the settee. She turned, her shoulder aching horribly, and watched as he grabbed his mother by the upper arms.

"Stop it!" he shouted in her face. "This ends now! Walter was going to kill her, and he already admitted killing George Snowden. I spoke with Scully in the stables and Mrs. Johnson in the kitchen. Aunt Catherine was in love with him. Furthermore, Fanny's father brought a letter from George Snowden detailing his elopement with Catherine. He didn't kidnap her."

Fanny knew she'd been right. Later, she'd be happy about it. Now she was too overwhelmed with a dozen other, darker emotions.

"That's a lie. Your father would be horrified by your allegiance to them." Her eyes turned pleading. "David, I'm your family, not her. She's no one from nothing."

David pulled his hands away with such force that the countess stumbled backward.

"She's everything," Snowden said with quiet steel. "My daughter will make a fine countess to your son."

Fanny stared at him, wondering if she'd heard him correctly.

The countess brought her hands to her face and started to cry. "I don't want to believe it."

Fanny saw the woman's pain, heard it in the anguished tone of her voice. With great effort, she stood and went to David's side. His arm came quickly around her.

"I'm sorry for your pain," Fanny said quietly. "But you can see the painting he made. I believe he was designing how it might look." Her stomach turned again, and she swallowed, trying not to heave as she had earlier. "I didn't mean to kill him. I was only trying to survive."

David's arm squeezed her, and he pressed a lingering kiss to her forehead. "Look at her, Mother," he said darkly. "She's been stabbed. By Walter. You can't dismiss that."

The countess lowered her hands and wiped her face. She focused on Fanny, her lip trembling. "I can't believe he could be capable of such a thing. Did he really say he'd killed Snowden?"

"Yes, and he planned to…kill me the same way." Her body shuddered, and she leaned into David. "I think I need to sit again."

"I want to get you back to Stour's Edge. Can you manage riding with me?" he asked tenderly, his face and voice so altered from the man who'd railed so violently at his mother a few moments ago.

"I think so." She really had no idea, but she was desperate to leave this place.

"It's time to let the past go," Jacob said. His calm declaration surprised Fanny, and seemingly everyone else as they all swung their heads to look at him. He looked toward his father and then toward the countess. "Let it all go. There's a chance to find some goodness with Fanny marrying her earl. Their marriage can't erase the past, but it's a hope for a better future."

A heavy silence descended for a moment before Snowden cleared his throat. He glanced toward Jacob. "I didn't know you had such a way with words."

Jacob delivered him a pointed stare. "Father, it's time to let it *all* go. And that includes Ivy."

Snowden nodded just once, his features a mix of sadness and determination.

West started toward the door. "I'm going to fetch the doctor. David, I'll see you back at Stour's Edge. One of you needs to get back soon before my wife tries to ride here, which would be terrible in her condition." West strode from the house.

"We'll go now," Fanny said. "I can't wait to leave."

"What about Walter?" the countess croaked. "We can't just leave him here."

"We can, and we will," David said. Fanny could feel his heart thundering in his chest. "I'll send a cart to fetch him."

David turned to Jacob. "Will you help me get your sister on my horse and lead hers back to Stour's Edge?"

Jacob nodded.

"I'm picking you up now, my love." David swept Fanny into his arms. She winced as pain shot through her anew. He carried her from the house and walked to his horse. "Ready?"

Jacob held out his arms, and David transferred her to her brother. Fanny looked up at him and smiled. "What happened to make you so nice?"

His gaze was so serious, so concerned, that she almost didn't recognize him. "We're family. I never liked the way that Mary—*Ivy*—left. I didn't like how you left either." He shot a disgruntled glower toward their father, who'd come outside after them.

"Hand her up," David called from atop his horse.

Jacob lifted Fanny and helped David settle her in front of him. His arms came around her to pick up the reins. It wasn't the most comfortable position, but at least she was in the embrace of the man she loved.

"Thank you, Jacob."

"You have a place at Huntwell, if you want it," David said. Fanny's heart swelled with love.

His cheeks flushed a light pink. "I'd like that, my lord."

"I'm going to be your brother-in-law. Call me David." He turned the horse and led them away from the lodge.

"I'm afraid I don't ever want to come back here," Fanny said, closing her eyes as she leaned against him.

"Good, because I'm going to burn it down."

"I'm so sorry about your uncle." She felt ill again, but tamped the sick feeling down. Maybe someday she'd be able to think of him without wanting to vomit. Today was not that day. "I didn't mean to kill him."

"I know, love. Please don't think about it. Or him. I'm so sorry this happened. I never imagined he could do something so horrific."

They were quiet a moment before she found a bit of happiness. "I'm so happy to hear that your aunt and my great-uncle loved each other. How did you find out?"

"Your father brought a letter written by your great-uncle. In it, he explained how he and my aunt fell in love and eloped to Scotland. He worked at a coaching inn, and it truly sounded as if they would have led a happy life together if she hadn't died birthing their babe."

Fanny heard the sorrow in his voice and felt it in her own heart. "Is that why my father and brother are here?"

"Yes. Your father found the letter and wanted to show me the proof of what had happened. But I had already interviewed a few retainers who were at Huntwell thirty years ago. The head groom knew your great-uncle well. He was quite a popular fellow on the estate—especially with the ladies."

This made her smile. "Was he?"

"Until he fell in love, according to Scully— my head groom. And since he saw Snowden and my aunt kissing in the stable, I think it's safe to conclude she was the recipient of his affection." He kissed Fanny's head, which was nestled beneath his chin. "Just as you are mine."

"Only our ending will be much happier than theirs." She felt sad for them but also hopeful for the future stretching before her and David.

By God, he hoped so. He kissed her again. "Yes, it will."

❧❧❧

WEARY IN BODY and soul, David eyed the bed in his room at Stour's Edge. After yesterday's events at the lodge, West had invited him to stay for as long as he liked. It had been late afternoon before they'd returned to Stour's Edge and well into evening before the physician had tended Fanny. She'd required a row of neat stitches to seal her wound, and was so far recovering well. They were to watch for fever, and David prayed she wouldn't develop an infection as his father had done. He didn't think he could survive it.

He didn't think he'd want to.

The sheer terror he'd experienced when he'd seen her bleeding had been the single worst thing he'd ever known. How had he ever thought he could marry someone else?

It didn't bear consideration.

David opened his door and peered into the sitting room to which his and Fanny's room adjoined. As expected, it was empty. Still, he'd had to look.

He made his way to Fanny's room and slowly opened the door. Scanning the interior, he saw Barker sitting beside her bed. It was late, and the maid was reading by the light of a single candle.

She looked up as he walked inside. Stifling a yawn, she rose. "Are you here to take a watch?" she asked.

No one cared if he and Fanny were alone together. For

one, she wasn't in any state to partake in impropriety. For another thing, they were as good as wed.

"Yes, I'll stay all night. Get some rest."

She nodded. "Thank you, my lord." She left, closing the door with a soft snick.

David stared at Fanny for a few moments before removing his dressing gown and sliding into the bed next to her. He turned to his side and put his arm around her waist.

She snuggled into him and sighed. "I'm glad you're back. I missed you today."

"Were you pretending to sleep?" he asked.

"No, I *was* sleeping. But you woke me."

"Damn, I didn't mean to."

She smiled against him. "It's all right." She opened her eyes and looked up at him. He was swept away by the brilliance of her blue-green eyes. "How was Huntwell? Did you get Jacob settled over there?"

He was to be the new apprentice to the steward. "Not yet. He decided he wanted to stay here for a few days. He's worried about you."

"The change in him will take a bit of getting used to."

"I can imagine. He's certainly acquitted himself quite well with all that's happened." David moved his hand up and stroked her braid. "He wants to take a turn watching over you tomorrow."

She laughed softly. "Everyone wants a turn. I look forward to when I can be alone again. Except for you. I want you here all the time."

He winced. "I'm sorry I had to leave today."

"Do not apologize. You had to go to Huntwell. What's to be done with your uncle?" She tensed, and he stroked her arm, careful to avoid her shoulder.

"He'll be buried at the church in town. I refused to

allow him to be buried next to my father. My mother admitted she and Walter had been having an affair the past several years. Apparently, Walter had been in love with her since before she wed my father. That's why he never married."

"How sad."

"I have no pity for him." Bitterness burned his mouth.

"He deserves it most of all," she said. "Who knows what drives someone to the madness that fueled his mind. Perhaps it was feeling lonely for so many years."

"None of it excuses his actions."

"No, it doesn't. I was merely trying to understand."

"Sometimes there is no understanding," he said flatly.

She nuzzled his chest. "What of your mother?"

"She's already moved to the dower house, but then I plan to set her up in a house in London where she can stay forever." He twined his fingers with hers, mindful not to move her arm at all. "She did say she regretted threatening you and hopes you can find it in your heart to forgive her someday. I told her she was not invited to our wedding."

Her eyes widened. "The wedding! You haven't had a chance to purchase the license, have you?"

"No, I've been too concerned about you. I'll go day after tomorrow, though there is no rush since the doctor said you must rest for a week."

She pouted. "That's far too long."

"Actually, it gives us time to invite our friends from London. I was hoping we could get married in a fortnight."

After exhaling, she pressed her lips together. "That makes far too much sense. But I shan't like it."

"Neither will I, my love." He leaned down and kissed her gently, a brief brush of lips.

She sighed and closed her eyes for a moment. Her left hand moved beneath the covers, finding his cock. She opened her eyes, and they held an accusatory glint. "You're wearing smallclothes."

"I thought it wise. I can't very well visit my betrothed in her sickbed without any clothes on."

"Well, that's very boring."

He laughed again. "Somehow, I don't think life with you will ever be boring."

Her eyes twinkled as she looked up at him. "Not if I can help it, although after the last few days, I would prefer a lot of *nothing*." Her hand stroked him through his underclothes, and he let out a soft groan. "Perhaps not *nothing*."

"You're a temptress," he breathed. Then he took her hand and moved it away from him. "And you're going to keep your hands to yourself for six more days."

"And you're cruel. But I suppose I can wait if I must." Her tone was rife with exaggerated resignation. "It's better than waiting a fortnight until we are married."

"We probably *should* wait for that."

She gave him a seductive smile and moved her hand right back over to the bulge in his smallclothes. "But we won't."

He grinned down at her before swooping down to capture her lips. "No, we won't."

Epilogue

THE DAY OF Fanny and David's wedding was marked with brilliant blue sky and bright, beautiful sunlight. The procession from the church in Clare to Stour's Edge had been intermittently lined with townspeople and tenants from the estate.

David had assured Fanny that their greeting at Huntwell the next day would be equally joyous. They had quite a celebration planned for their new countess.

But today, they would share their happiness with their close friends and family. That included Fanny's parents and John and his new wife, as well as Patience and her husband and daughter. Jacob was there, of course, and quite thrilled to be working at Huntwell.

They'd just finished the elaborate breakfast Ivy had overseen, which was an impressive feat for someone due to deliver a child within the next month or so. They now crowded the large drawing room, and it seemed the men had gathered at one side while the women were on the other.

Ivy held court on a settee with her dear friends Emmaline, Lucy, and Aquilla around her. Lavinia approached Fanny with a smile. "I'm just so happy for you!" Her gaze drifted toward her husband, Beck, and then she frowned. "But I wish Sarah was here."

"I know, I miss her too," Fanny said. "I can't imagine how she must be feeling. Is she still not seeing anyone?"

"No. Nor is Anthony. They're closeted in their parents' town house." Lavinia's face creased with sorrow. "I'm worried about them, but I know it will just take time.

Felix is there keeping an eye on them."

"I'll come to London the moment she asks," Fanny said, her heart hurting for her friend in her time of tragedy. "I feel terrible I haven't gone to see her."

Lavinia's eyes narrowed briefly. "Goodness, Fanny, you've been rather busy, what with getting married and nearly getting killed. How is your shoulder today?"

"A bit sore." She rotated it a couple of times, which seemed to help it from becoming too stiff. The doctor had taken the stitches out last week, which had greatly improved matters. However, David had decided they should refrain from any bedroom activities until after they were wed. She'd wanted to kick him. In fact, she actually had.

"You should take it easy," Lavinia said with great concern.

"Did David tell you to say that?"

"He might have, but I would have done so anyway." She flashed a smile.

Fanny looked toward her husband just as he happened to be looking at her in return. Her lips curved into a smile, and his did the same.

"Go," Lavinia whispered.

"What?" Fanny glanced at her.

"To your husband." Lavinia laughed softly.

Sending her friend a grateful smile, Fanny crossed the room toward David. Only she didn't have to go the whole way because he met her in the middle.

He offered her his arm. "May I escort you for a brief walk on the terrace, wife?"

"Yes, please, husband." She curled her hand over his sleeve, and he led her through the open door. "When will you start your book? You said you would after we were wed."

"I actually started it last night. I couldn't sleep." He sent her a sheepish grin.

"Me neither. I wrote up a list of tasks for the workhouse, starting with hiring an agent to find a suitable property."

"An excellent idea. I'll have Graham arrange it. He's eager to be of use since he was absent...before."

David clearly didn't want to discuss the horrid event with his uncle, and she was grateful to him for it. Graham had been in London tending to business for David and had been horrified by what had transpired. He'd been delighted to be here for their wedding, however. "I quite like him," Fanny said.

"Good, he likes you too. He's glad I didn't...follow my father's wishes."

He was referring to marrying Miss Stoke, of course. Fanny felt bad for her. She'd seemed to genuinely think David would marry her and had to have been disappointed when he'd said he wouldn't.

Honestly, it seemed a miracle that she and David had found their way to each other at all.

Fanny gestured toward a tree near the terrace. "Oh, look, a pair of doves."

He pulled her in front of him and wrapped his arms around her. "That must be a sign of good fortune."

"A confirmation that we were meant to be," she said.

He pressed his lips to her temple and whispered in her ear, "Written in the stars."

The doves took flight directly over their heads, and Fanny quickly stepped away from him.

"Why'd you do that?" he asked.

She watched the birds fly to a different tree, then went back into his arms, only facing him this time. "Birds like to...unload on you."

He laughed. "Just that one time."

She playfully arched a brow at him. "Which you richly deserved."

"I certainly did. Hopefully, now I deserve you."

"I think so." She slipped her arms around him. "It feels like we've been through a great many obstacles to get here."

"I would agree. Sometimes I doubted we would make it, but not because we didn't want to."

She stroked her hands along his back. "Yet here we are."

He kissed her, and her body stirred with desire. "Yes," he said, "and here we'll stay."

THE END

Thank You!

❧

Thank you so much for reading *The Duke of Kisses*. I hope you enjoyed it! Don't miss the next Untouchable - Felix, the Earl of Ware in *The Duke of Distraction*!

Would you like to know when my next book is available? Sign up for my reader club at http://www.darcyburke.com/readerclub and follow me on social media:

Facebook: http://facebook.com/DarcyBurkeFans
Twitter at @darcyburke
Instagram at darcyburkeauthor
Pinterest at darcyburkewrite

I hope you'll consider leaving a review at your favorite online vendor or networking site!

The Duke of Kisses is the eleventh book in The Untouchables series. *The Duke of Distraction* is coming up next! Catch up with my other historical series: Secrets and Scandals and Legendary Rogues. If you like contemporary romance, I hope you'll check out my Ribbon Ridge series available from Avon Impulse, and the continuation of Ribbon Ridge in So Hot.

I appreciate my readers so much. Thank you, thank you, *thank* *you*.

Books by Darcy Burke

Historical Romance

The Untouchables

The Forbidden Duke
The Duke of Daring
The Duke of Deception
The Duke of Desire
The Duke of Defiance
The Duke of Danger
The Duke of Ice
The Duke of Ruin
The Duke of Lies
The Duke of Seduction
The Duke of Kisses
The Duke of Distraction

Secrets and Scandals

Her Wicked Ways
His Wicked Heart
To Seduce a Scoundrel
To Love a Thief (a novella)
Never Love a Scoundrel
Scoundrel Ever After

Legendary Rogues

Lady of Desire
Romancing the Earl
Lord of Fortune
Captivating the Scoundrel

Contemporary Romance

Ribbon Ridge

Where the Heart Is (a prequel novella)
Only in My Dreams
Yours to Hold
When Love Happens
The Idea of You
When We Kiss
You're Still the One

Ribbon Ridge: So Hot

So Good
So Right
So Wrong

Praise for Darcy Burke's

The Untouchables Series

THE FORBIDDEN DUKE

"I LOVED this story!!" 5 Stars

-Historical Romance Lover

"This is a wonderful read and I can't wait to see what comes next in this amazing series..." 5 Stars

-Teatime and Books

THE DUKE of DARING

"You will not be able to put it down once you start. Such a good read."

-Books Need TLC

"An unconventional beauty set on life as a spinster meets the one man who might change her mind, only to find his painful past makes it impossible to love. A wonderfully emotional journey from attraction, to friendship, to a love that conquers all."

-Bronwen Evans, USA Today Bestselling Author

THE DUKE of DECEPTION

"...an enjoyable, well-paced story ... Ned and Aquilla are an engaging, well-matched couple – strong, caring and compassionate; and ...it's easy to believe that they will continue to be happy together long after the book is ended."

-All About Romance

"This is my favorite so far in the series! They had chemistry from the moment they met...their passion leaps off the pages."-Sassy Book Lover

THE DUKE of DESIRE

"Masterfully written with great characterization...with a flourish toward characters, secrets, and romance... Must read addition to "The Untouchables" series!"

-My Book Addiction and More

"If you are looking for a truly endearing story about two people who take the path least travelled to find the other, with a side of 'YAH THAT'S HOT!' then this book is absolutely for you!"

-The Reading Cafe

THE DUKE of DEFIANCE

"This story was so beautifully written, and it hooked me from page one. I couldn't put the book down and just had to read it in one sitting even though it meant reading into the wee hours of the morning."

-Buried Under Romance

"I loved the Duke of Defiance! This is the kind of book you hate when it is over and I had to make myself stop reading just so I wouldn't have to leave the fun of Knighton's (aka Bran) and Joanna's story!"

-Behind Closed Doors Book Review

THE DUKE of DANGER

"The sparks fly between them right from the start... the HEA is certainly very hard-won, and well-deserved."

-All About Romance

"Another book hangover by Darcy! Every time I pick a favorite in this series, she tops it. The ending was perfect and made me want more."

-Sassy Book Lover

THE DUKE of ICE

"Each book gets better and better, and this novel was no exception. I think this one may be my fave yet! 5 out 5 for this reader!"

-Front Porch Romance

"An incredibly emotional story...I dare anyone to stop reading once the second half gets under way because this is intense!"
-Buried Under Romance

THE DUKE of RUIN

"This is a fast paced novel that held me until the last page."
-Guilty Pleasures Book Reviews

" ...everything I could ask for in a historical romance... impossible to stop reading."

-The Bookish Sisters

THE DUKE of LIES

"THE DUKE OF LIES is a work of genius! The characters are wonderfully complex, engaging; there is much mystery, and so many, many lies from so many people; I couldn't wait to see it all uncovered."

-Buried Under Romance

"..the epitome of romantic [with]...a bit of danger/action. The main characters are mature, fierce, passionate, and full of surprises. If you are a hopeless romantic and you love reading stories that'll leave you feeling like you're walking on clouds then you need to read this book or maybe even this entire series."

-The Bookish Sisters

Secrets & Scandals Series

HER WICKED WAYS

"A bad girl heroine steals both the show and a highwayman's heart in Darcy Burke's deliciously wicked debut."
—Courtney Milan, *NYT* Bestselling Author

"…fast paced, very sexy, with engaging characters."
—Smexybooks

HIS WICKED HEART

"Intense and intriguing. Cinderella meets *Fight Club* in a historical romance packed with passion, action and secrets."
—Anna Campbell, *Seven Nights in a Rogue's Bed*

"A romance...to make you smile and sigh…a wonderful read!"
—Rogues Under the Covers

TO SEDUCE A SCOUNDREL

"Darcy Burke pulls no punches with this sexy, romantic page-turner. Sevrin and Philippa's story grabs you from the first scene and doesn't let go. To Seduce a Scoundrel is simply delicious!"

—Tessa Dare, *NYT* Bestselling Author

"I was captivated on the first page and didn't let go until this glorious book was finished!"

—Romancing the Book

TO LOVE A THIEF

"With refreshing circumstances surrounding both the hero and the heroine, a nice little mystery, and a touch of heat, this novella was a perfect way to pass the day."

–The Romanceaholic

"A refreshing read with a dash of danger and a little heat. For fans of honorable heroes and fun heroines who know what they want and take it."

-The Luv NV

NEVER LOVE A SCOUNDREL

"I loved the story of these two misfits thumbing their noses at society and finding love." Five stars.

–A Lust for Reading

"A nice mix of intrigue and passion...wonderfully complex characters, with flaws and quirks that will draw you in and steal your heart."

–BookTrib

SCOUNDREL EVER AFTER

"There is something so delicious about a bad boy, no matter what era he is from, and Ethan was definitely delicious."

-A Lust for Reading

"I loved the chemistry between the two main characters...Jagger/Ethan is not what he seems at all and neither is sweet society Miss Audrey. They are believably compatible."

-Confessions of a College Angel

Legendary Rogues Series

LADY of DESIRE

"A fast-paced mixture of adventure and romance, very much in the mould of *Romancing the Stone* or *Indiana Jones*."

-All About Romance

"...gave me such a book hangover! ...addictive...one of the most entertaining stories I've read this year!"

-Adria's Romance Reviews

ROMANCING the EARL

"Once again Darcy Burke takes an interesting story and...turns it into magic. An exceptionally well-written book."

-Bodice Rippers, Femme Fatale, and Fantasy

"...A fast paced story that was exciting and interesting. This is a definite must add to your book lists!"

-Kilts and Swords

LORD of FORTUNE

"I don't think I know enough superlatives to describe this book! It is wonderfully, magically delicious. It sucked me in from the very first sentence and didn't turn me loose—not even at the end ..."

-Flippin Pages

"If you love a deep, passionate romance with a bit of mystery, then this is the book for you!"

-Teatime and Books

Ribbon Ridge Series

A contemporary family saga featuring the Archer family of sextuplets who return to their small Oregon wine country town to confront tragedy and find love...

The "multilayered plot keeps readers invested in the story line, and the explicit sensuality adds to the excitement that will have readers craving the next Ribbon Ridge offering."
-Library Journal Starred Review on YOURS TO HOLD

"Darcy Burke writes a uniquely touching and heart-warming series about the love, pain, and joys of family as well as the love that feeds your soul when you meet "the one."
-The Many Faces of Romance

I can't tell you how much I love this series. Each book gets better and better.
-Romancing the Readers

"Darcy Burke's Ribbon Ridge series is one of my all-time favorites. Fall in love with the Archer family, I know I did."
-Forever Book Lover

Ribbon Ridge: So Hot

SO GOOD

" ...worth the read with its well-written words, beautiful descriptions, and likeable characters...they are flirty, sexy and a match made in wine heaven."

-Harlequin Junkie Top Pick

"I absolutely love the characters in this book and the families. I honestly could not put it down and finished it in a day."

-Chin Up Mom

SO RIGHT

"This is another great story by Darcy Burke. Painting pictures with her words that make you want to sit and stare at them for hours. I love the banter between the characters and the general sense of fun and friendliness."

-The Ardent Reader

" ...the romance is emotional; the characters are spirited and passionate... "

-The Reading Café

SO WRONG

"As usual, Ms. Burke brings you fun characters and witty banter in this sweet hometown series. I loved the dance between Crystal and Jamie as they fought their attraction."

-The Many Faces of Romance

"I really love both this series and the Ribbon Ridge series from Darcy Burke. She has this way of taking your heart and ripping it right out of your chest one second and then the next you are laughing at something the characters are doing."

-Romancing the Readers

About the Author

⭐️€•3⭐️

Darcy Burke is the USA Today Bestselling Author of hot, action-packed historical and sexy, emotional contemporary romance. Darcy wrote her first book at age 11, a happily ever after about a swan addicted to magic and the female swan who loved him, with exceedingly poor illustrations.

A native Oregonian, Darcy lives on the edge of wine country with her guitar-strumming husband, their two hilarious kids who seem to have inherited the writing gene. They're a crazy cat family with two Bengal cats, a small, fame-seeking cat named after a fruit, and an older rescue Maine Coon who is the master of chill and five a.m. serenading. In her "spare" time Darcy is a serial volunteer enrolled in a 12-step program where one learns to say "no," but she keeps having to start over. Her happy places are Disneyland and Labor Day weekend at the Gorge. Visit Darcy online at http://www.darcyburke.com and sign up for her newsletter, follow her on Twitter at http://twitter.com/darcyburke, or like her Facebook page, http://www.facebook.com/darcyburkefans.